Restored Hearts
~
Book 2

~ ~ ~

RECONCILIATIONS

Susan Elizabeth Ball

Reconciliations

Copyright @ 2022 by Susan Elizabeth Ball. All rights reserved. No part of this book may be reproduced, stored in, or introduced to a retrieval system, or transmitted in any form, or by any means—electronic, mechanical, photocopying, recording, or otherwise—without the prior written permission of the copyright owner. Contact Susan Ball by email at susan.ball5@aol.com

Unless otherwise indicated, all Scriptures are taken from the HOLY BIBLE, NEW KING JAMES VERSION (NKJV), Bible Gateway https://www.biblegateway.com/ which is in the public domain and may be used freely without restriction without prior permission. Note these works are in the public domain in the United States of America.

ISBN:

Reconciliations is a work of fiction. References to real people, events, establishments, organizations, and locales are intended only to provide a sense of authenticity and are used fictitiously. All other characters, incidents, and dialogue are created from the author's imagination.

Printed in the U.S. A.

~ ~ ~

Dedication

~ ~ ~

In loving memory to
Mom and Dad
For your devotion to God
And to one another
Through sixty years of marriage.

~ ~ ~

~ ~ ~

Therefore, if anyone is in Christ,
he is a new creation; old things have passed away;
behold, all things have become new.
Now all things are of God, who has reconciled us
to Himself through Jesus Christ,
and has given us the ministry of reconciliation,
that is, that God was in Christ reconciling the world to Himself,
not imputing their trespasses to them,
and has committed to us the word of reconciliation.

2 CORINTHIANS 5: 17 – 19

~ ~ ~

Prologue

A bright orange Spark turning left onto Riverside Drive caught Mark's attention as he stared out the window of his office. He was spending a few quiet moments in reflection before the ceremony began.

"How ironic," he said, chuckling.

The weatherman had promised a glorious spring day, and for once, it seemed the forecast was accurate. The sun shone brightly, glistening on the dewdrops that remained on the grass. The cherry blossoms were in full bloom, and the early daylilies planted along the sidewalk were beginning to open. It was the perfect setting for the celebration—an event that had not seemed even remotely possible when he was drawn into the lives of the celebrants eight months earlier.

"What's ironic, dear?" The question drew Mark from his reverie. He pointed out the window, as he turned his gaze toward his wife.

She spied the car and smiled. "I think it's a reminder that God moves in mysterious ways."

"He certainly does," Mark agreed. "But who would ever have thought that He would use a bright orange car to bring us here today?"

Chapter 1

Mark knew he was cornered when he heard the footsteps approaching. He had hoped to take a quick peek at the car and be on his way without encountering a salesperson. He should have known that was not going to happen.

"She's a great car," the salesman said. Mark turned, feeling a bit foolish. Here he was a grown man, nearly sixty years old, staring at the car like a teenage boy drooling over a Mustang. The salesman stuck out his hand. "Kevin Peterson."

Mark extended his own automatically. "Nice to meet you. Mark Vinson."

"It's open. Why don't you get behind the wheel? You'll be surprised by the amount of legroom."

The salesman opened the door and invited Mark to get in. Obediently, Mark climbed into the car. *"What am I doing?"* he thought. *"I can't afford a new car."*

It did have plenty of legroom and more headroom than he had expected.

"You can't beat it for the money," the salesman told him. The sticker price indicated that the car could be his for not much more than he had budgeted for a used car. "And, it gets excellent gas mileage. Would you like to test drive it?"

Mark looked at the salesman, then at the brand-new Spark, and finally back to the salesman.

"I guess so," Mark replied, wondering again how he got himself into this situation. He'd stopped in at Wilson Chevrolet to take a look at the used cars. He had no intention of purchasing a car today and certainly not a new car. Mark was only trying to get an idea of what was available and what kind of money he would have to put out to replace the twelve-year-old clunker he was currently driving. The old Cutlass had been a great car, but with more than 220,000 miles on the odometer, Mark knew it was on its last legs.

"I'll grab the key and be right back." The salesman headed into the showroom, leaving Mark to consider the merits of the compact sedan he was about to test drive.

When he pulled into the dealership, Mark had intended to head directly for the used car lot, but the new car's bright orange color—the salesman called it cayenne orange—had caught his eye. He should have resisted temptation and turned away, but with one glance, it had captured his attention. Mark had found himself making his way over to the car. The salesman had appeared by his side almost as soon as he exited his vehicle.

What was that guy's name? Mark normally had an excellent memory for names, but this one had flown right out of his head. He guessed it was the excitement of sitting behind the wheel of a new car.

Mark was still sitting in the car when the salesman returned with the key. While Mark drove, the salesman pointed out the various features of the car. "It's considered a subcompact, but it has much more legroom than other cars in this class. You can tell for yourself how well it handles. The back seats lie flat so you can transport larger items."

Mark had to agree with him. "It does drive nicely, and it's quite comfortable."

They made a loop down Route 1 to Route 3 and got on the interstate. Even at high speeds, Mark found the handling to be nimble. By the time they returned to the dealership, Mark knew that he wanted this car. Mark also knew better than to make a major purchasing decision without consulting both his wife and the Lord.

"So, what did you think?" the salesman asked, as the men exited the vehicle.

Mark handed him the keys. "I like it, but I'm not ready to make a decision today."

"Fair enough. Think it over for a few days. Here's my card. My hours are listed on the back." The salesman shook Mark's hand and walked away. Mark appreciated his no-pressure tactics.

Mark looked at the business card in his hand. "Kevin Peterson," he silently read. *Why does that name seem familiar?* Mark had the strangest feeling that he should know Kevin, yet he was certain he had never seen the tall, dark-haired salesman before. "Weird. Oh, well." Mark shrugged off the feeling and climbed back into his car. He would pray about the decision. "I hope the car comes in some colors other than bright orange," he thought as he drove away.

~ ~ ~

Kevin Peterson sought out his friend Josh Daniels as he entered the showroom. "I'm starved. Time for dinner."

Josh stuck his head into the business office and let the floor manager know that the two salesmen were taking their dinner break.

"How'd the test drive go?" Josh asked as he wove his way through traffic.

"Pretty good. He seemed to like it. I think he will be back, but you never know. He is definitely in the market for a new--or newer--vehicle. Did you see that junk heap he was driving?"

Kevin and Josh had been close friends since Josh joined the sales team at Wilson Chevrolet eight years earlier. Kevin had worked at the dealership for more than twice as long and for most of that time had been the top salesman. He knew how to read customers and varied his sales pitch accordingly.

In a few minutes, they had reached the Princess Anne Café, one of their favorite local eateries. The two friends settled into a booth and ordered soft drinks. While perusing the menu, Josh hit Kevin with some unexpected news. "Lisa's pregnant."

"Again? Haven't you two ever heard of birth control?" Kevin teased. From the smile on Josh's face, Kevin knew his friend was happy, and he was happy for him. He got up from his seat and grabbed Josh in a bear hug. "Congratulations, man. That's great. How many does this make? Four?"

The men sat back down. "Five. Lisa says this will be the last one. Of course, she said that after Joey was born, too. She always wanted a big family."

"Well, she certainly got her wish." The waitress returned with their sodas, and the men placed their dinner orders.

"What about you?" Josh asked, suddenly serious. "Did you ever want kids?"

Kevin squirmed. "I never thought much about it, one way or the other. Christine wasn't anxious to start a family." Kevin rarely spoke of his ex-wife who had divorced him three years ago. "If I had married Karen, I would have had step-children. I wasn't prepared for a ready-made family. So, I guess the answer is no, I have never had a strong desire to have children. Which is just as well, considering my luck with women."

Kevin had dated Karen Harper, a widow with three children, seriously for about six months, but they had ended their relationship several months ago.

"If you ever get remarried, your new wife might want children," Josh ventured.

"True. I guess I'll cross that bridge when I come to it. At the moment, though, there is no future Mrs. Kevin Peterson in the picture."

Silence reigned for a few moments as the men attacked their food. About halfway through his sandwich, Josh stopped eating and looked expectantly at Kevin. Kevin had the impression that Josh wanted to tell him something. He waited for Josh to speak. Josh hesitated and looked away.

"Spit it out," Kevin commanded.

Josh took a deep breath. "If Christine were in trouble, would you help her?"

Kevin stopped chewing and swallowed hard. "Why would you ask me that?"

"Just answer the question. Would you help her if she needed you?"

"If you mean financial trouble, no way. Absolutely not. I was more than generous with her in the divorce. If she can't handle her money, that's her problem." Kevin had been blindsided when Christine left him. It had taken him a long time to get over the hurt, and he had no intention of allowing her to hurt him again. And he was certain she would if he got involved in her life.

Josh shook his head. "No, I mean if she were in real trouble and had no one else to turn to. Suppose she was in a bad relationship with a creep who treated her badly. Would you help her get out of it?"

Josh had Kevin's full attention now. "You're not just supposing, are you?" Although Kevin tried desperately to sound nonchalant, he was dismayed by the concern he felt for Christine's

5

well-being. "You know something. What's happening with Christine?"

"I saw her the other day." Josh dropped his voice and looked around the restaurant as if he were afraid someone might overhear them. Kevin knew Josh well enough to realize that Josh would rather not say what he was about to share. "Lisa and I were shopping, and we ran into her. She was with a guy—Larry something or other. She said they're living together."

A scowl crossed Kevin's face. "Of course, she is. Christine has always been able to find a man to take care of her, at least for a little while. Unfortunately, she usually picks losers. He's probably just the next guy in a long line of losers."

"She seemed skittish like she was in a hurry to get away." Josh talked fast, as if to get it all out quickly. "And she kept tugging at her sleeve, pulling it down to make sure her forearm was covered. When she raised her hand to wave goodbye, her sleeve fell back, and I saw a large bruise on her arm."

"She probably bumped into something. Christine's clumsy. She was always banging into the dresser or the bedpost and getting bruised."

"No," Josh shook his head adamantly. "It looked like someone, I assume Larry, had grabbed her hard. I saw impressions of fingers on her arm."

Kevin tried not to look alarmed. There was no way he was getting involved in Christine's domestic problems. "Christine is a big girl," he said flatly. "She can take care of herself. If this guy isn't treating her right, she can pack up and move out."

"Yeah. I guess." Josh did not seem convinced, however. "I thought you should know. That's all."

"I appreciate your concern, but I'm sure Christine will be just fine."

Chapter 2

Karen Harper was staring at the computer screen in frustration. She wanted to pound it with her fist, but she knew that nothing would be accomplished by that feat except that she might hurt her hand or damage the computer. Besides, although she hated to admit it, it was not the computer's fault that she was unable to reconcile the firm's checking account balance with the bank's statement. Karen had made an error, plain and simple. It was a small error, only $7.02, but she needed to find it and correct it. After checking and rechecking each entry, Karen was starting to get a headache and her neck muscles were tense.

Engrossed in discovering her error, Karen was unaware of her boss quietly slipping into the room and standing behind her until she felt his hands on her shoulders. His touch startled her so that she jumped in her seat and gasped.

"You seem tense," he said as he stroked her shoulders and upper arms.

Karen did not turn to face him but continued to look at the computer. "You are aware," Karen said tersely, "that your behavior is inappropriate. I could charge you with harassment."

"Would this also be considered harassment?" he asked innocently as he began to massage her neck.

"Most definitely," Karen answered, without quite so much conviction.

"And this." He bent to kiss her on the back of her neck.

"Absolutely," she murmured.

Karen giggled and gave up all pretense of offense. She stood then and wrapped her arms around his neck, her lips finding his. Karen could scarcely believe that such a wonderful, kind, generous man as Greg Marshall had fallen in love with her. It had been a month since he had declared his intention to marry her, but Karen still awoke each morning wondering if it had all been a glorious dream. The diamond ring on her left hand provided her all the reassurance she needed that his love for her was real.

"What were you concentrating on so intently?" Greg asked.

"Balancing the checkbook. I made an entry mistake, and I can't find it. It's driving me crazy."

"Maybe you need to take a break from it. It's almost lunchtime. Is this the day Robin is taking you out?"

"Yes. It will be nice to get away from the office for a while," Karen smiled.

Karen normally packed a lunch and ate in the office. Robin, the office receptionist, was a long-time friend of Greg's and had become one of Karen's closest friends and confidants in the several months that the women had worked together. It had been nearly two weeks since Karen and Greg had announced their engagement, and Robin had yet to hear all the intimate details.

~ ~ ~

"Of course, you know that Greg's family and mine spent a lot of time together during the summer," Karen began after the two ladies had placed their lunch orders.

Robin nodded. "I remember you mentioned that Greg and the girls went with you and the boys to the National Zoo and King's Dominion."

"And several movies." Karen laughed. "Although I usually went to a kiddie movie with the younger kids while Greg and Trevor saw the latest action film."

"Greg had taken a sincere interest in Trevor for a while, I recall," Robin said.

"That started when Trevor was suspended from school back in April and I had to bring him to work with me. Greg invited him to go hiking and later took him fishing. Greg was the positive role model Trevor needed."

The server returned to the table with a basket of hush puppies and two glasses of ice water. Karen waited until she moved away to continue the conversation.

"Greg and I enjoyed each other's company. We were becoming more than just good friends, but neither of us admitted it until the night of the fair. Greg behaved just as you said—like a little kid trying to take it all in. I ate more junk food that night than I had probably eaten in six months, and he talked me into going on nearing every ride—including the double Ferris wheel. I was scared silly, so Greg rode with me and kept his arm around me."

Robin shook her head knowingly. She had shared with Karen previously that she had been to the fair with Greg and his late wife, Cindy, once several years ago. And once was certainly quite enough as far as Robin was concerned

Karen continued her story. "It was getting late, and Greg had bought everyone lemonade and soft pretzels. Kyle was sitting on Greg's lap. He called Greg daddy." Karen's eyes misted over as she recalled the conversation between her six-year-old and Greg. "He said, 'I'm tired, Daddy. Can we go home now?' It was so precious. And do you know what Greg did?" Karen's voice cracked as she asked the question.

"He hugged him and said, 'Sure, son.' Just like that, I knew he was the one—the one God had for me, and for my boys. When we got home, I wasn't sure what to say to Greg. But I didn't have to say anything. He kissed me and told me he wanted to be Kyle's daddy, and Trevor and Austin's too, of course."

"He didn't propose that night, did he?" Robin asked.

"No, he waited a couple of weeks. After the fair, we saw each other almost every night, usually with the kids. Most nights he came over for dinner or took the whole family out. After the kids went to bed, we talked for hours. He told me all about Cindy, and I told him about Jeff. Trevor had told him a lot about Jeff already, but I wanted him to hear it from me. Then one night he asked me to get a babysitter. He said we needed a night out to ourselves. He took me to the Log Cabin restaurant up on Route 1 in Stafford."

"I know the place," Robin said. "Chris and I usually go there for our anniversary. They have the best seafood."

Karen nodded her agreement. "I had the crab cakes. They were divine."

"I usually have the broiled platter," Robin interjected. "That way I get a bit of everything—shrimp, crab, scallops, and oysters. I love it all."

"Greg had reserved a table by the fireplace. There wasn't a fire, of course, but the staff had placed a mirror and at least two dozen candles in front of the fireplace, and they were all lit. It created a cozy, romantic atmosphere. After dessert, we were sipping our coffee when Greg pulled out a small box and got down on one knee. I couldn't believe it! Greg Marshall was proposing to me in front of everyone in the restaurant. I started to cry, and people around us started clapping and yelling out their congratulations. It was amazing." Tears were threatening to spill from Karen's eyes as she finished her story.

Chapter 3

Despite Kevin's assertion that Christine was no longer a part of his life and thus none of his concern, he found he could not stop thinking about her. She had hurt him deeply when she left him after he caught her with another man. His pain was increased when Kevin learned that Christine had been involved with two other men during the final months of their eleven-year marriage. Since their breakup, Kevin had one serious girlfriend while Christine had, according to the rumors, gone from one bad relationship to another. She was showing her true colors, and Kevin told himself he was glad to be rid of her. Yet the thought of some guy manhandling her disturbed him more than a little.

Kevin knew that Christine Miller was a wild child the moment he laid his eyes on her. That had been part of the attraction. They met at a bowling alley, the old one downtown that had been bulldozed a dozen years ago and replaced with an office complex. Kevin, three years out of high school, was bowling with a couple of guys from the Chevy dealership, and Christine was there with a group of high school girls with reputations for being fast and loose. Christine very much looked the part in her tight blue jeans, low-cut halter top, and high heels. Her bleached blond hair was permed in long curls; two barrettes held the curls out of her face. She was wearing too much makeup, too much jewelry, and too much perfume. She puffed on a cigarette with her left hand and held a bottle of cheap beer in her right.

One of the guys knew a couple of the girls and made introductions. Kevin thought Christine was the most attractive of the group. When he looked beyond her carefully sculpted façade, he realized that she was quite lovely. Christine seemed to have found him attractive as well. When the group began to break up, Christine asked Kevin if he would drive her home. Kevin was fully aware of what she was offering; she confirmed it when she suggested that he take the long way to her house.

"Let's drive down by the river," Christine purred, as she slid up against him in the front seat of his pickup truck and stroked his thigh with her hand. "I know a quiet place where we can park."

Afterward, Kevin had driven her home. Home was a dilapidated doublewide she shared with her mother, her mother's current live-in boyfriend, and a younger half-sister. The small yard was littered with trash. Two rusted cars were parked out front; Kevin was surprised to learn that they were operational. A short flight of steps led up to a small platform and the door of the trailer. To enter the trailer, one had to step over the cat curled up on the third step and avoid the pet dishes placed along the edge of the platform. A large bag of dog food was torn open and propped in the corner. Its contents were scattered on the steps and the ground. Kevin had never encountered such squalor, and he felt uncomfortable leaving Christine there. As it was her home, however, he had no choice.

"I had fun tonight," she told him as she climbed from the car. She handed him a scrap of paper with a phone number on it. "Call me sometime and maybe we can do it again."

Kevin put the paper in the glove compartment and said goodbye, knowing full well he would never dial the number and expecting never to see Christine Miller again. He had enjoyed the evening, but Christine was the kind of a girl that a guy enjoyed for an evening and moved on.

A few weeks later Kevin was surprised when Christine walked into Wilson Chevrolet. He spied her walking across the showroom toward him. Fortunately, she was dressed a bit more respectably than she had been the night they met. She had also toned down the makeup and her hair. She looked younger…and anxious.

Christine asked Kevin if she could talk to him privately. He showed her into his office. She sat in one of the two vinyl chairs used by customers when they filled out the paperwork for their new car purchases. She held her purse in her lap and played with the straps. Kevin leaned against the corner of the desk, wondering what she wanted, while his mind rampantly played out possible scenarios. He hoped she was not…

"I think I'm pregnant," she said without preamble.

Pregnant! Of all the possible reasons she could have had for coming to see him, being pregnant was the one he had most feared.

Kevin felt dizzy, but he managed to keep his composure. He did not bother to ask if she was sure the baby was his. He knew the risks he was taking when they had climbed into the bed of his pickup down by the river. He knew he should have taken precautions, but she had not seemed concerned about it and well, frankly, he had not been prepared; the thought that he could find himself in that situation never entered his mind as he had left his apartment to go bowling with buddies.

Kevin was not one to shirk his responsibilities. He paced his small office as he tried to think of how to respond. He barely knew the girl, but their lives would be forever linked by a hasty act committed on the night they met.

Ultimately Kevin knelt in front of Christine and looked her in the eyes. "What do you want to do? I'll be there for you, whatever you decide."

Her relief was visible immediately. She had tried to act tough, but Kevin had seen her vulnerability. He had the distinct impression that her family would be of no help to her and that he was the only person to whom she could turn.

"I don't know. I guess I should have an abortion."

An abortion would be the easy way out, Kevin knew, but he wanted no part in killing an innocent child.

"What about putting the baby up for adoption?" he suggested.

"I don't know what to do. Momma will kill me if she finds out."

"Let's go someplace where we can talk. I can take my break now, and we can discuss it over dinner."

The look in Christine's eyes alerted Kevin that she probably did not have any money, so he quickly added, "May I buy you dinner?"

It was the least he could do; after all, it was his fault, as much as hers, that they were in this predicament.

Over dinner, they had discussed their options. Christine was leaning towards having an abortion so that she would not have to confess her deeds to her mother. Although the more Christine shared about her family, the less Kevin thought her mother would care. It seemed that Christine was merely following in her mother's footsteps.

"Momma had me when she was 16," Christine told him. "Daddy was her first husband. She was fifteen and he was twenty-five when they got married. He left when I was two, but they didn't get divorced until I was eight. My sister has a different daddy. Momma couldn't marry him because she was still married to my daddy. She married Tim when I was nine and Bill when I was thirteen. I liked Tim, but Momma ditched him when she met Bill. Bill had a son, Eddie, who was four years older than me. I think Momma loved Bill, but she caught him in bed with Aunt Marlene and kicked him out. I was glad they left, but I was sad for Momma. She had been so happy with Bill. Of course, she didn't know about me and Eddie."

"What about you and Eddie?" Kevin was afraid to hear the answer, but he felt compelled to ask.

"Eddie came on to me when I was fourteen." Christine shared her confession flatly, as if she were relating an event she had merely witnessed. "He was very good-looking and very cool. I was attracted to him right away and let him know that I was available. At first, he just flirted with me and took me out for ice cream occasionally. Then one night when Momma and Bill were out, Eddie said he wanted to make a woman out of me. I let him. I liked it a lot. We did it every chance we got 'til Eddie got tired of me. He started dating other girls, but he still came to my bedroom when he struck out with his date. One night I told him no, that I didn't want him to use me like that anymore. He didn't listen. After that I hated him. A few weeks later Momma kicked them out. She says she will never get married again, cause it's cheaper to kick out a boyfriend than it is to divorce a husband."

"How many boyfriends has your mother had since she got rid of Eddie?" Kevin asked the first question that popped into his head.

"Several. I dunno. I don't try to keep track anymore."

"Have you dated many guys?"

"Yeah, I guess. I don't seem to have any trouble getting a guy's attention. It's keeping them around that's hard. Momma says guys find sex with a new woman exciting, and as soon as the excitement wears off, they move on. I guess she's right, 'cause my boyfriends have all moved on pretty quick."

Guilt washed over Kevin. Men had been taking advantage of Christine all her life and Kevin saw himself as just another in a long line of men willing to use her and then discard her. But Kevin knew he was not like the others. He had been raised with better values than the creeps Christine normally associated with. He would not abandon Christine in her time of need.

He looked across the booth at the eighteen-year-old girl facing him. A girl who might be carrying his child. A girl who had known nothing but betrayal and abandonment from the men in her life. He decided then and there that it was his responsibility to rescue her. He summoned up all the courage he could muster, looked her in the eye, and said gently, "Marry me."

To her credit, Christine shook her head from side to side. "No. I didn't come here to trap you into marryin' me. I came because I thought you should know about the baby. I don't want anything from you, except maybe help with paying for an abortion."

"I believe you," Kevin said gently. He was not giving up that easily. "Marry me anyway. I know I don't have to do this, but I want to. Please don't kill our child. I have a good job. You only have a few months until you graduate. We can make this work. Christine Miller, will you please marry me?"

This time Christine said yes. Five days later she stopped into the dealership again. Kevin saw that she had been crying. He steered her into his office and shut the door.

"You don't hafta marry me," she blurted out. "I'm not gonna have a baby."

Kevin eyed her questioningly.

"There never was a baby. I was just..." Karen looked down at the floor for several seconds. "late. Very late."

Kevin nodded to let her know he accepted her explanation. He realized he could bow out of the engagement gracefully, but was surprised to realize that was not what he wanted. He and Christine had spent time together each day since her announcement, and he found that he liked her. He also liked the idea of removing her from her current existence. He gathered Christine into his arms and gently kissed her forehead. "How about going out with me Friday night? Let's not break off the engagement. We'll postpone the wedding until after you graduate and see how things progress."

Christine burst into tears. She managed a shaky, "Okay."

Two months later, in the parking lot of the Outback, Kevin declared that he loved her, got down on one knee, and proposed properly. Three months after the proposal, Christine graduated. The two were married by a justice of the peace on the banks of the Rappahannock River with Kevin's parents and Christine's sister in attendance. Christine's mother was not invited to the ceremony.

Kevin hoped that by providing Christine with love and security, she would be able to overcome her difficult youth. In his drive to provide her with the material things she lacked growing up, Kevin became obsessed with working long hours and making money. He failed to give her what she had wanted most—his time and his attention. Given the way Christine had been raised, Kevin now realized that she equated a lack of attention with a lack of affection.

With the benefit of hindsight, Kevin could admit that he bore more of the blame than he had been willing to own up to at the time of their divorce. Christine had behaved as her mother had taught her. Instead of talking to Kevin and working to resolve their differences, Christine had simply moved on, looking for physical affection whenever an opportunity arose. At least that is what Kevin now believed.

Josh's questions at dinner had gotten Kevin thinking about children. He wondered if Christine had wanted a baby—if a baby would have made her feel more secure in their relationship. Except for the pregnancy scare, they had never discussed the possibility of children. For his part, Kevin figured he probably would have enjoyed children if they had come along, but he had never had a strong inclination to ask his wife for a child.

Chapter 4

Five days after he took the Spark for a test drive, Mark decided to broach the subject of buying a brand-new car with Janet, his wife of thirty-six years. When they had discussed the need to replace his Oldsmobile Cutlass, they had always talked in terms of buying a gently-used car.

"I went by Wilson Chevrolet the other day," Mark began after dinner Tuesday evening as they sat in the den. Janet looked up from the novel she was reading and gave him her full attention. "I wanted to see what they had on the lot in our price range."

"Did you find anything worth considering?" Janet asked. After so many years together, she knew her husband would only have brought up the subject if he had found a car he liked. He must really want it to have waited several days to tell her about it. Janet Vinson could never complain that her husband pampered himself; in fact, quite the opposite was true. Mark was hesitant to ever spend money on anything for himself that might be considered an extravagance.

"As a matter of fact, I did." Mark plunged right in. "It would be a great car for us. It gets excellent gas mileage. It looks small, but it had plenty of room for my long legs."

"How many miles does it have on it? How old is it?" Janet was anxious to know all the particulars.

"Well....um, actually, well, it's...brand new."

"Brand new? We can't afford a brand-new car. Mark, we agreed on what we could afford. What were you doing looking at brand-new cars?"

Janet rambled on for a good while before Mark was able to speak without interrupting her. "Janet, you know I wouldn't consider anything that we couldn't afford. I was headed for the used car lot when I spied a bright orange car. The salesman said the color was Cayenne Orange. The color attracted my attention, and I had to check it out."

"Bright orange! Mark, a minister can't drive around town in a bright orange car. The congregation would think that you had lost your mind."

"Well, of course, I wasn't planning on driving a bright orange car. It comes in other colors. At least, I'm sure it must."

Janet looked at him skeptically.

"I guess I should have asked about the other colors," Mark admitted. "I was hoping you would go down there with me tomorrow to take a look at it. We can find out what the other color choices are."

Mark sounded hopeful, and Janet hated to disappoint him. But she could not agree to let him buy a car they could not afford.

"What about the price? New cars are so expensive."

"The price is a bit higher than what we agreed to spend," Mark conceded. "We would have to take some money out of our retirement account. But when you consider the money, we will save on gas and repair bills, we may come out ahead in the long run."

Janet could see that this was important to Mark. "I suppose that there's no harm in taking a look. Do you think we can afford it?"

"Yes, dear. And maybe we can negotiate the price down a bit. Dealers expect to knock some off the list price so that customers feel like they got a good deal."

Mark sounded so optimistic that Janet simply said, "Of course, dear." She did not have the heart to say what she was thinking, *We'll be lucky to get out of there without paying a whole lot more than the sticker price.*

Janet had never in her life owned a brand-new car; however, she had heard horror stories of uninformed car shoppers who got talked into paying outrageous prices for all kinds of extras that were unnecessary. Mark was no pushover, but in his efforts to always think the best of anyone until proven otherwise, he sometimes let others take advantage of him. Janet would be there to see that it did not happen this time.

~ ~ ~

When Kevin Peterson arrived at work at noon the next day, he found Mark Vinson waiting for him, along with a woman whom Kevin assumed to be Mrs. Vinson. It had been nearly a week since he had test-driven the Spark. *Right on schedule,* Kevin thought to himself. He grabbed the keys before heading over to greet the couple.

"Hello, Mark. Want to take another look at the Spark?" He extended his hand to grasp Mark's. Kevin never forgot a customer's name or what vehicle they were considering.

"Yes. I'd like to introduce my wife, Janet. Janet, this is Kevin Peterson."

"I'm impressed," Kevin remarked. When Mark looked puzzled, he continued, "It's my business to remember your name, but it's rare for a first-time customer to remember mine."

"It's part of my business to remember names, as well. I'm the pastor of Riverside Christian Fellowship. People expect their minister to know their names, even if their attendance is sporadic."

"Well, Reverend, let's take another look at that car. By the way, we have a special discount for ministers and public servants."

Twenty minutes later, after another test drive for Janet's benefit, the reverend and the car salesman shook hands on a deal that made them both happy. Janet, who was given the honor of selecting the color for their new vehicle, had chosen a much calmer Blue Glow. Kevin informed them that he would place the order immediately and they should have their car in a week or so.

Chapter 5

The following Thursday Kevin called the Vinson home to inform them that their new Spark was ready to be picked up. Janet dropped Mark at the dealership and headed off to do some errands. The paperwork was nearly complete when the phone on Kevin's desk rang.

"Excuse me just a moment," he said to Mark, as he answered the phone. "Hello. Kevin Peterson here. How can I help you?"

"Kevin, it's Stacey Jeffries over at Mary Washington Hospital."

"Hi, Stacey. How's the Impala working out?"

"Great. Kevin, this isn't a social call." Stacey hesitated before continuing. "I wanted to let you know that Christine was brought into the emergency room a little while ago. She was seriously injured in an automobile accident."

Stacey paused, and Kevin drew a deep breath. "Is she going to be okay?"

For the second time in two weeks, Kevin felt himself being drawn back into Christine's life. He was quite certain that he did not want to get involved, and he was even more certain that Christine would not welcome his involvement. He realized that his heart was still vulnerable where Christine was concerned. It was not a feeling that he enjoyed.

"She's in bad shape, although I don't think her injuries are life-threatening," Stacey said softly. "I know you two aren't married anymore, but… I think you should come to the hospital."

"I don't know if that's wise." Kevin felt like he was in a lose-lose situation. If he went to the hospital, he risked getting hurt by Christine again. If he did not go, he would feel like a jerk. "I heard she's living with some guy named Larry. He should be the one with her at the hospital."

"If she is, we have no information about him. Her chart lists you as her next of kin and emergency contact. You are the only person we can legally talk to about her condition. She needs someone to be here for her, and I'm afraid you are that someone."

Kevin exhaled a long, slow breath before agreeing to come to the hospital right away. He hung up the phone and leaned back in his chair. He rubbed his eyes and then his forehead before lacing his hands behind his head.

"Is there anything I can do?"

The question startled Kevin so that he bolted upright in his chair. He had forgotten that he was not alone.

"I didn't mean to alarm you," Mark continued. "I couldn't help but overhear. I'd be happy to go with you to the hospital. Hospital visitation is one of the duties of a pastor."

While Kevin was tempted to decline the offer and state that he could handle things on his own, he knew that to be a lie. Instead, he nodded his head affirmatively. "Yeah. I'd like that. This is going to be rough."

As Mark was anxious to get behind the wheel of his new car and Kevin was looking rather pale, Mark offered Kevin a ride to the hospital.

~ ~ ~

Kevin sought out Stacey as soon as he arrived at the hospital. "They've taken her into the operating room to set her arm. She has multiple fractures in her left arm and wrist. She also broke her left leg, bruised a couple of ribs, and suffered a concussion. She is very fortunate in that she doesn't appear to have any internal injuries. That's all I know right now. You need to go to the admissions window. They have some papers for you to sign."

Kevin did as he was told, mechanically signing each spot that was indicated. When he was through, Stacey showed the gentlemen to the surgical waiting room and returned to her duties in the ER. Mark spied a beverage station set up in a corner of the room.

"I could use a cup of coffee." Mark rose as he spoke. "How about you?"

"Thanks. Black with sugar."

~ ~ ~

In the two weeks since meeting Kevin, Mark had figured out why his name seemed familiar. Karen Harper, a member of Mark's congregation, had mentioned Kevin's name many times during their counseling sessions last spring. She had sought the pastor's counsel regarding unresolved issues over the death of her first husband and about her then-current dating relationship with Kevin. Ultimately, Mark had counseled Karen to terminate her relationship with Kevin, as Kevin had not made Jesus Christ the Lord of his life and seemed to have no interest in doing so.

As they sipped the coffee and waited for any word on Christine's condition, Mark silently prayed. "Father, I know that I am not here with Kevin by chance. You arranged this encounter because Kevin needs You in his life. Christine needs You, as well. Father, I ask that You will give me wisdom in this situation. Help me to share your love and words with these hurting people. I ask that You touch Christine's body and heal it. But, more than that, Father God, I ask that You heal these two hurting hearts. Draw them to yourself, Lord. Please let me be clay in your hands that You can use to bring about your purposes."

~ ~ ~

It seemed like an eternity before Kevin heard his name being paged by the waiting room receptionist. He glanced at the clock on the wall and was surprised to realize that he and Mark had been at the hospital for only a little more than an hour.

"Mr. Peterson, your wife is out of surgery," the receptionist told him.

Kevin did not bother to correct her assumption.

"They've taken her to the recovery room. If everything progresses normally, she should be moved to a room shortly. The doctor will be out to talk to you momentarily."

A waiting room ambassador led Kevin and Mark to a private conference room to await the doctor. In short order, Dr. Reyes appeared and told Kevin that the surgery had gone pretty much as expected.

"Your wife's left arm was damaged extensively, but we have put it back together. It will take a few months to properly heal, and then she will need physical therapy to help her regain complete use of it. Her left leg was set in a cast and should heal in about 6 weeks. We called in a plastic surgeon to stitch up her face. We hope that it will heal without too much scarring; however, that remains to be seen. She may need additional plastic surgery in the future. Her other injuries are relatively minor and should heal fine. The major area of concern is the trauma she sustained to her head. We will watch her carefully for a couple of days to ascertain that she has nothing more serious than a concussion."

He paused and asked Kevin if he had any questions. "When can I see her?"

"She should be in her room shortly, but she will be heavily sedated. We'd like you to spend only a few minutes with her today. She needs to rest."

Dr. Reyes was nearly out the door when he turned back to Kevin. "I almost forgot the most important information." The doctor smiled for the first time. "The baby is fine."

Kevin felt as if he had been punched in the stomach. "Baby? Christine is pregnant!"

"I guess I ruined the surprise, uh?" Dr. Reyes's expression bore no trace of remorse as he walked back over to Kevin and stuck out his right hand. "You should be a father in about seven months, give or take. Congratulations."

Kevin automatically shook the hand that was extended to him, while feeling anything but celebratory. The physician exited the room without noticing Kevin's discomfiture.

Kevin stared at the floor, fighting the urge to flee the hospital without seeing Christine. He felt Mark's hand on his shoulder, and he felt oddly comforted by the gesture. They sat in silence for several minutes before a nurse came to escort them to Christine's room.

Kevin's shock in learning of Christine's pregnancy paled in comparison to that which he felt upon seeing her lying in the hospital bed. A gauze bandage was wrapped around her head and covered her left ear; auburn hair matted with blood stuck out from under the bandage and fell to her shoulders. Christine's right eye was blackened and swollen shut. Her face was bruised and crisscrossed with stitches.

"That can't be Christine," Kevin gasped.

"Oh, it's her, alright," the nurse assured him. "She'll look more like herself when the swelling goes down and the stitches come out. You can talk to her if you want. She won't be able to respond, but she might be able to hear you. I'll give you ten minutes."

Kevin was able to maintain control until the nurse was gone. Then the tears came in great, heaving sobs. Mark helped him to the chair that had been placed alongside Christine's bed and handed him a wad of tissues.

"Thanks." Kevin blew his nose and wiped his face. "I'm sorry," he whispered. "I didn't expect her to look like this. You should have seen her before. She was so beautiful."

"And she will be again," Mark said gently.

"Not like before. She'll have a lot of scars." A scowl crossed Kevin's face. "I wonder if Larry will want her when he sees her scarred face," he hissed. "I've seen enough. Let's get out of here."

~ ~ ~

Mark was beginning to suspect that Kevin harbored feelings for his former wife despite the tremendous pain she had caused him.

"I'd like to pray for Christine before we go," Mark stated as Kevin was exiting the room.

"Go ahead. I'll wait for you in the hall."

Mark prayed aloud, remembering the nurse had said that Christine might be able to hear them. He thanked God for sparing Christine's life and the life of the recently conceived child growing inside her. He concluded by asking God to continue to watch over Christine and to allow her to heal quickly.

When Mark dropped Kevin back at the dealership, he handed Kevin his card. "I'll check in on Christine tomorrow. Call me anytime if there's anything else I can do."

"I think I'll let Larry handle things from here on out. Thanks for being there today. Maybe I'll see you around." Kevin shook hands with the minister.

"I hope to see you in church sometime," Mark said optimistically.

Kevin shrugged as he walked away without responding.

As Mark drove home, Kevin was on his heart. "Heavenly Father," he prayed, "I ask that You wrap your protective arms around Kevin. He's hurting, Lord, and he doesn't know where to turn. He doesn't recognize his need for You. Please don't let him do anything foolish, but draw him to yourself. Thank You for loving Kevin and Christine far more than they will ever know. Thank You for bringing them into my life. I pray that You will use me in whatever way You choose to show them your great love."

~ ~ ~

Kevin left the dealership and headed for the nearest ABC store. He had not taken a drink since the night he discovered Christine in their bed with a copier repairman. He'd wanted to punch Mike Sloan in the face. Instead, he'd drowned his hurt in a bottle of scotch. Of course, getting drunk had not solved anything. His heart was just as bruised and broken the next day, only he had a major hangover to go with it. He'd vowed never to get drunk again. A vow he had fully intended to keep; that was, until his visit to the hospital. He had not realized that Christine still had the power to hurt him until the doctor's pronouncement that she was pregnant.

Kevin parked the car in front of the liquor store. He reached for the handle to open the door. Suddenly, he stopped. A haggard, middle-aged redhead stood on the sidewalk. She drew a last puff on her cigarette before tossing the butt and entering the store.

"Christine's mom," Kevin spat out between clenched teeth. "Just my luck. Darlene probably doesn't even know that Christine is in the hospital. There's no way I'm telling her."

Kevin started the engine and sped out of the parking lot. He'd avoided that woman like the plague when he was married to Christine, and he had no intention of speaking to her now. With no alcohol to dull his pain, Kevin headed home, took a sleeping pill, and went straight to bed.

"With any luck, I'll wake up to find it was all a bad dream."

Kevin had no idea that his nightmare was just beginning.

Chapter 6

Delightful aromas wafting from the kitchen greeted Mark as he opened the front door of the small cape cod home he and Janet had purchased when they moved to Fredericksburg twenty years earlier.

"Hi honey," Janet's cheerful welcome rang out. "I'm in the kitchen."

Mark walked into the kitchen to find Janet in the midst of preparing a feast. An apple pie and a pan of yeast rolls sat on the counter waiting to be baked. Janet was spreading breadcrumbs on top of a broccoli casserole. When she finished, she wiped her hands on her blue gingham apron and walked into Mark's open arms. Mark bent his head and kissed his wife softly on the lips.

"How's the new car?" she asked.

"Wonderful. How was your day?"

"Busy but good. And yours?"

"Eventful. It's good to be home." Mark kissed her again before releasing her. "Dinner smells wonderful. It looks like you've been cooking all day."

Janet removed a golden brown, roasted chicken from the oven and slid in the casserole. "I invited Greg and Karen to eat dinner with us. They should be here soon."

Upon learning that they would have dinner guests, Mark quickly decided to postpone telling Janet the details of his day; there was not enough time now to do justice to the story.

"What can I do to help?" Mark asked as he snatched a piece of crispy chicken skin.

"How about setting the table? Wash your hands first, and no more picking at the chicken." Janet smacked Mark's hand as he tried to pull a bit of meat off of a chicken leg. "When you're finished, you could whip the potatoes. I'm going to sauté some asparagus and make gravy."

Mark reached into the cupboard for plates. Janet was already washing the asparagus and snapping off the ends.

The doorbell rang before Mark got around to the potatoes. He opened the door and greeted their dinner guests. Greg Marshall and Karen Harper were not merely dinner guests. They were to be married in a couple of months and would begin their premarital counseling after dinner. Karen headed for the kitchen to help Janet finish the dinner preparations while Greg joined Mark in the living room. In short order, the women announced that dinner was served.

Mark blessed the meal. "Father in Heaven, we thank You for this bountiful meal You have provided. Bless the hands that prepared it and all of us as we partake of it. We ask for special blessings on Greg and Karen as they look forward to a life together with You at the center. In the precious name of Jesus, we ask these things. Amen.

"How is the house-hunting going?" Janet asked as she passed the chicken to Greg.

"We made an offer today on a house." Greg piled his plate high with chicken. "We should find out in a day or two if it's been accepted."

He passed the chicken to Karen and heaped mashed potatoes on his plate.

"Is it in the city?" Mark wanted to know.

Greg's mouth was full, so Karen fielded this one. "No, it's in Ferry Farms, quite near to the house I'm renting now. We felt that it was best for my sons to stay in the same school district."

Greg jumped in. "Karen's boys have been through a lot of changes in the past couple of years. They need the stability of continuing in the same schools. My girls won't have any trouble adjusting to a new house and a new school."

"That's true, but you will be further from Tom and Gretchen," Janet commented thoughtfully.

Tom and Gretchen Sullivan, Greg's in-laws, had been a tremendous source of help to Greg since the death of his wife more than three years earlier.

"Don't I know it!" Greg laughed. "Gretchen will not let me hear the end of it, but truthfully it is only a few minutes further. Gretchen can make it in under fifteen minutes. I don't think the extra distance will keep her away."

The diners all had a good chuckle at Greg's comments.

"Tell us about the house," Janet prompted.

Karen described the house, while Greg focused his attention on his food. "It has five bedrooms in the main part of the house and one in a separate in-law suite. We'll put Trevor in that one so that he can have some privacy."

Trevor was Karen's oldest child. At fifteen, he was significantly older than his brothers Austin and Kyle, who were almost ten and six, respectively.

"There's a bedroom for each child," Karen continued, "but Brittany and Bethany want to share, so we'll use one as an office."

Greg's nine-year-old twin daughters had always shared a room by choice. Greg often teased that they would probably continue to do so until one of them married.

The foursome finished eating and helped clear the table before Mark led the engaged couple to his study for their first of three counseling sessions. Janet set about doing the dishes and checked on the apple pie in the oven. It would be ready to serve by the time the counseling session was over.

Mark began the session with prayer, asking God to bless the couple's upcoming marriage and the blending of two families into one. Karen and Greg held hands as they sat together on the loveseat; Mark moved his swivel chair from behind the desk and sat facing them.

"In a situation such as yours, I would normally begin by asking how the children feel about the impending changes in their lives. In your case, however, the children tell me every time I see them how happy and excited they are. Even Trevor has confided in me that he can't wait until Greg is his father. I've seen very positive changes in Trevor over the last few months. How is he doing at school so far this year?"

Mark had spent many hours counseling Karen and Trevor last spring. As a result, the fractured relationship between mother and son had improved significantly. Karen had recommitted her life to Christ. And Trevor had accepted Christ's free offer of salvation. Although Trevor still had unresolved issues, he had made tremendous strides in the past six months.

"He's off to a great start—better than I even hoped for," Karen replied. "His grades have improved from last year. Of course, there was nowhere for them to go but up. He was fortunate to have passed the ninth grade."

Greg jumped in. "He's playing football. We were cautiously excited when he said he was going out for the team. It was a good sign that he wanted to try out, but we were nervous that he would become depressed if he didn't make the team."

Mark understood Greg's fears. Trevor had been withdrawn and depressed during his first year of high school, as a result of his father's death and his mother's decision to relocate the family. "From what I understand, your worries were for naught. I believe he told me that he made the varsity team."

"He did," Greg continued. "He's not a starter, but he should see a fair amount of playing time. The first game was last Friday. He had two tackles." Greg beamed; Mark thought that Greg could not be prouder even if Trevor were his own flesh-and-blood son.

"You could have heard us celebrating from a mile away." Karen was as proud of her son's accomplishments on the field as Greg.

"He had a big cheering section," Greg added chuckling. "Karen's parents drove up from Chester for the game, and Chad and Emily were there, of course. Tom and Gretchen came, too."

"My parents were so thrilled seeing Trevor play that they are planning to come to every home game of the season," Karen said. "They want to bring the Harpers with them to the next game."

Mark had never met the Harpers, but he knew they were Karen's late husband's parents. As recently as last spring, Karen and the Harpers had not been on speaking terms. Mark had been instrumental in encouraging Karen to restore that relationship; he was thankful that God had allowed him to be used in that capacity.

"Trevor told me recently that I made the right decision moving the family from Chester to Fredericksburg." The smile on Karen's face as she relayed that information touched Mark's heart.

"I'm glad that you two have decided to sell Greg's house and purchase a new home," Mark told the couple, as he guided the conversation to the heart of the evening's counseling session. "It will give you both a fresh start without Karen feeling as if she is an intruder in Cindy's house. You will have to strike a balance between keeping the children's memories of Jeff and Cindy alive without letting Jeff and Cindy become silent parties in your marriage. I have a few suggestions that I'd like to share with you, if you don't mind."

"We'd love to hear them," Greg spoke for the couple. "We have been concerned about that as well. I want to be particularly careful of Tom and Gretchen's feelings."

"My first suggestion may cause them some pain, but I believe that it is necessary. You need to put away some of the pictures of Cindy and Jeff. I suggest that you let your children have as many pictures of their parent as they want in their bedrooms. Outside of the bedrooms, you should limit those pictures to only one room, preferably a room you don't use every day. For most people, that's the formal living room. Since you will be packing everything for the move, it will be a matter of simply not unpacking all of the pictures."

The suggestion would be easier for Karen than for Greg. Pictures of Cindy were displayed in every room of his home, as he wanted to have her likeness close at hand. Karen had put most of Jeff's pictures away when she moved to Fredericksburg. Her marriage had been troubled near the end, and her grief over her deceased spouse did not touch her as deeply as Greg's had him.

"I'll let Gretchen have the pictures we don't display, and the girls can see them when they visit her." Greg went the extra mile to be considerate of his late wife's parents. His parents had died in an automobile accident while Greg was in dental school, and the Sullivans had loved him as their own son since his marriage to Cindy.

"I would also like to suggest that you buy new furniture for your master bedroom. Again, you don't want to be distracted by thoughts of your former spouses. As for the rest of the furniture, communicate your feelings to each other. Karen, if you hate his den couch, tell him. And, Greg, if you can't live without your easy chair, Karen needs to know that."

Greg turned to Karen, his face serious. "Karen, I can't live without my Lazy Boy." Unfortunately, he spoiled the effect by bursting out in laughter. "I've never been particularly attached to furniture. However, we will definitely be keeping all of the pieces Karen has refinished. Her dining room table, as well as the coffee table and end table in the living room, are works of art."

Karen beamed. Refinishing wood furniture had been a hobby of Karen's for years and recently, with her brother's and Greg's encouragement, she had begun a part-time furniture restoration business.

Mark spent the next forty-five minutes discussing the issues of raising children in a blended home. He cautioned the couple to present a unified front to the children when it came to setting and enforcing rules and discipline. He also elaborated on some of the challenges and joys they would have with children of both genders in the household, a situation that neither of them had experienced thus far.

"I think we've covered enough ground for one week. At our next session, I want to discuss finances. You've both been independent and in total control for a few years, so it may take some compromises to develop a workable plan. Now I think I smell Janet's apple pie."

Over hot apple pie topped with vanilla ice cream, Mark shared with his wife and friends his unexpectedly eventful day. The foursome spent time in prayer for both Christine and Kevin before ending the evening.

Chapter 7

Kevin awoke bright and early the next morning, sighed deeply as he stretched his arms wide across the king-sized bed, and turned to look at the radio-alarm clock on his bedside table. "Seven o'clock! What in the world? The alarm didn't even go off."

It had been years since Kevin had awakened at such an early hour without the ringing of the alarm clock. It took a moment for his mind to call forth the events of the previous day. When it did, a flood of pain and confusion washed over him. The pain he blamed on Christine; the confusion resulted from the fact that he was not feeling the ill effects of the hangover he had planned for this morning. Then he remembered that Christine's mother had spoiled that. "Well, maybe she did me a favor for once in her life."

Thanks to the sleeping pill, Kevin had his best night's sleep in months. He was not due at the dealership until noon, so he had an entire morning to do as he pleased. Unfortunately, a morning free of distractions was not what Kevin desired. He needed activity to occupy his mind and keep the unwanted thoughts of Christine at bay.

"I have time for a round of golf."

The sudden inspiration filled him with pleasure as he climbed out of bed and headed for the shower. "That's just the ticket to take my mind off Christine. Better yet, I can take out my frustration on the ball."

Kevin's mood improved considerably, at least until he turned on the news while eating breakfast.

"We're in for a rainy, miserable day. Be sure to take your umbrellas with you when you head out," he heard the forecaster say.

"So much for golf," Kevin muttered as he set his empty cereal bowl in the sink. "What can I do inside for the next three hours?"

The ringing of the telephone interrupted his one-sided conversation.

"Hello," he answered non-too-politely.

A cheerful voice—way too cheerful for this early in the morning, thought Kevin—responded. "Hello. Is this Mr. Peterson?"

"Yes, Kevin Peterson, here."

"Mr. Peterson, this is Mary Gregory at Mary Washington Hospital. I'm the accounts receivables clerk in the accounting department. I need you to come in today and make a deposit on your wife's care. Can I expect you this morning?"

"You want me to do what?" Kevin shouted back. "I'm not paying Christine's hospital bill."

"Sir, please don't shout at me."

"Sorry," Kevin mumbled.

The cheerful voice continued, "You need to pay a deposit to the hospital. You are responsible for your wife's treatment."

"Ex-wife." It was only by clenching his teeth that Kevin was able to spit out the words without shouting. "Christine is my ex-wife. She's responsible for her own treatment."

"Well, sir, you did sign an agreement yesterday taking full responsibility for her care."

"I did what?"

"Sir, you're shouting again. I'm going to have to ask you not to shout at me."

"Sorry," Kevin muttered, although he felt anything but sorry. "I don't remember signing anything like that. They handed me a stack of papers, and I just signed them."

"You didn't read them?"

"No, I was kind of in shock. I just did what the nurse told me to."

"Sir, you should never sign anything without reading it first."

"Don't lecture me," Kevin fumed through gritted teeth.

First, she reprimands me for shouting, now she's lecturing me about knowing what I'm signing. Of course, Kevin knew that none of this was Mary Gregory's fault. She was just the messenger. What was that saying? "Don't shoot the messenger because you don't like the message." Anyway, Kevin knew better. He was always saying similar things to his customers at Wilson Chevrolet.

"Well, I'm afraid that one of those papers committed you to pay for her care," Mary Gregory continued. "Of course, insurance will cover most of it. She does have insurance, doesn't she?"

"How would I know?" Kevin was careful to not shout, although he was certain that the frustration he was feeling was evident in his voice. "We've been divorced for three years. I haven't seen her in more than a year. I don't even know why I was called. She has a live-in boyfriend. He should be the one who was called. He should be the one picking up the tab for her hospital bill."

"I am sorry, sir." Kevin had the impression that Mary Gregory was truly sorry. "We don't have any information regarding anyone else to call. Her records indicate that you are her next of kin and that you should be called in case of an emergency. At any rate, I need you to come down to the hospital this morning and make a $200 deposit for her care."

"And if I don't?" Kevin asked to be obstinate, although he did not doubt that he would do as she had instructed. While he was angry about the hospital's demands, he had no intention of ruining his good credit record over a few hundred dollars.

"You wouldn't want to do that, sir," Mary Gregory responded, once again using her overly-cheerful voice.

"No, of course not," a subdued Kevin replied. "I'll be there in a little while."

~ ~ ~

Kevin heard someone call out his name just as he entered the hospital. He turned to see Mark Vinson behind him.

"Good morning, Kevin. I see you changed your mind about coming to see Christine. I'm on my way up to see her now. We can ride up on the elevator together."

"Actually, I'm not here by choice," Kevin answered. Mark looked puzzled. "The hospital called and said I have to make a payment on Christine's bill. Apparently, one of the papers they gave me to sign yesterday was a promissory note."

"That's rough," Mark said sympathetically. "You will see Christine while you're here, won't you?"

"I suppose I might as well. But first I'm going to stop at the business office and make my payment."

"Very good. I have to check in on another patient. I'll do that first and catch up with you in a bit."

"Mr. Peterson, I'm afraid I have some news that you might find a bit disturbing," Mary Gregory began. She seemed hesitant to continue.

"Go ahead. Hit me with it. I can handle it. I've had so much disturbing news in the last twenty-four hours that nothing will phase me now." Kevin believed every word that he had just spoken. Unfortunately, he was quickly proven very wrong.

"Well, here goes. We searched our records and found a court order requiring you to pay for Mrs. Peterson's medical expenses for a period of five years from your divorce or until Mrs. Peterson remarried. Mrs. Peterson hasn't remarried, has she?" Mary Gregory added, almost hopefully.

Kevin had completely forgotten about the court decree. Christine needed an emergency appendectomy shortly after moving out. She was still technically married to Kevin and covered by his medical insurance at the time, so Kevin had been coerced into covering the co-pay on the surgery. As Christine's job did not provide her with health insurance, she was worried about future medical bills. Christine's lawyer had convinced the judge in the divorce trial to issue the decree, and the judge had complied.

"No, she hasn't remarried." Kevin had fully expected that the hospital would realize their mistake and refund him the $200 in due course. Now it seemed that the money might be the first of many payments to the hospital. This was bad news, indeed, but nothing so earth-shattering as seeing Christine lying bruised and battered in the hospital bed or finding out that she was carrying another man's child.

"I'm afraid," Mary Gregory said gently, "that Mrs. Peterson doesn't have any health insurance, so you will be responsible for her entire medical bill."

That statement shook Kevin's composure to the core. He had no idea how much money a hospital stay could entail, but he was certain that he would spend the rest of his life paying off this debt.

Mary Gregory let that statement sink in before she continued. "There's more bad news."

Of course, there is, Kevin thought sarcastically. He managed, however, to avoid expressing that sentiment aloud.

"Mrs. Peterson is going to need round-the-clock care for about six weeks after she's released. With both limbs on her left side out of commission, she will need help with bathing, toileting, getting dressed, and meal preparation. She will need to go to a rehabilitation facility unless you can make other arrangements for her care. I don't have to tell you that a stay in rehab will not be cheap."

Kevin stared at Mary Gregory in stunned silence. *How could this be happening? This is worse than if we were still married. At least then she would be covered by my insurance.* Mary Gregory continued talking for several minutes but Kevin did not hear a word she spoke. When she was stopped and smiled at him, he handed her a check for $200 and walked blindly from the room.

"Don't you want your receipt?" he heard her call after him. He did not reply.

~ ~ ~

Mark entered Christine's room to find that she was awake, although not truly alert.

"Your preacher is here," the nurse attending to Christine announced.

"I don't have a preacher." Christine made no effort to look at Mark, much less greet him. Refusing to acknowledge him in any manner, she picked at the food on her tray and made a pretense of finding it completely engrossing.

"Am I interrupting?" Mark hesitated just inside the door, uncertain if he was welcome. He considered that it might be best to withdraw and await Kevin in the hallway.

"Not at all." It was the nurse who answered. "A visitor is just what the doctor ordered. It will do her a world of good."

The nurse exited the room, whispering to Mark on her way out that the patient was on heavy painkillers. Mark approached the bed, pulling the solitary chair closer to the patient's side.

"Please keep eating. I guess I should introduce myself. I'm Rev. Mark Vinson. I'm the pastor of Riverside Christian Fellowship. I'm a friend of Kevin's. I came by to see if I could be of service to you."

Christine eyed Mark suspiciously. "You're a preacher?"

"Yes."

"And you say you're Kevin's friend?"

"Yes."

"Kevin's never had any use for church. When did he get religion?"

"I don't believe that anything has changed in that regard. Kevin doesn't attend church, at least not that I know of. Anyway, he doesn't attend my church. But we are friends nevertheless. And I am here to help, if I can."

Christine nibbled on a bit of toast. Mark took that as a signal that he should continue.

"Is there anything I can do for you?"

"I dunno. What did you have in mind?"

"Would you like me to contact your family?"

"Why?"

"They should know that you're in the hospital."

"Like any of them would care.

"What about friends?"

"What about friends?" Either Christine was being deliberately difficult or the medication was making it hard for her to follow the conversation. *Maybe she is just plain obstinate.* Mark banished that thought as quickly as it popped into his head.

"Father, forgive me," he silently prayed. "Give me the wisdom to know how to reach her."

"May I pray for you?" he asked.

"What for?"

"That you'll recover quickly and feel better soon."

"Sure, whatever."

Mark took that as approval. He bowed his head and prayed aloud, "Heavenly Father, I thank You for protecting Christine from more serious injuries. I ask that You help her body to heal quickly and completely. In the name of your son, Jesus, I ask this. Amen."

Mark told Christine that he would be by to see her each day for as long as she was in the hospital. As he was leaving the room, he met Christine's doctor in the doorway. He waited in the hall until the doctor was finished with his examination and got an update on her condition.

Chapter 8

Mark looked around the lobby for Kevin as he left the hospital, but Kevin was nowhere in sight. Mark had lingered in Christine's room, awaiting Kevin's arrival, for as long as seemed prudent. Finally, he had no choice but to assume that Kevin had changed his mind about visiting Christine. He was thankful that he had not told her to expect a visit from Kevin.

Mark's cell phone rang when he was nearly home. He pulled into the parking lot of the convenience store he was passing and picked his phone up from the seat beside him. Kevin had explained that his new car came equipped with Bluetooth, but with all the activity of the past two days, Mark had not taken the time to connect his phone to it.

"Hmm, I don't recognize this number," he mumbled, even as he pressed the talk button. "Hello, Pastor Mark Vinson here."

"Mark, it's Kevin Peterson," an anxious voice on the other end told him.

"Kevin, what happened to you? I waited in Christine's room for as long as I could."

"I'm in jail! That's what happened to me."

"In jail?" Mark asked incredulously. He was glad that he had pulled over before taking this call. "Whatever for?"

"I'll explain later. I promise. Can you come down to the city jail and help get me out of here?"

"I'm on my way."

Mark reversed directions and headed to the jail. Upon his arrival, he inquired about Kevin and was shown to a small conference room. A distraught Kevin sat at one end of a rectangular wooden table. A man in an ill-fitting brown suit sat at the other end. Mark assumed him to be a member of the Fredericksburg Police department. He stood and introduced himself as Lt. Jamison.

"What's going on here?" Mark asked, taking a seat between the two men.

"They think I beat up Christine," Kevin answered.

"Why that's ridiculous," Mark told the investigator. "Christine was in an automobile accident. I was there when the police officer explained to Kevin how the accident occurred."

"It's true that she was in an accident and most of her injuries resulted from her car colliding into a tree. However, the doctors have informed us that some of her injuries are not consistent with the accident. She has several bruises on her upper arms, back, and even her face that were inflicted two or three days before the accident. Someone has been abusing her. We believe that Mr. Peterson could be to blame for his wife's bruises."

"She's no longer his wife."

"I've told them that, but they don't believe me," Kevin bellowed forcefully, jumping to his feet. Lt. Jamison moved quickly around the table, grabbed Kevin's arm, and shoved him back into his chair.

When it was quiet again, Mark continued. "They've been divorced for years. Kevin didn't have anything to do with Christine's injuries."

Mark was doing his best to defend Kevin against accusations that he knew to be unfounded.

"Three years," Kevin interjected. "We've been divorced for three years. I hadn't seen her in more than a year before yesterday. If anyone beat her up, it's that goon she lives with. Josh warned me about him, but there was nothing I could do. Besides, it was none of my business."

"Who's Josh?" Lt. Jamison asked. "And who's the goon?"

"Josh Daniels is my best friend. We work together at Wilson Chevrolet. I don't know who the goon is, but Josh saw him with Christine. He said Christine was afraid of the guy. She had a bruise on her arm when Josh saw them."

"Reverend, how long have you been acquainted with Mr. Peterson?" the lieutenant asked.

"Only a few weeks," Mark admitted. "However, I've had knowledge of him and his relationship with his ex-wife for several months."

Kevin looked shocked. "What do you mean, you've 'had knowledge of me'?"

Mark took on the composure of a pastor trying to calm a member of his flock. "I only realized it a couple of days ago. I counseled a woman you were dating last spring. Karen Harper. In the course of her discussing your relationship, she brought up some things you shared with her about your breakup with Christine. I fully intended to tell you about it after our, or rather my, visit to the hospital this morning."

Kevin nodded letting Mark know that he accepted his explanation, and Mark turned his attention back to the lieutenant. "Mrs. Harper verified that Mr. and Mrs. Peterson had been divorced for quite some time before she met Mr. Peterson. I believe that he is telling you the truth about not having seen Mrs. Peterson recently."

Just then a younger man entered the room. "It seems that the detainee is telling the truth. Here's a copy of the divorce decree. I called Hardy Construction, where Mrs. Peterson works. The owner, Jonathan Hardy, confirmed that Mrs. Peterson has been sharing a residence with his son Larry."

"He's the man you want," Kevin concurred. "Josh said the guy's name was Larry."

In short order, the lieutenant decided that he had no reason to question Kevin further and allowed him to leave. As he had only been brought in for questioning and no charges had been filed, there was no paperwork to process.

"Where are you parked?" Mark asked, as they exited the police headquarters.

"At the hospital," Kevin answered, shaking his head in frustration. "You will not believe the day I've had, and it's only 11:15."

"Why don't you tell me about it over lunch? My treat. How does some Allman's barbeque sound?"

"Sounds wonderful. I'm starved. I had an early breakfast."

~ ~ ~

The waitress arrived at the table with two large glasses of sweet tea and her order pad.

"Hey Pastor Mark," she said, setting the glasses in front of the two hungry men. "Y'all ready to order?" she asked.

"Hello, Wanda. Thanks for bringing the tea right away." Mark answered cheerfully. "I'll have the large chopped pork sandwich combo with fries and baked beans."

"You want slaw on your sandwich?"

"Of course."

"How about you?" she asked turning to Kevin. "What will you have?"

"The same."

Wanda left to turn their orders into the kitchen. "I hope you like sweet tea," Mark replied to Kevin. "Wanda always brings me tea as soon as I sit down. I guess she assumed you would want sweet tea, also."

"It's fine. How do you know Wanda?"

"I'm her pastor. She's attended Riverside for as long as I have been the pastor there. Now I want to hear all about your morning."

Kevin shared with Mark the details of his early morning phone call from Mary Gregory and their conversation at the hospital. "I had just left the business office and was headed toward the elevator when I heard someone say, 'That's Mr. Peterson, officers.' The next thing I knew, Lt. Jamison flashed a badge at me and said he wanted to ask me some questions. Then he said that he would be asking the questions at the police station. I thought I was under arrest, but I had no idea what they suspected me of doing. I have never been so scared as when they shoved me into the police car. I'm just thankful they didn't put handcuffs on me."

He stopped talking as Wanda approached the table with their lunches. "Thanks for coming to my rescue."

"You're welcome. It's all in a day's work," Mark answered.

Neither man spoke for a few minutes as they dug into their sandwiches.

"No one makes barbeque like Allman's," Mark murmured between bites. "Christine was awake when I went to see her this morning. I introduced myself as a friend of yours and prayed for her. Fortunately, I didn't mention that you were planning to drop in."

"Did she look any better today?"

Mark hesitated for a moment as he decided how to answer Kevin's question. He chose to be forthright. "Well, actually, I'd have to say that she looked rather worse than yesterday, although her coloring was better. She seemed more swollen, and she was clearly in pain."

Kevin grimaced at Mark's words. "I didn't think she could look worse than yesterday."

"The nurse said that it was normal, and the swelling should start to go down in another couple of days. The doctor will release her early next week if her pain is manageable and her head doesn't show signs of any more trauma."

"I don't know where she will go when they release her," Kevin sighed. "They told me she will need care for six weeks or so, depending on how quickly her bones knit back together, and I'm responsible for seeing that she gets it. I may have to pay for her to go to a rehabilitation facility. I don't know how I will be able to afford that."

"Is there anyone who can take care of her? What about her parents?" Mark's concern was genuine.

Kevin shared a little of Christine's background with Mark. "I don't know where she'll live after she's better. She certainly can't go back to Larry's house, given that he's been abusing her."

Even as Kevin was speaking, a plan was developing in Mark's mind. *What a wonderful opportunity to share God's love with these two hurting people*, he thought.

Aloud he said, "I have a couple of ideas that might pan out. Give me a day or two to see what I can come up with. In the meantime, worry will not make anything better."

~ ~ ~

After dinner that night, Mark gathered his wife in a warm embrace. "There's something I need to discuss with you," he told her.

Janet poured them each a cup of coffee, and the couple settled in their favorite easy chairs.

"How is Christine Peterson doing today?" Janet asked.

Mark loved that Janet knew him so well that she realized where the conversation was headed. He filled her in on his visit to the hospital and Kevin's ordeals.

"She's going to need a place to stay and a lot of help until she can get back on her feet, literally and figuratively."

"We have the space, and I'm certain our church members will help," Janet volunteered immediately.

"I was hoping you'd say that. I'd like you to meet her and extend the invitation. I think she will receive it better from a woman; from what Kevin has told me, she is not very trusting of men. Ultimately, it's Christine's decision, although I don't think she has any other viable options."

"We can go see her in the morning."

Mark stood and walked over to Janet's chair. He leaned down and clasped her face with both his hands.

"I'm a very blessed man to have such a wonderful wife," he told her before kissing her tenderly. Janet responded by kissing him back passionately. Mark pulled her out of the chair and up to bed.

Chapter 9

By the time Christine was released from the hospital, Mark Vinson's plan had been set in motion. Kevin had still not visited Christine, but as her "next of kin," the hospital had insisted that he check her out of the hospital. A very reluctant Kevin entered Mary Washington Hospital for the third time in less than a week at 9 a.m. Wednesday with Mark Vinson at his side. Kevin still did not know where they were taking Christine, but Mark had assured him that her care had been arranged.

As they walked down the corridor of the fourth floor toward Christine's room, Kevin steeled himself for his first conversation with Christine in more than a year. However, he only made it as far as the nurses' station before being stopped by a rather large black woman wearing navy nursing scrubs.

"You must be Mr. Peterson," she announced, as she stepped in front of him, effectively blocking him from continuing. "Good to see you again, Reverend." She smiled cheerfully at Mark, but her face bore a frown as she turned her gaze back to Kevin. "So, the errant husband finally makes an appearance."

"Ex-husband." Kevin tried to sound forceful without yelling.

"Ex-husband, is it? Well, husband or ex, I have orders to send you straight to accounting. Mary Gregory wants to see you. You have a bill to straighten out before Mrs. Peterson can be released."

Kevin exhaled a heavy, frustrated sigh and dropped his head in despair. Then he cast a glance at Mark. "I'd like to see this God you're always talking about make this bill disappear. I'll be paying on it for the rest of my life."

Mark laid a hand on Kevin's shoulder. "I serve a powerful God, my friend. Nothing is too big for Him to handle. You go ahead to accounting. I'll wait with Christine."

Mary Gregory was even more chipper than she had been on Kevin's previous visit.

"I didn't think it was possible."

"You didn't think what was possible?" Mary Gregory asked in her best oh-so-pleasant voice.

Kevin was startled by Mary Gregory's question. *Did I say that out loud?* He recovered quickly and replied honestly, "I didn't think it was possible to be so pleasant doing such an unpleasant job."

"Discussing financial arrangements with families under such trying conditions can be difficult, but I have so much to be grateful for that I can't help being happy."

Kevin wondered what she was talking about, but decided to let it go. He'd never known anyone so consistently cheerful, except for Mark Vinson. He wondered if there was a connection, but Mary Gregory was speaking again and he needed to pay attention.

"I have a few papers for you to sign before we can release your wife."

"Ex-wife." Kevin clenched his teeth to keep from yelling. He had no desire to be reprimanded again by Mary Gregory for raising his voice.

"Yes, of course, before we release Mrs. Peterson, I should have said. Now, if you will sign here," she pointed to an x, "and here."

"I'd better read this first," Kevin said firmly. He'd learned this lesson the hard way.

"Oh, that won't be necessary," Mary Gregory said gaily. "There's nothing disagreeable in these documents, I assure you."

Isn't this the same woman who chastised me about signing documents without reading them?

Kevin was in no mood to read all the fine print, and he was already in hock to them up to his neck, so it did not really matter at this point what the papers contained. He signed everywhere Mary Gregory pointed. After what seemed like a dozen signatures, she declared that he was through and gave him a release form to give to the nurse on the fourth floor.

Kevin thanked her. For what he wasn't sure, but he thanked her anyway and turned to leave.

"Just a minute, Mr. Peterson. You almost got away without this."

Mary Gregory held what appeared to be a check in her hand.

"Are you giving me money this time?" he asked, making a feeble attempt at joking.

"Just returning your $200 deposit." Mary Gregory handed him the very check he had written to the hospital a few days earlier.

"I don't understand." Kevin was completely bewildered.

"That's because you didn't read the papers you signed. You never know what you might be signing, if you don't read the fine print."

"But you told me..." Kevin's voice trailed off, as he saw the twinkle in Mary Gregory's eyes.

"Have a wonderful day, Mr. Peterson." He was almost out the door when she called after him, "And read those papers you signed."

Kevin made his second trip up to the fourth floor, this time with Christine's release firmly in his right hand. His left hand held the pile of papers Mary Gregory had given him. His footsteps slowed as he neared the door to her room. He could hear voices inside. Even though he normally frowned on eavesdropping, he paused at the door to listen before making his entrance.

"Pastor Vinson, I wanna thank you for doing this for me," he heard Christine say.

I wonder what Mark is doing for her. A stab of jealousy pierced Kevin's heart. *This is crazy*, he chided himself. Whatever Mark was doing for her was out of the goodness of his heart.

"Please call me Mark," the pastor replied. "And you don't need to keep thanking me. My wife and I are glad to help. God has blessed us, and we must bless others in return."

Kevin was thoroughly puzzled, but he decided that he should not delay his entrance any longer. He braced himself as he stepped into the room and found himself looking straight into Christine's deep blue eyes. For that half-second, all his anger at Christine disappeared and his heart stirred with the memory of how much he had once loved her. Then his eyes flitted across her face to the bruises now turning from purple to green that reminded him that they were caused by another man, a man who had shared her bed and her life in recent months—a man who had both impregnated her and beat her. His heart hardened and the smile that had almost formed disappeared as he regained control of his emotions.

"Hello, Christine." Even to his own ears, his voice sounded hollow and distant. He knew that Christine felt the coldness, too.

"Hello, Kevin. I suppose I should thank you for coming." Christine's voice was flat as she spoke.

"I wasn't given a choice."

Christine raised one eyebrow in question.

"They wouldn't let you go until I promised to take care of your medical bills." Venom flowed through his words, and Christine flinched as if she'd been slapped.

It was the effect Kevin had desired, but as he saw the hurt in her eyes, he rebuked himself for his actions. Christine had suffered enough lately, both from the accident and at the hands of the "goon," as Kevin had come to think of Larry Hardy.

Mark diffused the intense emotions coursing through the room. "Since they have released you, I think it time we get you out of here," he spoke kindly to Christine.

Kevin watched as a large male nursing assistant easily picked Christine up and gently placed her in the wheelchair held steady by the nurse Kevin had encountered earlier. Christine was dressed in a blue sleeveless sundress that hung loosely on her tiny frame; her shoulder-length auburn hair had been brushed back from her face and secured with two barrettes. Two vases of flowers had been loaded into the basket on the back of the wheelchair. She did not have a suitcase, or any other possessions, that Kevin could see.

"I'm ready; let's go," Christine said quietly.

The quartet left the room, with the nurse leading the way, Mark pushing Christine, and Kevin walking behind, feeling very much out of place.

~ ~ ~

The two men rode in silence, broken only when Mark indicated an upcoming turn. Kevin had met with several surprises already this morning, and there were more in store for him when the caravan reached the Vinson home. Mark felt it was best to allow Kevin a few quiet moments on the drive to absorb his shock. They were nearing the Battlefield Overlook neighborhood where Mark lived when Kevin finally gave voice to his most pressing questions.

"Where are we taking Christine? How much is this going to cost me? Why is Karen Harper here and helping with Christine? Who was the man with her?" The questions jumbled together as Kevin finally spit them out.

Mark indicated that Kevin should make a left-hand turn at the next intersection before answering. "We're taking Christine to my house. It will cost you nothing. Karen is helping because I asked for help and she volunteered. The gentleman with her is Greg Marshall; he is another member of my congregation who volunteered to help. My house is just ahead on the right. You'll recognize my new car in the driveway."

Kevin pulled into the driveway and cut the motor, but did not exit the car. He looked directly at Mark. "I need more information about what is going on."

"I know you do, and I will give it to you, but not right now. Right now, we are going to unload Christine and get her settled in. Then we'll talk."

Mark could sense that Kevin was not completely satisfied, but also that Kevin realized that he was right. They could not leave Christine sitting in Karen Harper's van while Kevin's curiosity was satisfied.

~ ~ ~

Kevin had been so surprised to see Karen help Mark and another man place Christine into the waiting gray van that he had completely forgotten his manners. He stood by stupefied and allowed the two men to gently lift Christine, while Karen held the wheelchair steady, then climbed in beside Christine, and strapped her in.

The man had seemed vaguely familiar to Kevin, but he had been unable to place the face. When Mark identified him as Greg Marshall, Kevin recalled that he was Karen's boss.

Kevin remembered meeting Greg at Karen's house on a snowy day last winter when Kevin and Karen were still dating. Karen had watched her boss's twin daughters for the day.

Kevin hopped out of his car and intercepted Greg before he opened the sliding side door of the van to unload Christine. He stuck out his hand.

"Hi, Greg. It's nice to see you again," he said automatically. "Thanks for your help."

Greg shook hands firmly and smiled back. "Glad to be of service. It's good to see you, too."

Kevin had the impression that Greg meant it.

Greg gently lifted Christine out of the van and into the wheelchair Mark had produced.

"*I should have done that,*" Kevin thought. Being around Christine had made him uncomfortable, but seeing Karen had immobilized him.

Within a few minutes, Christine was safely conveyed to the main floor guest room. Janet Vinson, whom Kevin had met at the dealership, arrived to make certain that their patient was comfortable and had everything she needed. Greg and Karen made a discrete departure, and Mark guided Kevin into the den for the promised explanation.

Mark and Kevin settled into the brown leather armchairs in Mark's office. "I suppose," Mark began, "that you are wondering why Christine is staying here."

"That's one of my many questions."

Before Mark could respond, Kevin gushed forth with a host of other questions. "What's up with the accounting department at the hospital? Why did the hospital give back my $200 deposit? What is going on here?"

"Well, let's start with why Christine is here. You seemed quite upset about having to come up with the money for her care during the recovery period. As a pastor, I naturally asked the Lord how my church could be of help to you. And the Lord impressed upon me that this was an opportunity for us to be Good Samaritans."

"Good what?" Kevin felt more confused than before.

"Have you ever heard the story of the Good Samaritan from the Bible?" Mark asked.

"I'm not very familiar with the Bible," Kevin answered, hesitantly at first. Then he decided to be completely honest with Mark. "My family never attended church. I don't recollect ever reading the Bible."

"That is, unfortunately, not all that uncommon in our nation. You should give it a try; the Bible is full of interesting stories as well as great wisdom."

~ ~ ~

Mark offered up a quick, silent prayer for wisdom to be able to tell the story in a way an unchurched car salesman could understand.

"Do you have any rivals you don't get along with?" he asked Kevin, fishing for someone to represent the Samaritan.

"If you mean rival car salesmen at other dealerships, no. There is a brotherhood among car salesmen, even competitors. We all know how tough it is to make a living in our business, and we respect each other."

"Hmm. Okay. That is nice to know, although it doesn't help me to make my point."

"If you want to know who my enemies are," Kevin ventured, "well, that's an easy question to answer. Eagles fans, Cowboys fans, and Giants fans, not necessarily in that order."

"So, you're a die-hard fan of the Washington Commanders."

"Of course. Aren't you?" Kevin eyed Mark suspiciously.

Mark had the distinct impression that if he said he was not a fan of the Washington football team that Kevin would remove Christine from his home immediately. Fortunately, Mark had cheered on the home team since moving to the area, and he quickly expressed his undying devotion to the team.

"Alright then. I'm going to tell you a parable, or rather a story, from the Bible, but I'll try to update it so you can relate to it."

"Suppose you are driving home late one night. Out near the Chancellorsville Battlefield, a carload of thugs forces you off the road. You smash your car into a tree and hit your head on the steering wheel. You are knocked unconscious. The thugs jump out of their car and, in a matter of minutes, steal everything of value, including your wallet and your cell phone. Then they race away into the night, leaving you for dead."

"After a few minutes, a doctor passes you on his way home. It's late and he's just come out of a ten-hour surgery in which he saved a man's life against all odds. The thugs didn't shut the passenger door tight, so the overhead light is on and the doctor can see someone slumped across the wheel. Ordinarily, he would stop and render assistance, but he is simply too tired. There's no cell phone signal at this spot, but he promises himself he will call 911 just as soon as he gets to a spot with a signal. He means well, but by the time he gets a signal, you are far from his thoughts."

"Another car passes by soon. The driver is a lawyer--a personal injury attorney. He slows down to assess the situation. Single car accident, no one else around, and no chance of a lawsuit. He decides that you are not his problem. He continues on his way."

"It's late and quiet. No other cars pass for a long time. It's one a.m. when the next car passes. The driver is a salesman from Philly—a major Eagles fan--who comes down to Culpeper on business about once a month. He'd driven into Fredericksburg to eat dinner and to catch a band at a local nightspot. The first thing he notices about the car on the side of the road is the big Commanders magnet. The second thing he notices is you slumped over. Without giving it a second thought, he pulls over and runs to the car. He checks your pulse. You're alive. He can see that you are injured from the large lump on your head and the blood running down your face. He tries the cell phone--no signal. He knows not to move an injured person, but he doesn't want to leave you while he goes for help. He decides to load you into his car and drive you to the nearest hospital, which happens to be back in Fredericksburg. Definitely out of his way, but what choice does he have? You need help and the quicker, the better."

"He gets you to Mary Washington Hospital and signs you in, giving them and the police as much information as possible. He pulls out his wallet and pays the hospital the $200 deposit they require to treat you. The doctors are optimistic that you will recover with your memory intact and that the police will be able to locate your family to take care of you. Just in case, the Eagles fan provides his name and address and offers to take care of your medical bills, if needed."

Mark paused for Kevin to absorb the story before asking, "Which of these men would you want for a friend?"

"The last guy, of course."

"Even though, as an Eagles fan, he is your sworn enemy." Mark's eyes twinkled, and Kevin chuckled with him.

"Jesus told the story of the Good Samaritan to illustrate a point. He had told his followers that they should love their neighbors as themselves. Someone asked him, 'Who are my neighbors?' This story was his answer. As followers of Christ, we are to follow his example and help those in need around us regardless of whether or not it is convenient, whether it will profit us or cost us, and whether they are friends or foes. In Jesus' version of this story, a Samaritan, that is a person from the region of Samaria, helped the injured man. Thus, the expression Good Samaritan."

"During our Sunday evening's church service, I shared your predicament with my congregation and asked for volunteers to assist Janet and me with caring for Christine. The response was overwhelming. Christine is welcome to stay here until she can get back on her feet. Pun intended. Members of the church will stay with her when Janet is at work and will provide meals, clothing, and whatever else she needs."

Mark had been talking for quite a while. He wanted to give Kevin a chance to absorb all that he had told him, so he excused himself from the room. He returned a few minutes later with two large glasses of cold lemonade.

"Is Karen a member of your congregation?" was the first question out of Kevin's mouth, asked even before Mark had regained his seat.

Mark had mentioned this earlier in the conversation, but a lot had transpired since.

"Yes. She became a member earlier this year. Greg Marshall is also a member. I should probably mention that Karen and Greg will be married in November."

Kevin's shock clearly showed on his face. "She certainly moved on quickly after me, didn't she? She was definitely shopping for a husband."

Mark decided to ignore the last comment and address Kevin's question. "Yes and no. I cautioned her to wait at least three months after your breakup before dating again, and she stuck to that. However, she and Greg had been good friends for quite a while. You might have been aware of Greg's involvement with Trevor as a male role model and father figure and that Karen frequently took care of Greg's daughters. Their families were bonding without them being consciously aware of the fact, although I must say the attraction was apparent to many outside observers. When the two did start dating in July, it did not take them long to realize that theirs was a match made in Heaven."

"Does Greg know about Karen's past?"

"Greg knows everything. Karen has repented, and God has forgiven her of her mistakes. Christians aren't perfect, Kevin. They make mistakes just like everyone else. The difference is that Christians have accepted Jesus' free gift of forgiveness and salvation. Greg accepts Karen as she is, a sinner saved by grace; a sinner whose sins have all been washed away."

~ ~ ~

The talk of sin and forgiveness was making Kevin uncomfortable, so he deliberately changed the subject. "Do you know anything about the hospital bill?"

"Yes."

Kevin waited for Mark to explain but after an awkward pause, he realized Mark was not going to offer an explanation.

"Will you tell me?"

"No. Not today. You've got quite enough to think about. Just know that the bill is no longer your responsibility."

"Did you pay the bill?"

"You obviously have no idea what a minister earns to ask that question." Mark smiled, even as he rolled his eyes. "My church did not pay the bill, either."

"Someone paid it."

"Yes, someone did pay it. Earlier today you said you wanted to see my God make the bill disappear. He had already arranged for the bill to be taken care of before you spoke those words. I do hope that you will acknowledge God's help and thank Him for it."

Kevin raised his eyebrows. "How do you know it was God's doing and not just a coincidence?"

"Have you ever had anyone mysteriously bail you out of a financial dilemma before?

"No, but still...why would God want to help me out?"

"He loves you, and He wants you to return his love. God sometimes does amazing things—miracles—to help us come face-to-face with His presence. God knows that when something happens that seemed impossible, we are more apt to acknowledge God's presence and His working in our lives."

"You said that someone paid the bill. So, are you saying that God "made" someone pay the bill?"

"Yes and no. God arranged circumstances so that someone decided to pay the bill for you."

"How?"

"God moves in mysterious ways. Why don't you just let it go for today?"

"Okay." Kevin was reluctant to move on, but he could see that pursuing this line of questioning was not going to get him any answers until Mark was ready to tell him, so he moved on. "What about Christine's care here? Her care is not your responsibility. I should at least pay for her food."

"I thought we covered that already. We—Janet, the church members, and I—are happy to help and to show you and Christine the love that God has shown us."

"That's kind of you, but I should do something," Kevin insisted, even as he asked himself why he was doing so. He could easily walk away from the situation and put Christine out of his life. *Why am I so anxious to be involved? Because I cannot walk away from my responsibilities and leave someone else to shoulder the burden. I think.*

"Since you persist, there are some things I would like you to do."

Here we go, thought Kevin. *He's going to ask me for a donation and probably twist my arm into joining his church.*

Mark drew a single sheet of paper from a folder on his desk and handed it to Kevin.

"This is a schedule of the times Janet and I will need help with caring for Christine. As you can see, we've had several women volunteer to sit with Christine, but we have some slots that haven't been filled. It would be a great help if you could tend to Christine on Mondays while Janet is at work."

Kevin looked at the schedule. "Nine a.m. until 4 p.m. is quite a long time frame. What if she needs help with…private matters?"

"Janet will take care of that before she leaves and whoever brings her lunch will help while she's here."

"What am I supposed to do while I'm here?"

"Talk to her, see that she takes her medicine, get her a drink when she's thirsty."

"Would I be here alone with Christine?"

"Most of the time, yes."

"I'm not comfortable with that. Christine and I do not get along since…the divorce."

"Of course, it might be awkward at first, but when you think about it, a few hours a week is not so bad. If we hadn't taken Christine in, you would have to arrange care for her 24 hours a day, 7 days a week."

"Are you trying to guilt me into agreeing?"

"If that's what it takes."

"Since I'll feel like a heel if I don't agree, you've talked me into it."

Mark was proving to have more backbone than Kevin had expected.

"We could also use your help for a few hours on Friday morning and Sunday morning. The ladies meet for Bible study on Fridays, and we all attend worship services on Sundays, so no one is available to be here with Christine."

"I guess I could do that," Kevin agreed.

"I've arranged for some of the men to help pack up Christine's belongings and move them into storage for the time being. I would like you to assist us."

Kevin eyed Mark questioningly. "We need you to identify Christine's things," Mark explained. "I don't think we can count on Larry to be of help in that regard."

"When will the move occur?" Kevin asked, knowing that he would also agree to this request if he were available.

"Tuesday morning. I knew it was one of your days off."

"Let me know where and when to meet you."

"Lastly, I would like you to contribute financially"

Here it comes. I knew there would be a donation involved.

"Christine needs to take some classes at the community college to improve her job skills. I'd like you to consider assisting her with the cost of tuition and books."

"What makes you think Christine wants to take college classes?

"I asked her."

"Oh." It had never occurred to Kevin while they were married that his wife had any ambitions beyond answering telephones in an office. Perhaps he should have asked her about her dreams. Kevin's conscience was pricked as he was reminded again that he had not been as perfect a husband as he had believed himself to be.

Despite his strong misgivings about spending so much time with Christine, much of it alone, Kevin had to admire Mark's cleverness. Mark had saved Kevin thousands, perhaps tens of thousands, of dollars by offering to care for Christine, without any strings attached. Yet, it was the lack of strings that led Kevin to insist on helping out. *That was exactly what Mark had counted on,* Kevin thought, *seeing as he was prepared with a list of ways I could help. I have to hand it to him. Mark may always be kind and cheerful, but he certainly is no doormat.*

Chapter 10

The ringing of his phone woke Kevin from a sound sleep. He knew without a doubt whose voice would greet him when he answered. Not wanting to ruin her 'surprise,' Kevin simply said "Hello" through a giant yawn.

His ears were assaulted with the off-key strains of his mother's voice singing, "Happy birthday to you. Happy birthday to you. Happy birthday, precious baby boy, Kevin. Happy birthday to you."

Kevin pretended to be both pleased and surprised. Marilyn Peterson telephoned her youngest child at precisely 7:16 a.m. each year on the anniversary of his birth, so it was only by exercising great restraint that Kevin was able to pull off the pretense of being caught completely off guard.

"Thank you, Mother. What a wonderful surprise," Kevin managed to say, as he did each year.

"I just called to wish my baby boy a happy birthday! Thirty-seven years ago today…" Kevin stopped listening but was careful to occasionally murmur "Yes, Mother," so as not to hurt her feelings. On her end of the line, in Sarasota, Florida, Marilyn droned on for several minutes, recounting in great detail the excruciatingly painful twelve-hour labor she had endured to bring her beautiful son into the world.

Being a dutiful and loving son, Kevin resisted the impulse to interrupt the saga and remind her that he had heard the story, in all its gory detail, on every one of his birthdays since the age of seven. Instead, he allowed her to continue until she was forced to stop for breath, and then he proceeded to thank her profusely for giving him life and for always being there for him. And since he was, indeed, a loving and grateful son, he had for many years ordered a bouquet of roses to be delivered to his mother on this special day. One rose for each year of his life.

When the tale of Kevin's arrival into the world had been fully told, Kevin steered the conversation to a less pleasant topic.

"Has the headstone for Grandmother's grave been delivered?" he asked gently.

His mother was still grieving the passing of her own mother in the spring.

"Yes, it was placed on the gravesite last Tuesday. Your father drove me over to the cemetery to put lilacs on her grave. Lilacs were her favorite, you know."

Kevin did know, of course. As his mother reminisced about his grandmother, Kevin pondered whether he should make mention of Christine's accident. His mother had never been overly fond of Christine. She would always believe that Christine had manipulated Kevin into marrying her, and she had been hurt that Kevin and Christine had foregone a large church wedding for a simple ceremony at the river. At least Kevin's parents had been invited to witness the nuptials, unlike Christine's mother.

When Kevin had informed his parents that his marriage was ending, Marilyn Peterson had responded with all the expected remarks about how sad it was and that she was only interested in Kevin's happiness. Kevin assured her that he and Christine had grown apart and that they were no longer compatible. He very carefully avoided any mention of the hurt Christine had inflicted on him. Marilyn would have never been able to forgive Christine for her infidelity, and despite all that had occurred, Kevin desired that his mother think well of the woman who had once shared his life.

In the end, Kevin decided that it would be best not to mention his ex-wife to his mother on his birthday. After a few more minutes, Frank Peterson took the phone to extend his own birthday wishes to Kevin.

"Your mother sent you a package in the mail. I got you something special, just from me. You won't be able to use it until November, however. Check your email. Bye."

Kevin hung up the phone and stretched his 6'3" frame across the bed. In a rare moment of introspection, he reflected on how lonely it was to spend one's birthday alone. He had no special woman in his life to greet him with a birthday kiss, bake him a cake, share a romantic birthday dinner with, or giggle with excitement as he opened the perfect gift that she had hidden from him for weeks.

When Kevin had begun dating Karen Harper last October, he had hoped that solitary birthdays and lonely holidays were behind him, but those hopes had not come to fruition. Karen had brought too much baggage into the relationship, and he was unable to trust her after she revealed that she had sought a divorce from her husband because she was in love with another man. Kevin had adopted a "once bitten, twice shy" philosophy after his marriage to Christine ended. He vowed never again to open his heart fully to a woman unless she had earned his complete trust.

Slowly Kevin pushed himself from the comfortable bed and prepared himself to face the day. And what a day he was facing. Today was his first day "caring" for Christine. Before he headed over to the Vinson home, a shower and breakfast were in order. And he would most certainly check his email. *What could Dad have sent?*

Chapter 11

Despite the unpleasantness of the task before him and the prospect of eating his birthday dinner alone, Kevin's disposition was cheerful as he made the twenty-five-minute drive from his home in Lake of the Woods into Fredericksburg. His father was responsible for Kevin's good humor. Kevin had opened the birthday email to find two tickets to the Washington/Dallas football game. Club level seats, no less. How his dad had scored those tickets, and at what price, Kevin would probably never know. Frank Peterson enjoyed his secrets. Kevin thought that he would ask Josh to accompany him to the game on the third Sunday in November. Unless Kevin happened to be dating a Commanders fan by then.

Kevin arrived at the Vinson's home at quarter to nine—fifteen minutes ahead of schedule. Janet let him in and informed him that Christine had eaten breakfast and was resting in the guest room. Janet gave him a quick tour of the main level of the house, showing him where to find anything she thought he might need.

"Christine took her antibiotics already, and she's had a pain pill. She can have another one after lunch if she needs it. She doesn't seem to be in as much pain today. Thursday and Friday were bad days, probably from being moved here from the hospital. She slept a lot over the weekend, and I think she is much improved this morning."

Kevin nodded and once again wondered what he had gotten himself into. Fortunately, Christine had a high pain tolerance, and she was never one to whine. Kevin assumed that her background had taught her to take life as it came without complaining.

"I've got to run. Emily Clark will be dropping off lunch for Christine and you around noon. Christine hasn't had much of an appetite. Try to coax her to eat; she needs the nutrients."

"I'll do my best," Kevin promised, and he truly meant it.

"Do you remember where her room is? Just down the hall, second door on the right. There's a list of emergency numbers on her nightstand and by the phone in the kitchen. Have a nice day. Bye." Janet was almost out the door when she turned and called out "Happy birthday!"

How in the world did she know it is my birthday? Kevin was so surprised that he nearly forgot to respond and wound up calling out a hasty "thanks" to the closing door.

The time had come for Kevin to face Christine. He was not looking forward to their first private encounter in several years. He rapped on the door and waited for her "come in" before entering. The shocked expression on her face left no doubt in Kevin's mind that she had not been forewarned of his visit.

"Hello, Christine." He hoped that his voice sounded devoid of animosity and didn't betray the butterflies in his stomach.

"Kevin! What are you doing here?" Christine tugged the bed covers up to her chin.

"I'm your nursemaid for the day." He strode into the room nonchalantly—he hoped—and took a seat in the chair next to the bed.

"You're kidding!" She looked from Kevin to the door and back, as though she fully expected Janet or Mark to appear and make Kevin leave.

"Afraid not." He stuck his long legs straight out in front of him and locked his hands behind his head. He hoped he looked relaxed, although he felt anything but that. "Look, I'm not crazy about the idea, either. Mark press...," Kevin's voice trailed off, as he stopped himself from saying "pressured." For some inexplicable reason, he did not want Christine to think that he was here against his will. She'd been through plenty in the last week, and Kevin saw no reason to cause her any more pain.

"Mark asked me to help out. There was no one else who could be here while Janet is at work. I have the time, so here I am. We might as well make the best of it."

Christine nodded her head meekly, refusing to meet Kevin's eyes. Her hands twisted the bedspread. Kevin knew that reaction-- Christine felt trapped. And, why wouldn't she? She had been brought to the home of strangers and had been taken care of for the past several days by people she'd never previously met. And then who shows up, but her ex-husband.

"Listen, Christine," Kevin tried again, more gently than before. "You're hurt, and you need help. I'm here. You might as well let me help."

"I guess so," Christine's quiet voice was little more than a whisper. Then she seemed to summon up some inner courage. She looked at Kevin and made an attempt to smile. "I do need the help. It's nice of you to come."

"Are they taking good care of you?"

Christine relaxed a little more. "Yes. The people are nice to me. But I feel kinda like I'm taking advantage of them. I don't even know them."

"They are good people, Christine, and they enjoy helping others. You are going to have to accept a lot of help until you get better."

"I know. I'm not used to people helping me without expecting something in return. Know what I mean?"

Kevin nodded while searching for something to say. It was going to be a long seven hours if they did not come up with a topic of conversation or some other distraction. He started to ask her how her job was going but quickly realized that she no longer had a job. He did not care enough to ask her about her family, and it was likely she had not spoken to her mother in some time. Did she have any hobbies? None that Kevin could remember, except cooking. Christine was a great cook and loved to try out new recipes. His mind wandered as he thought of the excellent meals he had enjoyed while they were married.

"How is life at the car dealership?"

Kevin jumped at Christine's question. Christine giggled. "Where were you just then?"

"I was trying to think of something to say. You startled me."

"No kidding. You jumped six inches off that chair."

"Yes, well, to answer your question, things are about the same at the car dealership. Josh gives me some competition for the top salesman, but I always win out."

"Of course."

63

Christine's bland response alerted Kevin that Christine still harbored some bitterness about the amount of time and energy he put into his job.

"Does Amy still work there?" Christine asked bluntly.

"Who?" Kevin was caught off guard by the question, and his mind raced to figure out to whom Christine was referring.

"Amy."

"Amy?" Kevin could think of only one Amy who had worked at the dealership. "Amy Adler?"

"I guess she's the one. She was working there when we split up."

"No. Amy only worked there a few months. She moved to North Carolina to manage a furniture store."

"Oh. Do you still talk to her?"

What's gotten into Christine? Kevin wondered. *She's never taken an interest in my relatives before.* "Occasionally. She got married a couple of years ago and had a baby last spring. She seems happy."

An awkward silence ensued. After several minutes Kevin broke the silence. "Do you want to watch television?"

"Uh, sure. But the television is in the den. You'll have to help me into the wheelchair."

Kevin looked from Christine to the wheelchair and back again.

"Have you been using the wheelchair already?"

"Yes, I use it to…to…to get to the bathroom. If you help me slide off the bed and into the chair, you could wheel me into the den."

"I know an easier way." Kevin lifted Christine off the bed, carefully supporting her broken limbs, and carried her into the den. He placed her gently in the overstuffed armchair and propped her legs on the large ottoman.

"Comfy?" he asked.

"Yes, but I could use a blanket."

Kevin handed her the remote control and returned to the bedroom to fetch a blanket. He covered Christine and settled himself on the couch on the other side of the room.

As Christine watched the morning talk shows, Kevin watched Christine. Christine's bruises had faded to a greenish hue and the swelling had gone down considerably. He wondered when the stitches would come out and how she would look. Kevin hoped that there would not be much scarring.

This isn't so bad, Kevin thought. This day might not turn out as badly as he had feared. He picked up a Sports Illustrated and happily occupied himself.

After Christine had watched "The View" and "Martha," she announced that she was tired of television and would like to go back to bed.

Kevin carried her back to her bed and arranged the coverlet over her. Christine had always been thin, but today she felt and looked even lighter than Kevin remembered. That was surprising given the extra weight from having two limbs in casts and the fact that she was pregnant.

Pregnant! The thought made bile rise in Kevin's throat. Why did he have to think of that? He was never going to survive several more hours alone with Christine. The opening of the front door halted the rising tide of discomfort.

"Hello," a voice called out.

"That must be our lunch," he told Christine.

"We're in the bedroom," he called out to the owner of the voice, whom he assumed to be Emily Clark.

His assumption was correct. Emily served lunch to the couple in the bedroom using TV trays as tables. Lunch consisted of homemade chicken salad sandwiches, pickles, grapes, and chocolate chip cookies still warm from the oven.

Her husband is one lucky man, Kevin thought as he savored the first bite of his sandwich.

Emily handed him a glass of lemonade, and he noticed the absence of a wedding ring. Kevin estimated that she was in her mid-twenties. *A little young for me, but then again, maybe not too young.*

"Do you attend Riverside church?" he asked, hoping to engage her in conversation so she would hang around for a few minutes. He was not anxious to be alone with Christine again just yet.

"Yes, I've been a member all my life." Emily smiled as she answered, and her smile lit up her whole face. "I hope you enjoy your lunch," she said to Christine. "Happy birthday, Kevin," she added and turned to leave the room.

"How did you know it's my birthday?" Kevin called out after her.

"Karen Harper told me." Emily popped her head back in the door.

"You know Karen?"

"I'm dating her brother Chad. Bye now."

So much for Emily as date potential. It was probably a bad idea anyway.

Kevin and Christine ate in silence for several minutes. It was Christine who broke the silence. "Happy birthday, Kevin. I've lost track of the days since the accident. I didn't realize it was today."

"You aren't required to remember my birthday anymore." The words came out with more bitterness than Kevin had intended.

Christine flinched as though she'd been slapped. "I'm sorry you have to spend your birthday with me," she said in the small, quiet voice that had always reminded Kevin of a wounded child. He realized suddenly that in many ways Christine was still the scared girl he had rescued from a life of abuse and poverty.

He was surprised when she spoke again, "I know there are many other things you would rather be doing today than sitting here with me."

Kevin did not respond. A truthful answer would only make Christine feel worse, and it was not like she'd asked for him to be here. He could not bring himself to lie, so he kept quiet and ate his lunch. An uncomfortable silence reigned for the rest of the meal. Kevin took their dishes to the kitchen and tried to think of some way to help the remaining hours pass more quickly. He found some board games on a shelf in the den. Christine liked Chinese checkers. Fortunately, it was among the games. The time passed quickly as they played several games.

"How do you know Mark?" Christine asked as Kevin was putting the game away.

"I sold him a car last month."

"He said you two are friends."

"I think Mark is friends with everyone. He was taking delivery of the car when the hospital called. He went to the hospital with me and has seen me through this whole ordeal. I don't know what I would have done if Mark hadn't been there for me this last week."

"Been there for you?" Christine was aghast. "You make it sound like you were the injured one. I'm the one who was in the car wreck."

"If you only knew what I've been through, thanks to you, since your accident. You need to rest. I'm going to watch some television." Kevin left the room before Christine could respond.

Kevin flipped mindlessly through the channels looking for anything to hold his interest. It seemed that there was nothing on daytime television worth watching. He was about to give up when he found the ESPN Classic channel. He peeked in on Christine a couple of times. She slept most of the afternoon.

The game he was watching was in the fourth quarter when the doorbell rang. Kevin looked at his watch. It was twenty minutes to three. Too early for his replacement. It was probably someone from the church dropping off more food. The doorbell rang again.

"Coming," he called out, tearing himself away from the football game on TV.

Kevin opened the door to find a forty-something woman wearing orange floral hospital scrubs.

"I'm the home health nurse. I'm here to see Christine Peterson."

Kevin let her in and showed her to Christine's room. Christine was still sleeping but stirred as the nurse called her name.

"I'm going to bathe her and check her injuries," the nurse told Kevin. "You can wait in another room until I'm finished."

"I'm thirsty," Karen said.

Kevin brought her a glass of apple juice, but he did not speak to her.

Kevin sat in the living room, while the nurse attended to Christine. He wondered if Mark had made arrangements for the nurse's visit. He wondered who was paying for her visits. *At least it's not me.*

On her way out forty-five minutes later, the nurse informed him that Christine's injuries were healing as expected.

"When will the stitches come out?" he inquired.

"She is scheduled to see the plastic surgeon on Thursday. He should take them out then. I'll be back on Wednesday. Take care of our patient."

Kevin noted that it was after 3:30 already. In less than thirty minutes, he could escape, having survived his first day of caring for Christine. He thought he should see if she needed anything, but he'd had enough unpleasantness for one day, so he flipped through the television channel looking for anything to capture his attention.

Janet and Mark arrived home within minutes of each other just before four. Kevin had planned to escape the moment the clock struck the hour signaling the end of his shift, but the Vinsons would not hear of it. Janet had planned a special dinner in honor of Kevin's birthday. Mark invited Kevin to keep him company on the expansive deck off the kitchen while he grilled steaks. Janet busied herself in the kitchen preparing baked potatoes, Caesar salad, and rolls.

"How was your day?" Mark asked tentatively.

"Not as bad as I expected, although…"

Mark eyed him questionably as Kevin's voice trailed off. "Although what?"

"Although she still knows how to get under my skin."

Kevin carried the platter of cooked beef to the table. He was surprised to see Christine already seated at the table in her wheelchair. Janet had obviously taken the time to help her dress for dinner. She was wearing a blue blouse that matched her eyes and a black wrap-around skirt. Her auburn hair had been brushed and make-up lessened the effects of the accident. She looked very much like the old Christine, so much so that Kevin forgot to breathe. He knew he was staring like a lovesick schoolboy, but he was powerless to turn away until Mark broke the spell.

"Let's pray and eat before the food gets cold."

The meal passed quickly as Mark and Janet shared the happenings of their day. Janet had purchased a carrot cake for dessert. Kevin passed on blowing out the candles.

As Kevin drove home, he reflected on his day. He decided that, all in all, it had been a satisfactory birthday. Tomorrow would bring challenges of its own; he would assist Mark and Chad in moving Christine's belongings out of Larry's house.

Chapter 12

The next morning Kevin met Mark in the parking lot of Riverside Christian Fellowship. Kevin wondered if Mark had chosen the site so that Kevin would become more familiar with the church. He kept anticipating that Mark would pressure him into joining the church, but so far Mark had made no such suggestion.

Another man was standing in the parking lot with Mark when Kevin arrived.

"Kevin, I'd like you to meet Chad Butler. Chad, this is Kevin Peterson."

Chad grinned broadly and extended his hand to grasp Kevin's. "It's nice to finally meet you. I've heard a lot about you." In answer to Kevin's questioning look, Chad continued, "Karen talked to me about your relationship."

"I hope you won't hold that against me," Kevin replied, in a tone he hoped was interpreted as only half-serious.

Chad chuckled and nodded affirmatively, "Not at all. You helped Karen more than you will ever know. She'd dated a couple of real jerks before you came along. She needed someone who would treat her with respect."

"Thanks," Kevin was pleased to know that Karen had spoken well of him.

"Shall we go?" Mark was climbing into the back of Chad's Dodge crew cab pickup.

Mark called out directions to Chad. Kevin realized that he had no idea where Christine had been living for the last year. When she had moved out of their home in Lake of the Woods, she had moved into an apartment paid for by Mike Sloan, the man she hoped to marry when she left Kevin. Six months later, Mike dumped her and she moved into a dingy apartment near the river with an old friend from high school. When the friend kicked her out to make room for her latest boyfriend, Karen had moved into a decrepit trailer in the Thornburg area. From there, Kevin assumed that she had moved in with Larry—not that Kevin was keeping track of her whereabouts. It was just that friends had a way of letting him know where she was and what was going on in her life.

Christine had been on a downhill spiral since she left him. "It serves her right," Kevin thought spitefully. "One of these days she'll realize how good she had it with me. Then she will regret leaving me and try to come crawling back."

Kevin felt the stabbing in his heart that was becoming all-too-familiar again. He knew she was never coming back, and, even if she did, he would not take her back. Would he? No, of course not. He'd learned the truth about Christine Miller the hard way. So, why did he feel like he was not completely free of her?

Chad stopped in front of a traditional colonial house in a newer neighborhood. Kevin had paid no attention to the area as they drove and was unsure where they were. The subdivision looked like every other neighborhood built during the height of the housing boom a few years earlier. An enterprising developer had bought a tract of land, cleared all the trees, and built eight houses on every acre. He probably sold them as fast as he got them on the market.

The house in question, Larry's house, was certainly a step up from Christine's other places of residence of late. Larry, however, had proven to be just another in a long line of sleazeballs Christine allowed into her life.

Kevin noticed a police cruiser parked in the driveway. He was surprised to see Lt. Jamison step from the car.

"I asked the lieutenant to meet us here," Mark explained, "in case Larry decides to give us any trouble."

"Will Larry be here?" Kevin had not considered that possibility.

"It is his house."

"He should be in jail." Kevin spit out the words angrily.

"Yes, he should be," Mark agreed. "Christine refuses to press charges. She insists that the bruises are from the accident and a fall she took a few days earlier. Without her testimony, there is no case against him."

"Let's get going," the lieutenant urged. "The sooner we get started, the sooner we get out of here."

The front door opened as they climbed the three steps to the covered porch. A large man, obviously Larry, stood in the doorway with his arms folded across his chest. He was easily six-five and probably weighed on the upside of two-fifty, Kevin figured. Larry seemed eager to play the bully, but one look at Lt. Jamison and he quickly stepped aside and allowed the foursome to enter.

Kevin had no desire to make Larry's acquaintance and apparently, Larry's feelings mirrored his own.

"Get her stuff and get out," he grunted at the group. "And make sure you don't take any of my stuff. If any of my stuff is missing, I'll have you arrested for stealing."

"Where are Christine's belongings?" Mark managed to ask before Larry stormed away.

"All over. You didn't think I was going to pack her stuff for you, did you?" Larry laughed, clearly delighting in being as obnoxious as possible.

Mark looked at Kevin. "She has a living room set I bought her on our fifth anniversary. And a bed and dresser Mike Sloan bought her when she left me. She took a couple of lamps. That's all the furniture I know of."

"Let's start in the living room and then move to the bedroom."

It took about an hour to pack up the bed, dresser, couch, love seat, and coffee table. Chad's truck was nearly packed to the hilt. He thought they should unload the furniture into the shed where it would be stored and come back for the rest, but Lt. Jamison believed it was best to take it all in one trip.

"We can fill up the back seat of the police car and tuck some stuff around the furniture. I don't think Larry will take kindly to us coming back."

They assumed all the woman's clothing, jewelry, and make-up were Christine's. They found a box of DVDs in the den; Kevin recognized most of them as ones Christine had taken when she moved out. Not even Kevin had any idea as to what other possessions Christine might own.

"I think we'd best just take these things and let Larry keep the rest," Chad offered.

"Surely she has some books and knickknacks, probably some kitchen items," Mark suggested.

"Maybe," Kevin said doubtfully. "She wasn't much of a reader, but she loved to cook. She's been moving around a lot, so she may not have acquired much. I think this is the best we are going to be able to do."

"Anyone hungry?" Chad asked as they packed the last items into the pickup. "Emily invited us over for lunch. You're welcome, too, Lieutenant."

Lt. Jamison begged off, but Mark and Kevin eagerly accepted the invitation. Lt. Jamison made arrangements with Mark to drop off the boxes and clothes loaded in his police car later in the day.

They were climbing back into Chad's pickup when Larry came out the front door carrying a cardboard box. "This is Christine's. I don't know what's in it. She brought it with her, and she never unpacked it." Larry handed the box to Mark and disappeared back inside his house.

"Well, you just never know, do you?" Mark placed the box on the back seat and climbed in beside it.

~ ~ ~

Chad phoned Emily to let her know they were on the way.

"That went surprisingly well," Kevin commented to Mark, as Chad chatted on his cell phone with Emily. "I expected Larry to give us a lot of grief. But he pretty much stayed out of our way."

"You can thank Lt. Jamison for Larry's cooperation."

"How so?"

"Lt. Jamison paid a visit to Hardy Construction last week. Let's just say it was a highly unpleasant experience for Larry, and I'm certain that he did not want a repeat performance."

"Repeat performance of what?" Chad had just ended his conversation with Emily.

"Of his encounter with Lt. Jamison," Mark told him.

"I've had my own encounter with Lt. Jamison," Kevin chimed in, "and I can vouch for how unpleasant he can be."

"Your visit to the jail was a picnic compared to what he put Larry through. I guess I have to tell the whole story." The smile on Mark's face informed the others that he did not find that particular task to be disagreeable.

"Lt. Jamison showed up at the construction office just after nine, when it was most likely to be busy. He brought two uniformed officers with him and what he claimed to be a warrant for Larry's arrest for assault and battery. Before Larry knew what was happening, he was handcuffed and shoved into the back seat of a police cruiser."

"I'd have paid to see that." Kevin was enjoying the visual of Larry being humiliated in front of his father and coworkers.

"By the time they arrived at the station, Larry's father had contacted a lawyer and was threatening to sue the entire city police force. Lt. Jamison was not intimidated by his threats and made it very clear that the jail inmates consider abusers to be scum. A man who would beat a pregnant woman would find jail a very miserable place. With the current charges of assault and battery, Larry was facing three to five years behind bars. If Christine would lose the baby, a voluntary manslaughter charge would be filed, adding up to another possible ten years. By the time the lieutenant was finished describing Larry's life behind bars, his father was willing to agree to anything to keep his son out of jail. That's why you no longer owe Mary Washington Hospital your life's savings, Kevin. Lt. Jamison also got Mr. Hardy to agree to pay for the home health nurse and all medical bills incurred during the pregnancy and delivery. Additionally, Larry has agreed to deposit $10,000 in a bank certificate to help with the child's college education, if Christine will allow him to sign away all custodial rights to the child."

Chad turned the truck into a grocery store parking lot. "Emily needs me to pick up a couple of things," he explained. "It's pretty amazing that Lt. Jamison got Larry's father to cough up the money. Still, I think Larry got off pretty easy."

"He did, and he knows it. Lt. Jamison threatened him with more repercussions if he didn't cooperate with us today."

Mark and Kevin waited in the truck while Chad went into the store.

"I saw quite a different side of Lt. Jamison today than the first time I met him," Kevin mused thoughtfully.

"That's because he thought you were the abuser that day. He told me that he goes after wife beaters with a special vehemence. His sister was married to a guy who beat her. She hid it from the family for a long time. Eventually, he hurt her so badly that she is permanently disfigured. He'll spend the rest of his life in jail, but the lieutenant's sister will never be whole. Lt. Jamison is on a mission to rescue as many women as possible from scum like Larry."

"If he really wants to protect women, he should lock Larry up. Guys like that don't change. He'll beat the next woman, too."

"I agree, and so does Lt. Jamison. Unfortunately, we cannot convince Christine to testify against him. There are no witnesses, and therefore, no case. Of course, Larry doesn't know that Christine is refusing to press charges. If he did, he wouldn't have paid the hospital bill."

"Maybe she'll change her mind."

"I doubt it. Lt. Jamison, Janet, and I have all tried our best to convince her that he is dangerous, but she won't even consider it. I'm not sure if she's afraid of repercussions from Mr. Hardy, or if she doesn't want the father of her child to be in jail."

Or maybe she really loves him. Kevin's stomach tightened into a knot. He reminded himself once again that he had no interest in Christine or what happened to her.

~ ~ ~

The three men arrived at Emily's bungalow tired and hungry from their morning's work. Emily greeted them at the front door with a big smile, along with a hug for Pastor Mark and a peck on the cheek for Chad.

"Right this way, gentlemen." Emily led the trio into her cozy kitchen. The table was set and glasses of iced tea awaited them. "I'm making meatloaf sandwiches. They'll be ready in about two minutes."

"It smells wonderful," Kevin commented. Four sandwiches stuffed with thick slabs of meatloaf and cheddar cheese were browning on the large griddle sitting on the counter.

The iced tea quickly disappeared. Emily set a bowl of red grapes on the table and refilled the glasses, while Chad put away the groceries.

Emily took a peek at the underside of the sandwiches. "I think they're ready."

In only a moment, the food was being served. Emily joined the three men at the table, and Mark asked the blessing. As they all savored the delicious sandwiches, the men filled Emily in on their morning.

"What will you do with Christine's furniture?" Emily asked Mark.

"Chris and Robin Jennings have offered to store it in their shed. We will take it over and unload it after we eat."

Kevin jumped up as he felt something soft rub against his leg.

"Oscar, stop bothering him," Emily scolded.

Kevin looked down into the face of the largest and fattest cat he had ever seen. The cat was grayish-blue except for his four white paws and a patch of white on his chest.

Kevin's face turned a deep crimson, but he joined in the hearty laughter around the table. He reached down and stroked the cat.

"I've never seen a cat this size. He must weigh twenty pounds."

"Closer to thirty. He's the laziest cat in the world," Emily told him matter-of-factly. "And he eats everything in sight. That's why he's so fat."

"It looks like he's good for something," Kevin commented, as he held up a dead mouse.

"Oscar! Not in the house. Bad cat!"

Oscar did not seem the least bit bothered by Emily's rebuke. He found a spot of sun, plopped down, and began to lick his paws. Kevin tossed Oscar's gift into the trash and headed to the bathroom to wash his hands.

Chad began clearing the table. "By the way, Emily, the deli was out of honey maple turkey. I bought you a pound of smoked turkey instead."

"But Felix doesn't like smoked turkey!" Emily admonished him.

Chad stopped midway between the table and the sink. He turned to Emily, still holding a pile of dirty dishes. "The turkey was for Felix?" he asked incredulously.

"Of course," Emily replied, seemingly unaware that anyone would find that surprising.

Chad set the dishes in the sink and walked back to the table where Emily and Mark still sat. Kevin returned from the bathroom and joined them.

"Who's Felix?" Kevin asked, taking his seat.

Emily smiled at Kevin. "Felix is my other cat. He's around here somewhere."

Emily looked around the kitchen. Not spying Felix, she rose to go in search of him.

"Not so fast, young lady." Chad stepped in front of Emily, effectively blocking her path. He stood a head taller than Emily and looked down at her, both hands on his hips. "Let me get this straight. You had me stop at the grocery store to buy fresh deli meat for your cat?"

Chad sounded a bit perturbed. Emily shrugged and nodded, all the while smiling coyly at Chad. Chad was not satisfied.

"Whoever heard of a cat eating honey maple turkey?" Chad continued his questioning.

"Felix likes it. He's a very finicky eater."

Chad could not believe his ears. "Honey maple turkey! For a cat, of all things! That stuff is nearly $12 a pound."

"I know," Emily tried to placate Chad. "But he doesn't eat that much. He hates cat food. It's not my fault that he's so picky." Emily smiled sweetly.

Chad was not buying the innocent act. He decided to interrogate the witness. He leaned down, so that his nose was nearly touching Emily's and asked, "How did you happen to discover Felix's preference for honey maple turkey?"

Emily chewed on her lower lip. She knew that Chad had her there. If she had not started giving him nibbles off her sandwiches, Felix would never have acquired this particular taste.

"Okay, I admit I let him try it." Chad crossed his arms over his chest, as if declaring victory in the argument. "But Felix has never liked cat food," Emily continued.

Mark and Kevin had quietly watched the interaction between the young couple, trying hard to stifle the laughter that threatened to spill out. Mark, however, was not ready to declare the conversation over, even if Chad was. He had some questions of his own, and it seemed as good a time as any to jump into the fray.

76

"How did you learn that Felix doesn't like cat food?" Mark asked.

"Well, you know how cats stick their face in their bowls to eat?" Emily asked.

She looked at Mark, and he nodded.

"Felix won't do that. As a kitten, he started picking up bits of food in his paws. He would take a tiny bite and fling the rest of it off his paws onto the walls. I got tired of cleaning cat food off the walls, but he needed to eat. So, I tried hand feeding him. Twice a day I would hold him in my lap and feed him his cat food. It was really disgusting." Emily wrinkled her nose for emphasis.

The three men murmured their agreement.

"One day I decided that I would rather feed him something more appetizing, so I gave him a bite of my sandwich. After that I would give him bites of whatever I was eating. Pretty soon he showed a definite preference for honey maple turkey. I've been buying it for him ever since."

As if on cue, Felix wandered into the kitchen. In sharp contrast to Oscar, Felix was a sleek Siamese cat. His body was light in color, while his face and extremities were a dark chocolate brown. He looked up at Emily and let out a loud, raspy yowl.

"What in the world was that?" exclaimed Mark, "I've never heard a cat make a noise like that."

"He's talking to me. That's his way of telling me he's ready for his lunch. He's not going to be happy to find out that Chad didn't buy him any honey maple turkey." Emily glared at Chad, and Felix yowled for emphasis.

Chad held up his hands and pled his innocence. "It's not my fault. I tried to buy the stuff; the store was out of it."

Chad walked over to the refrigerator. "I'm going to see if he will eat the smoked turkey," he announced.

"You can try, but I've never gotten him to eat it."

"Did you know you have a package of honey maple turkey in here?" Chad asked, as he poked around in the refrigerator.

"Yes, but that's several days old. Felix only likes fresh deli meat."

"Of course, he does." Chad's voice held more than a trace of sarcasm. "What are you planning to do with the 'old' turkey?"

"I'll eat it, or I'll feed it to Oscar. Oscar eats anything."

As Emily had predicted, Felix turned up his nose to both the smoked turkey and the past-its-prime honey maple turkey. Oscar finished the cat food in his bowl, then wandered over to Chad and happily ate both slices of meat that Felix had rejected. Full and happy, he curled up for a nap.

Felix, in contrast, was hungry and unhappy. He stood by Emily's chair looking up at her and let out a series of yowls. Emily offered him a bite of meatloaf. Hunger won out over persnicketiness, and he ate the offered food.

"We'd better get over to the Jennings and unload Christine's things," Mark said, rising from the table. "Thanks for lunch, Emily. It was delicious and most entertaining."

"You're welcome. I'd best go to the grocery store and buy some honey maple turkey for Felix."

Chapter 13

Mark was exhausted by the time Christine's furniture was safely stowed in the Jennings' storage shed. He wanted nothing more than to take a hot shower, eat supper, and climb into bed. He had a nagging suspicion that those plans would not come to pass, but he could not quite put his finger on the cause of the feeling until he turned onto Dogwood Avenue and spotted Greg Marshall's car parked by the curb in front of his house.

"That's it. Karen and Greg are coming over for their second counseling session. I suppose I can muster enough energy for that. Then dinner, shower, and bed in quick succession."

All such thoughts were banished as the reverend entered his front door and was assaulted by cries of "Pastor Mark. Pastor Mark." Mark found himself in the eager embraces of the Marshall twins and the youngest two Harper boys. With both hands full, he was unable to return their hugs.

"Here. Let me take those." Greg removed the two pots of deep rose-colored mums from Mark's raised hands.

"Thanks. Hi, kids." Mark gave each one an affectionate squeeze.

Janet appeared from the kitchen in a flour-covered apron. Mark kissed her gently before handing her the bag draped over his right wrist. "These are fresh tomatoes from Chris' garden. And he sent you a plant." Mark nodded in Greg's direction. "The other one is for Christine. I'm sorry I didn't remember Karen would be here. I'm sure he would have sent one for her as well."

"She's already received hers," Greg told him. "Chris sent in one for each of the ladies in the office with Robin this morning. The women were thrilled."

Janet relieved Greg of both plants and headed back into the kitchen.

Now that his hands were free, Mark shook hands with Greg and Trevor.

"Where is Karen?" he asked looking around.

"She's helping Christine get dressed for dinner."

Mark bent down to Brittany's level. "What a wonderful surprise to find you in my house. Are we having a party?" he teased.

"We're invited for dinner," she proudly announced.

"Wonderful," Mark told her. Although he was still sweaty and his muscles were sore from the day's exertion, the delight of having a house full of the children was re-energizing him.

"We made dessert," Bethany told him, blushing.

"I can't wait to eat it. Maybe we can eat dessert first tonight."

"Pastor Mark!" both girls reprimanded. "That's not allowed."

"Oh, alright. I guess I'll have to eat my dinner and save room for dessert."

Janet popped her head out of the kitchen. "Dinner will be ready in about twenty minutes, Mark. You have just enough time to take a shower. That's not a suggestion, by the way."

Mark came down the stairs, his hair still damp, to find dinner ready to be served. He took his place at the head of the table and surveyed the group seated around it. It had been a long time since ten people had crowded around their dinner table. The last time was probably four years ago. Janet's parents were still alive and had spent Thanksgiving with them. Jenny, the Vinson's only child, had flown in from California with her husband, their three children, and her mother-in-law. It had been a wonderful week. Sadly, Janet's parents had died within three months of each other the following year, and Jenny had decided that traveling over the holidays was too much hassle with three children. Since adding a fourth child to her family, Jenny's visits back East had become almost non-existent. Large family meals around this table were a thing of the past, which made nights like this especially gratifying.

Janet had prepared fried chicken and all the usual fixings. The freshly-picked sliced tomatoes were the perfect complement to the meal.

"How's the football team doing?" Mark asked Trevor between bites of chicken.

"Not too good. We're 1 and 3 right now."

"Trevor's doing outstanding, though," Greg supplied. "He sacked the quarterback last week and caused a fumble the week before."

"Trevor's the best one on the whole team," Brittany chimed in.

Karen beamed, and Greg looked shocked. A naturally shy child, Brittany never offered an opinion publicly without considerable prodding.

"I bet he is," Mark agreed.

Mark was once again struck by God's perfect planning. Putting these two hurting families together and using them to bring healing to each other was nothing short of a miracle in Mark's opinion. He breathed a silent prayer of gratitude to the awesome Lord he served.

Christine was quiet throughout the meal, although she politely and succinctly answered questions posed to her directly. Kyle Harper was particularly curious to know if her broken limbs hurt.

"They hurt a lot for the first few days, but they don't hurt at all now."

"Will it hurt when the doctor takes the casts off?"

"I don't think so, but I'm not sure. I've never had a cast before."

"How did you break them?"

"I wrecked my car."

"Is that how you hurt your face?"

"Yes."

"Do you have stitches?"

"Yes, under the bandages."

Mark noted that Christine answered each one of Kyle's questions patiently. It gave him hope that she would be patient with her own child. Kevin had shared a great deal of Christine's background with him, and he was very concerned about the lack of good role models in her life. He prayed that she would bond with Janet, Karen, and other women in the church who could mentor her in the role she would have thrust upon her in the spring.

After dinner, Trevor volunteered to help Janet with the cleanup. The younger children went into the den to play Chinese checkers with Christine. Mark took Karen and Greg into his office for their second pre-marital counseling session.

"How are things in the orthodontic office these days?" Mark asked the couple once they were comfortably settled on the overstuffed brown leather couch in his office.

"Work is fine, but everyone's personal lives are a bit hectic," Karen answered. "Jenna's wedding is Saturday, Katie's baby is due at Thanksgiving, we're planning our wedding, and Robin will be out for at least a week when Chris has his hernia surgery."

"That reminds me. I need to mark his surgery on my calendar. He told me the date, but I didn't write it down. I think he said it's scheduled for the last week of September."

"That sounds about right," Greg interjected. "Jenna will be on her honeymoon next week, and then Robin will be out for a week. Katie is going to stay home with her baby, so I need to start interviewing for a new hygienist. Right now, however, I've got an ad in the paper for someone to replace Karen."

"Replace me!" From the shocked look on Karen's face, Mark deduced that this was the first Greg had mentioned this news to her. "What do you mean, replace me?"

"Just what I said. I have to hire someone to replace you." Greg clearly did not have a clue as to what was going on in Karen's head.

"Are you firing me?" Karen's face was angry as she stared down at her husband-to-be.

Greg was puzzled by her reaction. "What? No! I'm marrying you. After we get married, you'll be staying home to take of the kids and the house."

"Do I have a say in that or are you laying down the law?"

It finally dawned on Greg that he had made a major blunder. He ran a hand through his hair, expelled a deep sigh, and tried to regroup. "I guess I just assumed you would want to stay home after we're married." His voice was so humble that Mark could almost see Karen's anger fleeing her.

"Oh." Karen's voice was barely audible. She gave Greg a weak smile. "It hadn't occurred to me to quit working. After all, I only work while the kids are at school."

"That is true, but taking care of a family of seven will be considerably more work than caring for four. I assumed that you would want to be free to chaperone field trips and have more time to work on your restoration projects."

"I hadn't thought of it before." Karen's tone was subdued. "I would like to be able to volunteer in their classrooms and go on field trips. And I definitely would like more time to work on my projects. I had been planning to talk to you about cutting back my schedule to three days a week."

Mark had been an unintentional observer of what he correctly assumed to be the couple's first spat. He felt the time had come for him to intervene.

"May I make a few observations here?" Mark waited until they both nodded their consent before proceeding.

"Greg, you had Karen's best interests at heart when you put the ad in the paper, but you failed in the communications department. You should have discussed your concerns before deciding to replace Karen. And Karen, you assumed that you would keep working without consulting Greg on his wishes. You've both been single parents for several years now. You've made family decisions without any input from a partner. That has to change now. You should confer with each other on every major, and many minor, decision. You will have to be partners in raising and disciplining the children, spending decisions, and a whole host of other issues that will arise every day. Greg, as the husband, you have to set the example."

"You're right. I was out of line to make a decision like that without even consulting you, Karen. Will you forgive me?"

"Of course." To prove she meant it, she leaned over and brushed a kiss across his lips. "Let's talk about it some more later and make a decision together."

Mark spent the rest of their session discussing the importance of managing their finances in a way that would accomplish their shared goals, yet allow each one some independent expenditures. Afterward, they joined Janet, Christine, and the children for dessert.

The Marshall-Harper clan had picked fresh peaches over the weekend, and Karen had helped the girls to make peach cobbler for dessert. Janet warmed the cobbler and served large bowlfuls topped with scoops of vanilla ice cream. Everyone declared it to be the best peach cobbler ever. Brittany and Bethany were quiet, but words were not needed. The big smiles on their faces let everyone know how happy the compliments made them.

Chapter 14

Kevin arrived at work at noon on Wednesday after having spent much of his two days off with Christine or in doing things for Christine. He was relieved and happy to be back in familiar territory. He looked forward to the satisfaction of making a sale.

"How was your birthday?" Josh asked him as he walked into the showroom.

Kevin's response was to pull out his father's email. Josh quickly scanned the sheet. "Tickets to the Dallas game! Now that's a great present! You are taking me, aren't you?"

"Is there anybody else?" Kevin grinned, delighted in being able to share his good fortune with his best friend.

"Thanks, man. I'm going to owe you big time."

"You're paying for the parking *and* the food."

"It's a deal."

Josh left to speak with a returning customer. Kevin went to his office to complete some paperwork. Soon Josh popped in and took a seat across the desk from Kevin.

"How was the, uh, um, babysitting?"

"Not as bad as I expected, but not the way I wanted to spend my birthday. Pastor Mark's wife made me a great birthday dinner, even considering that Christine was there."

"So, what did you two do all day?"

"Mostly I ignored her unless she needed something. She watched television all morning, and I read Sports Illustrated. I did play a board game with her for an hour. After that she wanted to talk, but I wasn't in a mood to listen, so I told her to take a nap while I watched some TV. Man, there is nothing on in the middle of the day. I finally found ESPN Classic and watched a replay of Super Bowl 22. That was a sweet game."

"Redskins over the Broncos 42 – 10," Josh chimed in. "That was sweet. Doug Williams was on fire. Greatest game in Redskin history. I will never get used to calling them the Commanders."

Kevin agreed with Josh's sentiment before changing the subject. "I met Larry yesterday. Well, met isn't the right word. I was at his house picking up Christine's stuff, and he was there. We didn't speak. I don't think he knew who I was."

"How did that go?"

"Larry was on his best behavior because we brought a cop with us. Hanging out with Mark and Chad was okay. They're nice guys. Chad's girlfriend made us lunch. She's a knockout. Too bad she's taken."

"Even if she weren't taken, you don't want to get mixed up with another religious type. She'd probably turn out to be another Karen."

"Karen's a real nice lady," Kevin snapped defensively, perhaps a bit too defensively.

Josh's eyes widened in surprise to Kevin's reaction. "You were singing a different tune a few months ago. As I recall, you said she was 'an adulterous hypocrite who couldn't be trusted.'"

"Yeah, alright. I know what I said." Kevin got up from his desk and walked over to the window. He stared out the window without speaking. Josh waited him out. Finally, he turned back to face Josh.

"I was hurting at the time. I said a lot of things that I didn't mean. When I found out she wanted to leave her husband for another man, I put her in the same category as Christine. Now that some time has passed, I can see that she's not like Christine at all. Her husband had cheated on her for years. He caused her a lot of pain. Then she met someone who made her feel special—someone who valued her. It's no wonder she fell for the other guy."

Josh was listening to him, but he said nothing.

Kevin leaned back against the window. "Chad is Karen's brother. He actually thanked me for treating Karen so well when we were dating. Can you believe it?"

"Yes. Yes, I can believe it." Josh stood up and jabbed his finger in Kevin's direction for effect. "Kevin, you've always been a gentleman where the ladies are concerned. You treated Karen like a queen. You showered her with gifts and took her to nice restaurants. You even spent a whole day playing in the snow with her children."

"True. I also put a lot of pressure on her to sleep with me."

"Only after you had been dating for months. By today's dating standards that almost qualifies you for sainthood."

"Not everyone thinks that way. I felt like scum when Chad said I had treated his sister better than any other man she had dated. At that moment, I was glad she said 'no'. I don't think I could have looked him in the eye otherwise."

"I don't know what has gotten into you. Man, you're changing. I think you're hanging around with that pastor and those church people too much." Josh opened the door to exit the office. "I liked the old Kevin better."

Kevin pondered Josh's words for several minutes. Kevin had always considered himself a gentleman and a nice guy. He treated everyone he met with kindness and respect, and he tried to always do the right thing. Since he met Mark Vinson, however, he had begun to see himself in a new light. While his morals were certainly higher than those of the guys he worked with, and light years ahead of goons like Larry Hardy and Mike Sloan, Kevin found himself lacking in comparison to Pastor Mark and Chad. He wished he could live up to their standards.

Kevin was pulled from his introspection by the appearance of Leonel Yantz in the showroom. Leonel was a repeat customer who had become a good friend over the years.

"Hey Kevin," Leonel shouted from across the showroom. "It's your lucky day." Leonel, never one to be shy about what he wanted, waved a check in his left hand. "I've come bearing money. Where's my car?"

Leonel had been toying with the idea of buying a Corvette for months. He'd first looked at it back in January and had planned to buy it when he got his tax refund. Before the refund arrived, his wife lost her job and the car purchase was tabled until their financial situation improved. He dropped by every few weeks to look at the Corvettes on the lot and drool over them. Last week he had spied a bright red one that had just arrived and vowed that it would be his, even if he had to rob a bank to get it. Kevin had not heard any reports of a local bank robbery, but Leonel had come into some money.

Kevin pointed across the showroom to the sports car. "It's right there waiting for you, my friend." He stuck out his right hand to shake Leonel's and grabbed the check with his left. "I'll hang on to that for you," Kevin joked. He was surprised to see that it would easily cover the cost of the Corvette.

In short order, Leonel had signed all the papers and endorsed the bank check to Kevin. Not wanting to give him any change back, Kevin had talked Leonel into a few extras. "That was too easy, Leonel. You didn't even make me work for my paycheck today."

"Easy come, easy go." Leonel was smiling like a kid in a candy store.

"Easy come? What did you do? Win the lottery?"

"Almost. Bianka got a great job that she loves. It pays twenty percent more than her old job. Then her grandmother died and left us a nice bit of change. Bianka said I could use half to buy the Corvette if I'd go on a cruise with her." Leonel looked none too pleased about going on a cruise. "What could I say?"

"Yeah, that's rough, man. I feel for you. Trapped on a ship with a couple of thousand beautiful women in bikinis and all the great food you can eat. I tell you what. You stay here and sell cars, and I'll take Bianka on the cruise."

Kevin's stomach started growling, informing him that it was time for his dinner break. His first thought was to see if Josh was free to grab a bite to eat with him. He hesitated as he remembered Josh's earlier comments. Josh must have been hungry, too, because he came looking for Kevin a moment later.

"Hey, buddy," he began hesitantly. "Listen, I'm sorry about what I said earlier. I'm just worried about you. You're spending so much time with Christine. I don't want to see you get hurt again."

"I appreciate that. A few times I felt myself getting drawn in by her. She can look so defenseless and vulnerable. I have to keep reminding myself of her true colors."

Josh nodded, and Kevin decided to put the incident behind him.

Chapter 15

The Friday morning women's Bible study group began to gather just before nine o'clock in the home of Donna Clark. Emily Clark had arrived thirty minutes earlier to assist her mother in arranging chairs in the spacious family room, brewing a pot of coffee, and setting out plates and cups on the dining room table.

Lark Nelson, the Bible study leader, was the first of the guests to arrive. Lark entered carrying her Bible, her leader's guide, and a basket of home-baked blueberry scones still warm from the oven.

"Robin won't be able to make it today," Lark told Donna and Emily. "Jenna, one of the dental hygienists she works with, is getting married tomorrow, and Robin is helping with the last-minute preparations."

"Robin did mention that last week," Donna replied, taking the basket from Lark. "Jenna is fortunate to have Robin's help. No one is better at wedding details than Robin."

Donna removed the red gingham dishtowel and placed the basket of scones at the head of the table. Emily placed the butter dish and a container of soft cream cheese near them.

"You're right," Lark agreed. "Robin is the best. I don't know if I would have survived Savanna's wedding without her help. At times I felt so frustrated I wanted to crawl into my bed and have a good cry. Then Robin would show up and the pieces would all come together perfectly."

Donna put her hand on Lark's arm. "I think it was a great role-changing experience for both of you. Being the big sister, you were used to coming to Robin's rescue. The wedding allowed Robin to come to your aid and to be seen in a whole new light in your eyes."

The women were soon joined by the other regular attendees of the Bible study. Gretchen Sullivan arrived with Lark's mother,

89

Ruth Shepherd, and a peach pie. Wanda Beach was right behind them with a bowl of watermelon balls. Kim Perez and Savanna McAfee, Lark's daughter, arrived with their babies in tow to the delight of everyone in attendance.

"Janet said she would be a bit late," Donna announced. "She has to wait with Christine until Kevin arrives. Let's bless the food and enjoy some of this bounty while we wait for her."

Everyone quieted down while Donna prayed. Her amen was followed almost immediately by the whistling of the teakettle, bringing a round of chuckles from the group of ladies. Emily filled a carafe with steaming water and carried it to the table, along with a basket of teabags.

The ladies had filled their cups and plates and were settled in the family room by the time Janet arrived. She fixed herself a cup of English breakfast tea and selected a scone and some watermelon, then joined the other women.

Gretchen was filling the group in on Karen and Greg's new home purchase. "They are supposed to close by the end of October. That will give them about two weeks to move Karen and her boys in before the wedding. Chris and Tom have arranged with the men's ministries to move Greg and the girls' belongings in after the reception. That way the girls can stay in the house while Greg and Karen are on their honeymoon."

"Will you and Tom stay at the house with them?" Wanda asked.

"No, Karen's parents will be there. I'm looking forward to having the time to get to know them better."

"Wanda, I'm glad you were able to get off today," Gretchen commented.

"Me, too. It's been a whole month since I had a Friday off." Wanda made it to the Bible study whenever she was scheduled to be off from her waitress job at Allman's Barbecue.

"How are you holding up?" Lark asked Janet who had taken the seat next to her.

"It's certainly challenging having another person in the house all the time," Janet said after a few moments. Lark got the impression she was taking extra care to choose the right words. "I'm glad that we can help Christine, and I'm especially grateful for all the help you all are providing, but…" Janet's voice trailed off.

Lark placed her hand gently on her friend's shoulder. "It must feel like Grand Central Station with so many people coming and going all day."

Tears pooled in Janet's eyes, even as she smiled at Lark. "Thanks for understanding."

"The couple of times I've been over, I've sensed that Christine is a hard person to get to know. I haven't been able to engage her in conversation at all."

"I know what you mean. She's polite and answers any questions I ask her, but she makes no attempt to get to know us at all. She never asks any questions or offers any information about herself. Of course, she has only been with us a little more than a week, and she was heavily medicated at first. I'm hopeful that she will begin to feel comfortable enough to let us befriend her."

"I think she could use some friends," Emily chimed in. "Has she had any visitors?"

"Only Kevin, and I think he only comes because Mark twisted his arm. I don't think she gets along with her mother, and she hasn't mentioned any other family members. She appears to be quite alone."

As the women finished their refreshments, Lark asked them to share their prayer requests. The group spent several minutes in prayer before turning their attention to their study. Janet asked God for Christine's and Kevin's salvation and Christine's healing. Lark prayed that God would give Janet and Mark wisdom as to how best to minister to Christine's needs. Silently, Lark committed herself to ensuring that Janet and Mark were provided with time to focus on one another.

~ ~ ~

Kevin looked at his watch. Ten minutes before eleven. His relief caregiver would be here any minute, and he could be on his way. Kevin had kept his guard up even more today than Monday. Josh was right; he had to be alert or Christine could ensnare him in her web again. She was looking particularly beautiful, now that the stitches were removed and her bruises had faded. Kevin had to continually remind himself that Christine had caused him far too much pain to ever let her get close again.

He sat beside her bed and played Chinese checkers with her, but he resisted all of her attempts to engage him in conversation. She had asked him about his job, his poker buddies, even football, but Kevin stayed true to his plan. He answered each question tersely, letting her know he was not visiting with her of his own accord.

Christine surprised Kevin when she announced that Mark had filled her in on Kevin's experiences at the hospital and the city jail. "I'm so sorry you've been dragged into my problems, Kevin."

Kevin had the impression that she was being sincere. A crack opened up in his protective armor. "It's alright," he mumbled. "I suppose it's not your fault. You didn't plan any of this."

"Of course not. I do feel terrible that you were almost arrested, though."

The crack closed, as Kevin was reminded once again of Larry and the trauma he had put Christine through.

"Not terrible enough to put the true culprit behind bars," he snapped.

Christine looked shocked and turned her head to face the opposite wall. Kevin began putting the game away.

Kevin was relieved to hear the front door open and close. Noises from the kitchen informed him that his replacement had brought lunch and was depositing it in the kitchen for the time being. Approaching footsteps signaled the end of his shift, as he had come to think of his forced visitations with Christine. Not a minute too soon, he thought.

Kevin watched the bedroom door eagerly, ready to make his escape. He was surprised to see Karen Harper walk through the door.

"Karen. What a pleasant surprise."

Kevin stood as she entered. *What a pleasant surprise? Where did that come from? I'm beginning to sound like Mark. Josh is right; I am spending too much time with these people.*

"Hi, Kevin. It's nice to see you, although it's not a surprise for me. I knew you'd be here." She stuck out her right hand to shake his.

Kevin accepted her hand and leaned forward to place a kiss on her cheek. That seemed to surprise her.

"Are you here to sit with Christine?" he asked.

"Yes. Hello, Christine." Karen smiled broadly at the other woman. "You're looking much better than when I saw you on Tuesday."

"Thank you. I got my stitches out yesterday."

"Did Janet style your hair today? It looks lovely."

"Yes. Thank you."

"I've got to go," Kevin said abruptly. He was having enough trouble ignoring Christine's beauty without having Karen point it out "Bye Christine. Good-bye Karen."

"Wait a sec, Kevin. I'll walk out with you." The two left the bedroom. "I brought you an apple pie. It's in the kitchen."

Apple pie had always been Kevin's favorite. He was touched that Karen remembered.

Karen held out the pie for Kevin to take. "It's a late birthday present. I hope you had a nice day."

"I did. Thank you."

As he turned to leave, he was hit with the realization of how much he missed having Karen Harper as a friend. They had become good friends chatting over the Internet before dating. He had assumed the friendship was over when the romance fizzled. This encounter presented an opportunity to rekindle their friendship. He searched his memory banks for something he could comment on to extend the brief conversation.

"Are you still refinishing furniture?" He hoped he did not sound desperate.

"Yes. It's turned into a small business." Karen's smile told him how much she appreciated him asking about her hobby.

"Isn't Friday your day to work on the furniture? You're giving up a lot of your free time to be here."

"Yes, but Christine needs help. And I'm only staying a few hours. It's a small sacrifice to help someone in need. I'm cutting back my days at the orthodontic office so that I will have more time to devote to the business."

"It's nice of you to help Christine." Kevin meant it. He did not know of any other women who would care for their ex-boyfriend's ex-wife. Then again, everything about this experience was new and strange to Kevin.

"Enough about me. How are you? How's the car business?"

"Great. I finally sold Leonel that Corvette."

"It's about time."

An awkward silence followed. Finally, Kevin mustered up the courage to say the words he knew he had to. "I heard you're getting married. Congratulations. I hope you'll be very happy."

"I will be." Karen smiled and laid a hand on Kevin's shoulder. "Greg is the person God had for me. I know He has someone special for you, too. I hope you find her soon."

"So do I."

Kevin felt the burden of loneliness heavy on his shoulders as he backed his car out of the Vinson's driveway. Inside that house were the only two women he had truly cared about romantically. One had rejected him cruelly, and the other had moved on to find her true love.

~ ~ ~

Karen fixed lunch for herself and Christine before returning to the guest room. As she approached the room, she heard talking. She assumed the voice belonged to Christine since she knew of no one else in the house, but she did not recognize the high squeaky pitch. Karen peered cautiously into the room before entering. What she saw made her laugh out loud.

Muffin, the Vinson's cocker spaniel, had climbed into the bed with Christine.
Christine was gently scratching the dog's neck with her one good hand. "You're such a good little girl, aren't you?" Christine was telling Muffin.

Karen's laughter startled Christine, so that she jerked and, in turn, startled Muffin. Muffin scrambled to the end of the bed and assessed the situation before deciding that all was well. She crawled back into Christine's lap.

"I brought lunch." Karen held a thick wedge of chicken pie in one hand and a glass of ice water in the other. "Shall I move Muffin out of the way so you can eat?"

"No, please leave her. I can manage."

Karen set the food on the nightstand and grabbed the bed tray from the floor. She arranged the food for Christine, and then went back to the kitchen to fetch her own lunch. She pulled up a chair near the bed.

"This is delicious," Christine told her. "Did you make it?"

"Yes, it's an old family recipe handed down from my grandmother to my mother to me. It was one of the first dishes my mother taught me to cook. It's very easy and quick. Soon I will teach Bethany and Brittany to make it."

"What was so funny when you walked in?"

"You. Well, actually your voice. Have you noticed that everyone's voice takes on a high-pitched tone when they talk to babies and pets?"

"Do they? I've never noticed that. Of course, I haven't spent much time around babies or pets in a long while." Christine's eyes took on a wistful, faraway look. Karen thought she caught a glimpse of regret in them. Not wanting to make Christine uncomfortable, she made no comment about it.

Both women seemed content to eat their lunches without speaking for a while. When Karen returned from putting their dishes in the kitchen, she felt she needed to say something to break the ice. Christine beat her to it.

"You and Kevin seem pretty cozy. How do you know each other?"

"We met on the Internet about a year ago." Karen answered truthfully without elaborating, hoping the answer would satisfy Christine. It did not.

"Friends or lovers?"

"Friends at first. Then we dated for a while. We were *never* lovers." Karen emphasized the last statement, feeling it was important for Christine to know the truth about their relationship.

Christine looked skeptical, but did not question Karen's integrity.

"I had heard he was seeing someone. I guess that was you."

"Yes."

95

"And now you're engaged to that guy you were here with the other day? What's his name?"

"Greg. Yes, we're engaged."

"You move pretty quick, don't you?"

Karen chose to ignore that last remark.

"We have another connection," she said instead. Christine looked interested, so Karen continued. "Mike Sloan. I met him on the Internet before I met Kevin. We dated for a year."

"I don't have to ask about that relationship. Mike wouldn't have hung around for a year if you weren't putting out."

"I've made a lot of mistakes. Getting involved with Mike Sloan was one. Unfortunately, it was not my worst one."

At that Christine raised her eyebrows in surprise, then nodded her head in agreement.

"I know what you mean. I wish getting involved with Mike was the biggest mistake of my life." She shrugged a little, as if to say, "Oh well, what can you do?"

"I'm so glad that God allows us to move beyond our mistakes and start anew. I got a new chance when I repented of my sins, my mistakes."

"You've done *what* with your mistakes?"

"Repented."

Christine looked puzzled. "What does that mean?

Karen recognized that God had provided her with an opening to share her faith with Christine. She was thankful that she was prepared. "To repent means to be sorry for the mistakes that you've made and to ask God to forgive you. When we do that, God does forgive and He gives us a new start. To be truly repentant, we have to turn away from our sin and try to live a better life with God's help."

"So, you said you're sorry and you got another chance?" Christine asked.

"Yes."

"Another chance at what?"

"At living a life pleasing to God, and another chance at happiness. After I repented, God brought Greg into my life."

"And your past mistakes, your past relationships, don't bother Greg?" Christine sounded skeptical.

"Oh, I'm sure Greg would have preferred that I didn't have skeletons in my closet, but he doesn't hold my past against me. He accepts me just as I am."

The conversation was interrupted by the ringing of the doorbell. The home health nurse had arrived to check up on Christine and to bathe her. After the nurse left, Christine took a nap and Karen had no further opportunity to speak with her. She was grateful for the seeds that had been planted in Christine's heart and prayed that God would allow them to take root.

Chapter 16

The following week passed quickly for Kevin. He visited Christine on Sunday morning before going to work, while Mark and Janet were at church. Kevin carried Christine to the recliner in the den, and they watch an old movie on television, eliminating the need for conversation.

The movie idea was so successful, to Kevin's way of thinking, that he stopped at a Red Box and rented two DVDs to watch on Monday. A visit from the home health nurse was sandwiched in between the movie viewings. By the time the second movie ended, Christine was ready for a nap. Shortly thereafter, Janet Vinson arrived home. Kevin filled her in on the day's activities and left quickly.

~ ~ ~

Janet popped a roast in the oven for dinner and brewed herself a cup of green tea. When Mark arrived home, he found her sipping tea and reading her Bible at the kitchen table. He leaned down and embraced her in a bear hug.

"Hello, Sweetheart." Mark traced kisses along his wife's neck. "Something smells wonderful. What's cooking?"

"I stopped at the grocery store and picked up a roast for dinner," Janet replied, as she stretched her neck to give Mark better access. "I should get started on the vegetables to go with it."

"I'll help."

Janet got out a bag of potatoes. "How about peeling six of them for me?"

"How is our patient today?" Mark asked as they worked.

"She was asleep when I got here. Kevin said they had watched a couple of DVDs. The nurse had come earlier. She told Kevin that Christine is progressing as expected."

"Is Kevin gone?"

"Yes. I invited him to stay for dinner, but he said something about it being poker night."

~ ~ ~

Chad and Emily dropped by after dinner. Chad wanted to show Mark the plans for a house he was renovating on Sophia Street. The men disappeared into Mark's study, leaving the ladies to visit in the living room.

"When is your baby due?" Emily asked Christine.

Janet eyed Christine apprehensively. So far Christine had not mentioned the baby, and Janet had been reluctant to broach the subject.

"I'm not sure," Christine answered hesitantly. "I think around the end of March."

"Are you feeling okay? Have you had any morning sickness? You don't look like you're showing yet. Are you starting to feel bigger?" Emily peppered Christine with questions.

Surprisingly, Christine did not seem to be bothered by Emily's curiosity. She answered, much to Janet's surprise, that she had not yet experienced morning sickness and that she did not feel pregnant yet. Of course, she was not sure what to expect.

Janet deftly changed the subject and inquired of Emily about her grandmother. Emily said that she was adjusting as well as could be expected to her new living quarters.

"My grandmother recently had to be put in a nursing home," she explained to Christine. "We avoided it for as long as we could. I moved back to Fredericksburg last spring to help take care of her. I live in her house. We had hoped that my being there would allow her to stay in her own home. She was doing well until she fell during the night on her way to the bathroom and broke her hip. Now she needs round-the-clock care."

Emily turned to Janet. "Her doctor has told us not to expect her to leave the nursing home. She seems to be going downhill pretty quickly since she's been there. That was hard for Mom to hear, but at least she has time to prepare herself for the inevitable."

"How old is Mrs. Heflin?" Janet asked.

"She turned 87 a few weeks ago."

"It's marvelous she was able to be on her own for so long," Janet told her.

"Yes, we feel very blessed that her health had been relatively good until her fall. Still, it will be hard to let her go when the time comes."

"Of course. It always is. The assurance that you will see her again in Heaven will make it easier, however."

"It certainly will," Emily agreed.

~ ~ ~

Christine wondered how they could know for certain that they would see Mrs. Heflin in Heaven. She supposed Mrs. Heflin had been a good person. Janet and Emily, and well, everyone she had met since coming to the Vinson's home, seemed to be good people. Of course, they would be welcomed in Heaven when they died. Christine had no such assurance. She was certain that there was no place in Heaven for someone like her.

Chapter 17

On Friday Kevin arrived at the house with another DVD in hand. By filling their time together with movies, Kevin was able to avoid any significant interaction with Christine. Kevin decided to bring a DVD to watch each time he came to sit with Christine. The plan went smoothly until the following Friday, when he was surprised upon his arrival to find a houseful of women.

Donna Clark's mother-in-law needed surgery, so Donna and her husband Bill, had gone to Abingdon to be with her. They would be gone for several weeks, depending on how the surgery went and how quickly the elder Mrs. Clark recovered. Janet had offered to host the Bible study while Donna was away. Unknown to anyone else, Janet was conducting an experiment of sorts. She was hoping that Christine would be drawn into the group by the love and camaraderie of the women and, ultimately, might be persuaded to join them in their study.

Most of the members of the study group were involved in assisting with Christine's care and had met her at least briefly. And while Christine seemed genuinely touched by their efforts on her behalf, she did not attempt to let any of them, other than Emily Clark, get to know her at all. Kim Perez had come by on Wednesday with her infant daughter to drop off a pecan pie. Kim proudly showed off her child to Christine, but Christine had shown little interest in the child and made no attempt to converse other than to succinctly answer the few questions Kim asked her.

Janet was bothered by Christine's lack of interaction with the baby.

"It isn't normal," Janet had told Mark at dinner that evening, "for a pregnant woman to have no interest in an infant. I was sure Christine would want to hold the baby, but she barely looked at her. I wonder if she even wants her baby."

"That's an insightful question, dear. She may not be sure about that herself, or perhaps she's afraid. This is her first child after all. And her mother is not around to help her through the experience."

Janet had latched on to Mark's words and committed herself to filling the role of surrogate mother to Christine.

"You know, Mark, I've been treating Christine as a guest in our home, when I should have been treating her as a member of the family. I thought that by not pressing her into conversation I was giving her the space she needs. Instead, I've been allowing her to keep us at arm's length. I'm going to repent right now and, beginning tomorrow, I'm going to start getting to know the real Christine."

Janet wisely realized she could not be everything that Christine needed. She prayed that the wonderful women of her church would also be able to penetrate the shell that Christine had around her heart and be able to provide Christine with the friendships and maternal love that was desperately missing in her life.

~ ~ ~

The ladies were meeting in the den, where the only television was located, so Kevin went back to playing board games with Christine in her room and trying to avoid any real conversation. Janet introduced the ladies who had not previously met Christine and Kevin, but otherwise, the group kept to themselves.

Kevin was content with the routine that had developed—old movie on TV on Sunday, DVDs on Monday, and games on Friday. Kevin told himself that he was valiantly keeping up his defenses and protecting his heart from opening up to Christine. The façade lasted only until the fourth Friday of his caregiving.

The day started innocently enough. Kevin greeted the women of the Bible study group as he entered the house. The women, in turn, insisted on serving coffee and cherry cobbler to Kevin and Christine. The friendliness of the women, along with the hot coffee and warm cobbler, broke down Kevin's defenses.

Kevin decided that he would put forth a little effort to be kinder to Christine. It couldn't hurt to converse with her so long as he avoided any personal topics, could it? Besides, he'd been dying to share his introduction to Felix and Oscar, Emily's cats, with someone. He thought Christine would appreciate the story.

Kevin set up the Parcheesi board on the TV tray next to Christine's bed.

"I met two fellas at Emily's house a couple of weeks ago that you would like," he commented as Christine took her turn.

"What's so special about them?" she asked warily.

"They're named Oscar and Felix, just like in that old sitcom. You know the one, don't you?" Kevin took a turn.

Christine stared blankly at Kevin, so he decided he should elaborate. "One guy was a total slob, and the other guy was a fussy, neat freak who drove everyone crazy."

"Right. I remember. It was called the 'Odd Couple'."

"Yes. These guys are just like them. The slob, Oscar, is fat and lazy and eats absolutely anything. Felix is the fussy one. He lets everyone know when he's unhappy, and he only eats honey maple turkey fresh from the deli."

"Stop teasing me. No one eats turkey for every meal." Christine caught Kevin's only free pawn and sent him back to the start.

Kevin failed to roll a five and was unable to move a pawn into play. "Felix does. Except for the day I met him, the deli was out of the turkey he likes. He was quite unhappy. He let out a loud yowl. I've never heard anything like it."

Christine rolled double fives and moved two pawns onto the board. "He yowled? What do you mean?"

"Yowled. Yelled, screamed, whatever."

"He yelled at Emily!"

"Not yelled. Yowled. He yowled at Emily, and he kept it up until Emily found another deli that had the turkey."

"Why did Emily have to buy him turkey?" She rolled again for her bonus turn.

"Because he's Emily's cat." Kevin enjoyed a chuckle at Christine's expense as he rolled the dice. A one and a three came up. Kevin still had no pawns on the board. Meanwhile, Christine had one pawn nearing home and two others on the board.

103

"Kevin!" Christine swatted Kevin on the arm as she scolded him. "They're cats! You really had me going." Then she joined Kevin in a good laugh.

"What kind of cats are they?" Christine wanted to know as their laughter subsided.

"I knew you would want to know so I asked Emily. I wrote it down so I wouldn't forget." Kevin pulled a slip of paper from his shirt pocket. "Felix is a chocolate point Siamese. He looks like those two cats from 'Lady and the Tramp.'"

"I remember them. They caused a lot of trouble and blamed it on Tramp."

"That's right. He's long and thin with large, pointed ears and slanted eyes. Oscar, on the other hand, is huge. His fat belly drags the ground when he walks. Emily says he weighs nearly thirty pounds."

"Thirty pounds!" Christine exclaimed. "That's as big as Muffin. I've never seen a cat that big."

"Funny that you should make that comparison. Emily says his breed is a RagaMuffin. He's a blue and white RagaMuffin."

"Is he really blue?"

"Well, I'd say he's more a silvery gray. He has white paws and a little patch of white on his chest."

"I won," Emily exclaimed, as she moved her last pawn into home.

"I was distracted," Kevin protested.

"You distracted yourself with all your talking. I'd love to see those cats."

"I'll ask Emily to bring them over. I don't think Mark and Janet would mind."

"Muffin might." While they played the game, Muffin had sat contentedly across Christine's legs. Christine pulled the dog into her lap and stroked her head. "What do you think, girl? Would you like a couple of cats to come over for a visit?"

"It would be funny to see Muffin's reaction to a cat that is bigger than she is."

Kevin heard the kitchen door open and close, signaling the end of his shift. The Bible study group would be breaking up soon.

"That's probably Karen coming for the afternoon shift," he told Christine.

Karen had prepared lunch the past few Fridays and stayed with Christine while Janet cleaned up from the Bible study and ate lunch with Mark, so Kevin naturally assumed that Karen would do so every Friday.

They heard the rustling of shopping bags in the kitchen, followed by footsteps in the hall.

The woman who appeared in Christine's room, however, was not Karen. Kevin recognized the petite, African-American woman and searched his memory banks for a name to put with the face.

"Hello, Kevin. It's nice to see you again. I don't know if you remember me."

Robin! The name popped into his head just as he stretched out his hand to shake the one she extended to him.

"Of course. It's nice to see you again, Robin. You watched Karen's children on Valentine's Day so that we could go out."

"That's right. Chris and I had a great time making pizza with the boys."

He had not made the connection between Robin and Chris, so he was thankful that she added that last bit of information.

"Have you met Christine yet? Christine, this is Robin Jennings. She works with Karen in Greg's orthodontic practice. Your belongings are stored in her shed until you get a place of your own."

"I haven't had the pleasure," Robin said, as she extended her arms to gently hug Christine. "I've been busy helping a friend with her wedding, and I made a quick trip last weekend to visit my granddaughter. I am delighted to be able to finally meet you."

Christine allowed Robin to embrace her. Just a few weeks ago, she would have shrunk away from such intimate contact with a total stranger, but it seemed to Kevin that Christine was getting accustomed to being hugged by everyone--man, woman, or child-- that she met from Riverside Christian Fellowship.

Kevin prepared to take his leave as the two women exchanged pleasantries.

"Not so fast, young man." Robin stopped him with her best 'mom' voice. "You're not going anywhere until you have lunch. I brought ham biscuits and potato salad."

~ ~ ~

Three ham biscuits and one large serving of potato salad later, Kevin was on his way to work.

Robin cleared the dishes and took them to the kitchen. She returned with a plate of brownies and two cups of coffee.

"Janet had some errands, so I'm going to stay with you for a while," Robin told Christine, as she placed the tray on the bedside table. She offered Christine a brownie.

"I think you've met some of my family. My sister Lark leads the Bible study."

"Lark is an unusual name," Christine remarked.

"Our father loved songbirds, so he named all his children for them. In addition to Lark and me, we have two brothers, named Jay and Finch, and a sister Wren."

Christine nodded but made no reply. Robin was determined to draw Christine into a conversation. "Would you tell me about your family? Do you have siblings?"

"I have a half-sister," Christine answered, without offering up much information.

Robin was not to be deterred. "Are you close to her?"

"No, not really. She lived with her father's parents a lot of the time when we were growing up. It's been a few years since I've seen her."

No use pursuing that avenue. Robin tried another approach. "I have a granddaughter, Nicole. She will turn one about the time your baby is due."

No comment from Christine.

"I understand that this will be your first child."

"Yes."

"How long were you married to Kevin?"

"Eleven years."

"If you don't mind me saying so, that's a long time to be married and not have children."

"Kevin can't father children."

"What do you mean? I can't father children!"

Robin's mouth flew open, and Christine cupped her good hand over hers. They turned in the direction of the voice and found Kevin standing in the doorway. His face was flushed, and he looked shocked, or maybe furious. Robin was not quite sure.

"Kevin, what are you doing here?" Christine stammered. "I mean, back here. I mean, you just left to go to work."

"Say what you mean, Christine," Kevin demanded, anger evident in each word. "You want to know what I'm doing eavesdropping on your private conversation. For your information, I wasn't spying on you two, although I'm sure you have plenty of interesting things to discuss. I just came back to get my reading glasses. I left them on the dresser." He nodded to his right.

The two women followed his glance and found the glasses to be right where he indicated.

"There they are. Take them and go." Christine's voice was stronger and more in control. Robin sensed that she was trying to intimidate Kevin to leave without forcing her to explain her statement.

"I asked you a question, and I want an answer." Kevin's voice left no doubt that he was not going to leave without a full explanation.

Christine stuck out her chin and folded her arms across her chest. "You can't father children. What part of that don't you understand?"

"Why would you say that?"

"We were married for eleven years, and you never got me pregnant." Christine seemed to feel that was sufficient evidence to prove her assertion.

"We were never trying to have a baby. You always insisted that you didn't want children and used birth control pills."

"I forgot to take them about half the time."

Robin was feeling trapped as an unwitting observer in the drama being played out by the former couple. She desperately wanted to escape the room, but Kevin was blocking the only exit.

Kevin seemed flustered by Christine's assertion, but he quickly regrouped. "Did you just now come to the conclusion I'm...I'm..." Kevin's voice trailed off, as he could not bring himself say the word.

"Sterile," Christine supplied. "No. I've known for years."

Kevin's glare informed Christine that she should continue her tale.

"I used to freak out whenever I forgot to take the pill. I just knew I would wind up pregnant, but I never did. After a while, I figured out that it wasn't going to happen and stopped worrying about it."

"You never shared any of that with me."

Christine shrugged, but said nothing.

"Why did you assume it was my fault?"

"I'd been pregnant before, so the problem had to be with you."

Christine made the announcement matter-of-factly, as though it was not a big deal. Robin could see that she did not realize what she had revealed. Robin took a deep breath before daring to look Kevin's way. Clearly, this last revelation was also news to him. He staggered back a step as though he'd been punched. He propped himself against the doorjamb and stared hard at Christine and then at the floor.

Christine took a nibble of a brownie. She apparently had nothing more to say, and it was a long while before Kevin trusted himself to speak. Robin silently prayed for the two of them.

Robin heard Kevin exhale deeply. When he finally spoke, his voice was measured and wary. "When were you pregnant, Christine?"

Christine stopped eating and looked at him. "Before I met you."

"When?"

"When I was fifteen."

Kevin shut his eyes and exhaled. Robin had to stop herself from gasping. *Fifteen! She was just a child.*

"Who was the father?" Kevin asked.

Robin was amazed by the gentleness and calm she heard in Kevin's voice.

Christine's voice was flat and emotionless as she answered. "His name was Craig. He was one of Momma's boyfriends."

"How did your mother's boyfriend happen to get you pregnant?"

Christine could not look at Kevin or Robin. She kept her eyes on her plate and stroked Muffin, as she quietly replied. "He would come on to me when Momma was at work, but I always told him to leave me alone. One day Momma caught me necking with a boy from the trailer park. She called me a slut--like she had any room to talk. We had a terrible fight. When she left for work, Craig said he wanted to 'comfort' me."

Christine's voice began to quiver as she relived the event so long hidden in the past. "I wanted to get even with Momma, so I let him. Just that one time. He moved out maybe a month later. I didn't know I was pregnant until after he was gone."

"You never told me this before," Kevin said gently.

"I never told anyone," Christine whispered. Robin had to strain to hear her.

"That guy should have gone to jail." Kevin's voice was hard with anger.

"It was my fault," Christine cried out defensively. "I wanted to hurt Momma, so I let him."

"Christine," Kevin's tone became tender again, as he tried to calm her, "you were a child. He was a grown man. What he did was wrong."

Christine did not answer. She sniffled, and Robin was sure she was fighting back tears.

Kevin did not speak for several seconds. He seemed to be processing all that Christine had revealed. Robin knew what thought was running through his head—Christine never told anyone she was pregnant.

His voice was firm but gentle when he next spoke. "What happened to the baby?"

Christine was quiet for such a long time that Robin was sure she was not going to answer. When she did speak, her words were halting, "I went to a place…a clinic…downtown. I told them I didn't have any money…I didn't want to have a baby. They took care of it."

This time Robin did gasp. Kevin, on the other hand, seemed to expect the response and handled it better than Robin. He walked over to the bed, sat down on the side, and pulled Christine close. At his touch, the tears began to flow. Kevin held her head to his chest and rocked her in his arms.

"You could have told me, Christine. You could have told me," he whispered over and over.

When Christine's tears stopped, Kevin released her and straightened up. "I've got to get to work. Are you alright?"

Christine nodded, but said nothing.

Kevin reached out his hand and ran his fingertips along her chin. "Don't think about it anymore. It's all in the past."

He cupped her face in both of his hands. "I really have to go. I'll see you on Sunday." He pressed his lips to her forehead before leaving.

When the women were alone again, Robin took a seat on the bed and patted Christine's arm.

"I know that was difficult for you. But it was good for you to talk about it. It's not healthy to keep everything bottled up inside."

Christine did not respond, so Robin continued.

"We have a support group at church for women who've been abused physically or sexually," she said gently. "Unfortunately, it's a common occurrence. It might be good for you to be able to talk to women who have experienced the kinds of things you have."

Christine shook her head no. "I don't know if I could do that. They might want to know about the baby. I couldn't tell them that."

"You wouldn't have to tell them you were pregnant. But, trust me, if you come, you will not be the only woman in the group or the church, for that matter, who's had an abortion. Every member of the church was a sinner before they got saved. Everyone has done things they regret. Jesus helps us to move beyond our mistakes and to live a fulfilling life. He wants you to be part of his family, Christine. He has a wonderful plan for your life, if you will just allow him to work in you."

"I'll think about it."

"And I'll pray about it."

Chapter 18

Tears stung Kevin's eyes as he steered his Jeep Cherokee through the subdivision. His stomach churned. He felt ill. As he neared the entrance, he pulled the car over and made a beeline for the drainage ditch. Back in the car, he dialed the number for Wilson Chevrolet and informed the sales manager that he was taking a sick day.

Then he dialed Mark Vinson's cell phone number. "It's Kevin. Can you meet with me?" he asked as soon as Mark answered. The two men arranged to meet at the Princess Anne Café.

Mark had secured a table and placed his lunch order by the time Kevin walked in. The waitress hurried over to take Kevin's order.

"Just a cup of coffee, please." In response to Mark's questioning look, he said, "My stomach is bothering a bit right now."

Kevin then launched into an abbreviated retelling of the events that had just transpired in the Vinson's guest room, pausing only when the waitress returned with Kevin's coffee and Mark's blue plate special.

"I'm ready to order," he told the waitress. "I'll have the special. It looks good."

"Got your appetite back?" Mark teased.

"Now that I've gotten that off my chest, I'm feeling better. Scum like Craig and Larry make me sick. They should both be in jail, but neither of them is because Christine is too weak to make them pay for their crimes."

Mark chewed his food thoroughly before replying. "Think about the situation from Christine's point of view. What would have happened if she told her mother about Craig? Do you honestly think she would have had Craig arrested?"

"No, probably not."

"At best, she might have kicked Craig out. More likely, she would have blamed Christine and punished her. She was a poor excuse for a mother, but at fifteen, Christine needed her and wasn't willing to risk further damage to their relationship. By the time Christine found out she was pregnant, Craig was out of the picture."

The waitress returned with Kevin's lunch. Suddenly ravenous, he dug into his food. Mark chuckled watching him, then continued with his analysis.

"I have a harder time understanding why she won't press charges against Larry."

Kevin swallowed. "I think she's trying to save her job."

"You can't be serious."

"I am. She mentioned that she was going to have to get back to work soon or that Mr. Hardy would replace her."

"When was that?"

"This morning. I think she plans to return to work and act like nothing is out of the ordinary."

"I'll have a talk with her. I discussed the situation with her a few weeks ago, but she was on a lot of pain meds at the time. She may not even remember us talking. Mr. Hardy was pretty clear that he never wants to lay eyes on her again. He acted as if Christine were out to get them. Of course, Larry wants nothing to do with her. But, even if they were to welcome her back, she'd have to be insane to work there again."

Kevin knew the pastor was correct; convincing Christine of that might be more difficult. "She's worked there for a long time, and it's the only real job she's ever had. There's not a chance that Mr. Hardy will give her a reference. She doesn't have a lot of skills. It's hard to make enough answering phones to pay the rent, much less buy food and everything else she will need."

"All the more reason for her to take some classes at the community college," Mark replied, reminding Kevin of his promise to help with her tuition. "She's taken care of for now. We'll deal with the job situation when she has recuperated. In the meantime, I will be praying that God will provide for her needs."

Mark's grin let Kevin know that he was reminding him of God's provision for the hospital bill. Kevin should probably thank God for that, but he was not exactly sure how to go about it.

Over hot fudge sundaes, Mark dropped another bombshell on Kevin. "Christine needs to see a counselor," Mark stated assuredly.

"What kind of a counselor?" Kevin asked. The only counselors he could think of were school counselors and marriage counselors; neither of them could help Christine at this point in her life.

"A Christian mental health counselor."

"You think Christine is crazy?"

"No, of course not. I think Christine suffers from low self-esteem. She comes from a dysfunctional family where she learned to equate love with physical desires. She doesn't know how to truly love or accept love. Her mother's example taught her that a woman needs to be in a relationship with a man, even if he mistreats her. Christine will never be able to maintain a healthy, loving relationship until she learns to value herself and realizes that she deserves to be loved."

"A counselor can raise her self-esteem?" Kevin was skeptical.

"A counselor can help," Mark assured him. "Getting acquainted with God will help, too. When we realize how much God loves us, we can't help but feel valuable. Christine needs to hear God's Word and get to know Him personally."

Kevin looked doubtful; he continued eating without responding.

"Christine will be attending church with us this Sunday morning, so you won't need to stay with her. You can visit her in the evening, if you like."

That comment generated a response from Kevin. "Christine is going to church? Voluntarily?"

"She doesn't know it yet. I'll inform her tomorrow."

"She won't go."

"Oh, she'll go alright."

"Would you like to bet on it?" Kevin was confident that this would be easy money.

"A bet, umm. I'm not a wagering man. However, I think I might just take you up on it. No money will be involved, of course."

Kevin thought a bet had to involve money, but he did not want Mark to know that. "Of course," he agreed. *I wonder what is involved in this bet?*

"Here's the deal," Mark told him. "If Christine goes to church this Sunday, then you have to attend the following Sunday."

"I'm scheduled to work that day. I could probably arrange to be off another Sunday in a few weeks." *What have I just agreed to?*

"That's fine. If she doesn't go, then I'll..." Mark's voice dropped off as he tried to think of a comparable sacrifice.

"You'll play golf with me on Monday," Kevin declared.

"Golf! I'm terrible at golf."

"Good. I'm not."

"Fine. It doesn't matter what I agree to, anyway," Mark assured him. "This is one bet I'm sure to win." Kevin was having the same thought.

~ ~ ~

After the dinner dishes were cleaned up and Christine was settled in the large comfortable recliner in the den watching television, Mark asked Janet to take a walk with him.

"What's on your mind?" Janet asked, before they reached the end of the driveway.

He looked at her quizzically. "Does it show that much?"

"I doubt Christine noticed, but I certainly did. Christine seemed to be in another world at dinner, also. If I didn't know better, I would have thought that the two of you were keeping something from me."

"In a way, we were." Mark reached out to take hold of Janet's hand. "I had lunch with Kevin. Christine revealed some long-held, dark secrets today. Kevin interrupted a conversation she was having with Robin and demanded that she tell him the whole story. Christine is carrying more baggage than even Kevin was aware of. She's tried to handle things on her own, when she should have been in counseling. I suspect past hurts and abuses have caused her to make self-destructive choices."

"The kind of choices that destroyed her marriage and led her into a relationship with Larry." Janet's remark was more of a statement than a question.

"Exactly."

"Can you elaborate?" Janet was Mark's closest friend and confidante; however, she recognized that there were times when parishioners confided to Mark private things that he could share with no one, including his wife. She had learned to give Mark space to share what he could and to be understanding about the secrets he had to keep.

"I'm sure Kevin wouldn't object. It's not exactly a secret any longer. Robin witnessed the drama, although we can trust her to be discreet. I should speak with her soon to get her reaction."

The couple walked around the block three times while Mark shared Kevin's story with Janet.

When he was done, Janet's heart was as heavy as his own. "Christine needs a woman to talk to. How about turning the counseling over to me this time?"

Mark felt a big burden lift from his shoulders. He knew Janet could help Christine far more than he could. "Thanks," he said, as he gave her shoulder a gentle squeeze.

Chapter 19

Karen Harper invited Christine to spend Saturday at her house with the Marshall twins, Gretchen Sullivan, and Robin Jennings for a 'girls' day. Greg Marshall, Tom Sullivan, and Chris Jennings were chaperoning a father-son campout sponsored by the men's ministry at their church. They had picked up the three Harper boys after school on Friday and would return mid-afternoon on Sunday. The three men had been nearly as excited as the boys when they departed.

Gretchen and Robin picked up Christine on their way to Karen's house. The two girls were already there, having spent Friday night with their soon-to-be new mother. The women were planning to bake cookies, work on Christmas crafts, and primp. Bethany and Brittany had picked out a new nail polish and wanted their fingernails and toenails painted. Christine was thrilled to be invited as Robin promised her a pedicure, and Gretchen was going to cut her hair and add highlights. The women were on a mission to show God's love to Christine and to demonstrate how much fun they could have without compromising their values.

The Vinsons were delighted by the arrangements. They hoped that the more time Christine spent with those wonderful women, the more she would come to know and trust them. Christine's exterior had been toughened by years of abuse and betrayal—penetrating it would take more than just prayer. It would require a significant investment of time to show Christine what true friendship involved and allow her to see the love of Christ in their lives.

~ ~ ~

As soon as Christine was out of the house, Mark and Janet hopped in their car for some much-needed 'couple' time without any distractions. Mark set his cell phone on vibrate, and Janet turned hers off altogether. They both strongly believed that their long and happy marriage had prospered in part because they regularly made time to be alone as a couple and to share their innermost thoughts and feelings. Mark and Janet took advantage of their first free day since allowing Christine to move in to drive to the Shenandoah Valley and pick apples. Late September was the optimal time for picking a wide variety of apples for eating, cooking, and baking.

"I'd like Christine to attend church with us tomorrow," Mark stated before the car was completely out of the driveway.

"You would like it or you are demanding it?" Janet questioned.

"Christine is living under our roof for the present time, and under the circumstances, she has to adapt to our rules. And one of my rules is that everyone who resides under my roof goes to church every Sunday."

Janet had known exactly what Mark was going to say and struggled to remain quiet until he was finished. While Janet certainly wished that everyone attended church regularly, she did not agree with Mark in forcing someone to attend who did not want to be there. Mark's stubborn adherence to his number one rule had served to drive a wedge between the couple and their daughter during her teenage years, the effects of which they were still feeling all these years later.

Jenny had cheerfully been in church every time the doors opened until her senior year of high school. That year she started working part-time as a waitress at a local restaurant. She often worked late on Saturday nights and was exhausted on Sunday mornings. She pleaded with her father to be allowed to sleep in and skip the morning worship service with the provision that she would be present at the evening prayer service and the Wednesday night Bible study.

Mark had taken a hard stance. "A preacher's child has to set an example for other young people in the church through her actions and by regular church attendance."

Mark firmly believed that if he allowed Jenny to skip the Sunday morning service, soon other young people in the church would be missing services for less noble reasons. It was a sacrifice on Jenny's part to get by with less sleep on Saturday night, but one he felt she should willingly make. And if not willing, well, the sacrifice had to be made anyway.

Jenny, always a compliant child, went to the services, but Janet sensed a change taking place in her heart. The change was subtle at first and went unnoticed by Mark. Jenny loved to sing, particularly praise songs. Her melodic voice carried through the house as she worked on homework or did her chores. Within a few weeks of the confrontation over church attendance, Janet began to notice that Jenny was singing less frequently and with less enthusiasm, until after a few months she ceased singing altogether. At church, Jenny appeared to her mother to merely be going through the motions of following along in the Bible during her father's sermons. Although she stood during the singing of hymns, she typically had her arms folded across her chest and made no effort to join in.

As the year progressed, Janet noticed that Jenny volunteered to work in the nursery or to teach children's church nearly every Sunday. When she mentioned this to Mark, he interpreted it as a sign that she was eager to serve wherever she could. Janet, on the other hand, saw Jenny's service as a way to avoid listening to her father's sermons.

By the time graduation rolled around, Jenny had given up all appearance of being at church willingly. Members of the congregation began to comment to Janet about Jenny's behavior. Janet pleaded with Mark to stop forcing Jenny to come to church. Janet believed that Jenny's attitude was having a negative impact on younger children in the church. Mark would not hear of it; she still lived under his roof and she would attend church, even if it made her miserable. It was one of the few times in their role as parents that Mark and Janet had been divided.

Janet had been secretly relieved when it was time for Jenny to go away to college. The stress caused by the tension between her husband and her only child had become unbearable. Jenny chose a college as far from home as possible—Pepperdine University in Malibu, California. Mark was thrilled that Jenny had chosen a Christian college and elected to major in social work. He took the decision as further evidence of her commitment to serve the Lord through helping others. Conversely, Janet recognized that Jenny knew her father would only support her decision to move all the way across the country if she were enrolled in a Christian college.

Janet feared that the physical distance between them reflected the growing differences in Jenny's beliefs and their own. Her fears were reinforced during the two visits home that Jenny made during her freshman year. Jenny came home for a month at Christmas and a week at the close of the school year. She announced then that she had a job lined up in Malibu and would be spending the summer there. Mark insisted that Jenny attend church the one Sunday she was home and Jenny complied, although Janet could see that she was going merely to avoid a confrontation with her father.

Janet's worst fears were validated when Jenny announced at the end of her sophomore year that she was getting married to Peter MacKenzie. Peter had no use for religion, believing it to be a crutch of the weak and the weak-minded. He valued achievement, success, and individual freedom to choose the values that fit one's lifestyle and preferences. Consequently, now that Jenny and Peter had a family of their own, their children attended church only when Jenny brought them for a visit with Pappy and Memaw. Those visits were becoming increasingly infrequent.

"You're quiet," Mark commented, drawing Janet from her moment of reflection.

"I'm sorry. I was thinking about Jenny. I feel like we did her a disservice by forcing her to go to church when she needed her rest."

"You mean *I* did her a disservice. It was me who insisted that she get up and go to church. I know that you disagreed with me, but I still think it was the right thing to do."

"And I still disagree. But what's done is done. I just don't want to risk turning Christine away from God by insisting that she go to church if she doesn't want to."

Mark reached over and patted Janet's hand. "Perhaps you're right. We'll offer to take her and if she doesn't agree, I promise to let it go for now."

"Thank you." Janet rewarded him with a big smile.

The rest of the drive passed pleasantly with no more tension between the couple. The sun was high in the sky by the time they arrived at the apple orchard in Markham. Mark stopped at the entrance for sturdy bushel bags and a picking pole.

"Would you like a map of the orchard?" the attendant asked Mark.

"Thanks, but we have one."

"We'll take another one, please," Janet interjected before Mark could drive away without one.

Mark accepted the map and headed off to the right, as Janet directed him to the trees bearing Granny Smiths.

"I've written our plan for the day on this map," Janet explained. "I'll need another one to plan out our trip next year."

"I should have known," Mark teased.

Janet was an organizer by nature and, true to form, had planned out how many of each type of apple they would pick and knew just where those apples were to be found.

They began by picking a full bushel of Granny Smiths. Granny Smiths were the best apples for frying; they also made the best apple butter, in Janet's opinion. As he plucked apples from the tree using the picking pole, Mark envisioned them sizzling in a sea of melted butter in the big skillet. He was certain that he would awaken to the wonderful aroma of cinnamon and brown sugar in the morning, as a special reward for his hard work today. If he were especially fortunate, Janet would fry up a pan with dinner tonight. After all, fried apples were not just for breakfast. Within the next several days, Janet would cook all of the Granny Smith apples and can most of them to be enjoyed all winter long.

Next on Janet's list were Galas and Fujis; these were the couple's favorite varieties for snacking. Then they were off to gather some Stayman's. Like the Granny Smiths, most of these would be prepared for storage in the coming week. The Stayman's, however, would be made into applesauce and frozen until needed. The Vinsons ended by picking Yorks for baking into pies. The sweet apples stored well and actually got sweeter in storage.

"That's it," Janet told Mark, as he loaded the Staymans into the trunk of the car.

"It's a good thing, because I'm beat and starving," Mark responded.

"I don't know how you could be starving. I've seen you eat at least three apples."

Janet's teasing reprimand notwithstanding, it was time for lunch. They purchased hot dogs, chips, and sodas from the concession stand. The country store had a nice selection of locally-made jellies, as well as syrup made on the premises. Janet bought jars of blackberry and raspberry preserves and canned peaches. The peaches would become bubbling cobblers.

"I need to buy red and yellow delicious apples for Marge Carter," she told Mark. "She is going to use them in the meals for the homeless this week."

Riverside Christian Fellowship participated with other local churches in providing meals to homeless persons in the area. Seven teams, made up of volunteers of one or more churches, prepared and delivered meals every night of the week. Marge led a group made up of members of Riverside and First Methodist. Marge liked to include fresh fruit with the meals whenever possible.

Mark loaded the apples into the car while Janet paid for all their purchases. While he was grateful that his work was done, he knew that Janet's had just begun. She would spend countless hours in the coming week preparing, canning, and freezing the fruit. Mark marveled that she actually seemed to look forward to picking apples each fall.

~ ~ ~

Mark and Janet returned home in the late afternoon with their apples to find that Christine was still out of the house. Janet set about making an apple pie for dessert and a batch of apple sauce for the freezer, while Mark mowed the yard. It was nearly dinner time before Gretchen and Robin dropped Christine off.

"Your hair looks wonderful," Janet told Christine, as she set the table for dinner.

Christine blushed. "Thank you. All the credit belongs to Gretchen."

Janet had prepared a simple dinner of chili and cornbread, so that they would have plenty of room for warm apple pie. Conversation was light and happy over dinner as they shared the details of their busy day. Christine had no idea apples came in so many varieties. Janet enlightened her and described in some detail how she determined which type of apples to pick and how they would be used.

"Besides getting a new hairstyle, what did you do today?" Mark asked Christine.

Christine extended her right hand and wiggled her fingers. "Karen painted my fingernails, and Robin gave me a pedicure. Gretchen helped the girls make peanut butter cookies and oatmeal raisin cookies."

"They sent a tin of cookies for you, Mark," Janet informed him. "They're in the kitchen."

"We stopped by Emily Clark's house on the way home. I got to meet her cats." From the twinkle in Christine's eyes, the Vinsons were assured that the visit with Felix and Oscar had been a special treat for Christine.

While Janet cleared the dishes and cut three wedges of apple pie, Mark broached a delicate topic with Christine. "Kevin mentioned that you are anxious to get back to work."

"Yes. I need to go back before Mr. Hardy decides to replace me."

"I'm afraid that he already has. He feels that having you there would be uncomfortable for Larry." Mark tried to be honest with Christine while not revealing any more than was essential. "You don't need to worry about money or finding another job right now. You need to concentrate on healing and protecting your child. When you're well, we'll see what we can do about finding you a job."

Just then Janet returned with the pie and three steaming mugs of decaf coffee.

"I wonder how the campers are doing?" Mark mused.

"I'm certain they're having a wonderful time," Janet responded. "I hope Chris doesn't overdo it. He has his surgery on Monday. Chris is having a hernia repair," she explained to Christine.

"Robin mentioned that today. She said Emily will fill in for her at the dentist's office."

"Orthodontist office," Mark corrected.

"Yes. Robin had to give Emily the key, so that's why we went to Emily's house."

Further conversation was tabled by the ringing of the phone. Mark went to answer it.

"There's something I would like to ask you," Christine said to Janet, as soon as Mark was out of the room.

Janet nodded to Christine to ask.

"It's about church. I used to go to church on a bus when I was a kid. I really liked it."

Christine paused without having asked a question. When the pause lingered, Janet decided to try to extend the conversation. "I'm glad you liked it. What happened that you stopped going?"

"We moved to a different trailer park. The bus didn't come there, so I didn't have a ride. Momma said I'd had enough church teaching anyway. I think she only sent me to have me out of the house for a few hours. I thought about going after Kevin and I got married, but he worked on Sundays and I didn't want to go by myself."

"That's too bad. Perhaps you would like to start going again?" Janet asked hopefully.

"That's my question. I was wondering, if it wouldn't be too much trouble, if I could go with you to church tomorrow?" Christine asked Janet haltingly, apparently worried that she might impose on her hosts.

"Too much trouble? Don't be ridiculous. We were hoping that you would want to go with us. I'll wake you up in plenty of time."

Mark came back into the dining room. "Jenny is on the phone," he told Janet. "She would like to speak to you."

"Who's Jenny?" Christine asked after Janet had left the room.

"She's our daughter. She lives in San Diego with her family."

"That's far away."

"Much too far for my liking."

"Do you see her much?"

"No, hardly ever, actually. Janet and I fly out there for a week after Thanksgiving, and we go for two weeks in the summer. That's it. With four children, Jenny says it's too difficult for them to come here."

"You don't get to see them at Christmas?" Christine sounded aghast.

"No, I'm afraid not. They haven't come here for Christmas in several years."

"Why don't you go there for Christmas?"

"I have to be here. Christmas is a busy time at the church."

123

"Oh."

From Christine's reaction, Mark guessed that she was unaware of all the activities of a church during the Christmas season. He decided he should explain further.

"We have to put on the church Christmas dinner, the deacons' Christmas party, and the staff Christmas luncheon. There's also the Christmas cantata, the children's program, and the Christmas Eve candlelight service. We provide Christmas baskets with food and small gifts for people who need help, and we buy Christmas presents for less-fortunate children. I'm lucky to be able to take off the week after Thanksgiving."

"Can't someone else do some of those things?"

"Well, I don't do them all by myself…" Mark stumbled around for an appropriate response. "We have committees to plan and do most of the work. But I need to be at all the events. I am the senior pastor."

"It seems like an awful lot of parties and programs. Maybe you could skip one or two and visit your grandchildren at Christmas."

"I don't think…" Mark hesitated. He had started to say that it wasn't any of Christine's business, but that did not seem appropriate. "I mean, it's not…" Mark searched but he could not find a polite way to ask Christine to not interfere in matters of his family.

"Aren't your grandchildren important to you?"

"Of course, they're important. They are more important to me than anything." Mark knew he sounded indignant, but Christine had touched a tender nerve.

"If they are so important, you should spend Christmas with them. When I was a kid, seeing my grandparents was the best part of Christmas. I bet your grandchildren would give anything for you to skip a Christmas party and visit them instead."

"But, what about the Christmas Eve sermon? Someone has to preach." There, Mark thought, I've got her now.

"You said you're the senior pastor. Is there a junior pastor? Or something like that? Maybe he could preach for you." Christine seemed determined to counter each of Mark's arguments.

"Well…I guess he could…" Mark's voice trailed off.

"It's probably none of my business, and I don't know anything about how a church works. I'm only saying, if you were my grandfather, I would hate the church if it kept you from spending Christmas with me."

Mark shoved his chair back from the table and strode determinedly from the room.

"I need to speak with Jenny," he stated, as he took the phone from Janet's hand, oblivious to the fact that Janet was in mid-sentence.

"Jenny, your mother and I would like to spend Christmas week with you this year, if that is alright with you and Peter."

Mark was not certain who squealed the loudest, Jenny or her mother. He only knew that he would have trouble hearing for the rest of the evening.

Chapter 20

As Kevin was preparing to leave the dealership at closing time on Sunday evening, he received two more surprises in a day that had been filled with surprises. One came in the form of a message handed to him by the receptionist as he headed to his office just before six.

"You had a call while you were with your last customer."

Kevin assumed it was business-related and threw the message on his desk to be dealt with on Wednesday. He picked up the phone and dialed Vinson's number.

Kevin's day had started with a telephone call from Janet Vinson. Kevin had been surprised to hear Janet say that Christine would be attending the morning worship service with her and Mark. She'd also asked Kevin if he would come by after work so that Janet could attend the evening service. Kevin gladly agreed; he had not admitted it to Janet, but he was happy to postpone seeing Christine again, even if only for several hours. He had no idea what to expect after Friday's emotional scene.

"Well, he did it." Kevin muttered, hanging up the phone. "A bet's a bet. Mark found a way to get me to church."

Finding himself with a few extra hours, Kevin decided to spend the morning outdoors. The sun was warm, the early fall morning promised a beautiful day, and some physical activity would do him good. Kevin had tossed and turned the last two nights, and he hoped that burning some energy this morning would enable him to sleep better tonight.

Kevin grabbed a rake from his shed and headed to the front yard. He filled seven large trash bags with leaves and hauled them to the curb to be picked up Monday morning. That's when he spied the lovely blond with long legs lounging on the front porch of the house across the road.

Kevin made it a point to know his neighbors, particularly those who lived closest to him. Being a good neighbor was important to him. He never knew when someone in the neighborhood might be in the market for a new car.

Kevin knew the Simmons had moved out last month, but he seen no signs of anyone moving in. So, he was surprised by the presence of the new neighbor and even more so by her pleasing appearance. He definitely needed to get to know her.

"Who's the new lady?" he asked Bob Newton, his next-door neighbor. Bob was also spending the morning raking the leaves that had fallen recently.

"I haven't met her yet. Lacey talked to her when she moved in a couple of weeks ago. Said she seemed nice enough. She's certainly easy on the eyes. I seem to recall Lacey mentioning that she's single." Bob gave Kevin an encouraging grin. "You should go for it, buddy."

"I just might," Kevin grinned back. "I think I just might, at that."

An introduction to the neighbor had to wait, though, as Kevin headed inside to get a shower and dress for work.

The workday had dragged by slowly. Traffic in the shop was light. A few people stopped in to take a look at the new models that had recently arrived, but no serious shoppers. By four o'clock, Kevin had given up on making a sale, or even meeting a good prospect. Thus, he was very pleasantly surprised when a regular customer showed up and announced he wanted to trade in his 2-year-old Trailblazer for a brand-new model. Kevin happily placed the order for him.

The long workday had finally come to an end, and Kevin was starved. He planned to grab a bite to eat on his way to visit Christine.

"I wonder if she needs dinner," he pondered, waiting for her to pick up the phone. The phone went unanswered. After the fifth ring, the answering machine picked up.

"That's strange."

"What's strange?" Josh asked, startling Kevin.

"I didn't hear you come in," he told Josh.

"I guess you've started talking to yourself. I've heard that's the first sign of senility. Christine must be driving you crazy. So, what's strange?"

"Christine isn't answering the phone. Mark and Janet are probably at church, but Christine should be there."

"Maybe she's in the bathroom," Josh offered.

"No. She can't get out of bed without assistance. She's supposed to be there by herself until I get there."

"Well, she's going to be by herself for a while longer. Mr. Wilson wants to have a short meeting before we take off."

"I hope she's alright." Kevin rose and followed Josh out of the office and down the hall to the small conference room where Mr. Wilson and the other salesmen who worked on Sundays waited.

"I know you all are anxious to get home," Mr. Wilson began, "so I'll keep this short and to the point. I've decided to close the dealership on Sundays from now on."

That announcement was Kevin's other surprise. From the collective gasp, he assumed he was not the only one caught off guard.

When the murmuring ceased, Mr. Wilson continued. "We've noticed for quite some time that we get a lot of lookers on Sundays and very few buyers. Now, I realize that some of the lookers do come back later to buy a vehicle, but not enough to justify staying open. I'm looking forward to having one day a week when I don't have to think about the business. From the sales numbers, none of you will suffer without your Sunday shift. However, you are welcome to add another day to your schedule if you feel you need the hours. Just clear it with Roy. I don't want you all coming in on the same day. Now let's get out of here."

"Whew," Kevin said to Josh, as they filed out of the room. "I didn't see that coming."

"Are you going to add another day?" Josh asked him.

"I don't know. Maybe not. My sales totals are great, and if Sundays aren't contributing much, then I must be doing pretty good on the other four days a week. How about you?"

"I guess I'm going to start coming in on Saturdays. I hate to miss the kids' soccer games, but my sales numbers have been low lately as it is. Last month's commissions barely paid the monthly bills, and I'm going to have another mouth to feed soon."

Kevin decided to try Christine once more before heading over to the Vinson's. As he dialed the number, he glanced at the phone message he had left on his desk. It was from Mark telling him not to come over, as Christine would be out for the evening.

"Out for the evening! What does that mean? It sounds like she has a date." When Kevin was done ranting, he peeked at his watch. "6:25."

The Washington Commanders had the night game, and suddenly Kevin was free to watch it. He ran out of the office, no longer caring where Christine was or what she was doing.

Chapter 21

Christine awoke Monday morning to the smell of cinnamon and brown sugar wafting through the air. She let out a big yawn and had a good stretch before ringing the bell at her bedside to let Janet know she was awake.

Janet hurried to assist Christine with her needs and wheeled her into the kitchen.

"Breakfast is almost ready," she told Christine, as she settled her at the rectangular kitchen table. "I hope you like fried apples. I'm making scrambled eggs and biscuits to have with them."

As Janet busied herself with setting the table and dishing up the food, it occurred to her that Christine had barely spoken a word since she woke up. She glanced at Christine who was toying with her silverware. Janet had been paying close attention to Christine's body language lately and recognized Christine's silence and fidgeting as manifestations of being uncomfortable.

Did something at church upset her, Janet wondered, as she took her seat. When she asked the blessing on the food, she silently added a request for wisdom.

"Did you sleep well?" Janet asked, fishing for some hint of what was disturbing Christine.

"Yes, very well." Christine answered pleasantly, but she avoided looking into Janet's eyes.

"Did you enjoy the church services yesterday?"

"Yes."

"What did you like the best?"

"The music was nice."

"Did you understand Mark's sermon?"

"Most of it. He's a good preacher."

It did not seem to Janet that anything at church had upset Christine. Not that Christine was giving her any help in deciphering what was troubling her. Janet could not think of any way to draw

Christine out, so she decided the best approach was to simply ask her.

"Is something bothering you?" she asked.

"No, well…, um, sort of." Christine looked around the kitchen. "Is Mark having breakfast?"

"He ate earlier. He had an early morning appointment."

"Oh." Christine sounded almost relieved to Janet's ears.

Did Mark do something to upset Christine? Janet waited for Christine to offer some explanation of what had "sort of" upset her. When no information was forthcoming, Janet decided to change the subject.

"Would you like some apple butter for your biscuit?" Janet passed the half-empty jar to Christine.

"It's delicious," Christine told her.

"That's the last jar of the apple butter I made last fall."

"You made this?" Christine asked incredulously.

"Yes, it's quite simple. I'm going to make a new batch after breakfast. Perhaps you would like to help me and learn how to make it."

Christine nodded and the smile on her face told Janet that she was excited about the prospect.

"Don't you have to work today?"

"I was supposed to work, but Kevin called to say he's not feeling well. He sounded like he has a bad cold. So, I took the day off. I'm glad to have time to start cooking some of the apples I picked. Today we'll make several batches of apple butter—I like to use them for Christmas gifts. On Wednesday, I'm planning to cook and can the rest of the Granny Smith apples for frying during the winter months."

Christine did not reply. Rather, she reached for another biscuit and scooped apple butter on it. At least she's eating, Janet thought, even if she's not talking.

"By the way," Janet told her, "I forgot to thank you for the other night."

"Thank me? For what?" Christine seemed genuinely puzzled.

"For whatever you said to Mark that got him to agree to spend Christmas in California."

131

"Oh." Christine's voice sounded small, and she stared at her plate. After a moment, though, Janet's words seemed to sink in.

"You're not mad at me for interfering?" she asked.

"So that's it; she thinks we might be upset with her. Janet reached over and patted her hand.

"Of course not, dear. I'm grateful for what you said. I've been trying to talk Mark into spending Christmas with the grandkids for months. You accomplished what I could not."

Christine relaxed visibly.

Soon the breakfast dishes were cleared away, and it was time to make the apple butter.

Christine watched as Janet washed and quartered several large apples and put them in a large pot to cook. While they cooked, Janet retrieved small jars from the dishwasher and prepped the next batch of apples.

When the first batch of apples was cooked, Janet put them into the food mill and showed Christine how it worked. In spite of the cast on her left arm, Christine was able to use it to hold the mill steady and crank it with her right hand.

"It feels good to be doing something useful," she told Janet.

"There's nothing worse than feeling useless," Janet agreed.

Janet noticed a fleeting look of self-doubt cross Christine's face.

"I'm not much use these days," Christine said softly.

"Well, you certainly are being a big help to me today. I'll get more accomplished with your help than I would by myself. Plus, I'm enjoying having your company while I'm working."

The apples were reduced to a smooth pulp, so Janet emptied the contents of food mill into a large bowl. She washed the mill and refilled it with the next batch of cooked apples.

"I'm not good at many things," Christine said, as she began to crank the mill again. "I am a pretty good cook. At least Kevin always seemed to enjoy my cooking."

Janet stirred sugar, cinnamon, and cloves into the apple pulp before replying. "He told me what a great cook you are. I'm sure you have many other talents, as well."

"Not really. At least none that you can earn a living doing. About all I can do well is answer the phone and schedule appointments."

Janet put the seasoned mixture onto the stove to cook and stirred a second pot of simmering apples.

"Don't count yourself short, dear. God gave each one of us many talents. In fact, I was reading the other day that most people have between 300 and 500 talents."

"That can't be," Christine exclaimed.

"I know it sounds like a lot, until you stop to think about all the things you can do."

"Like what?"

"Well, like seeing. That's an ability that not everyone has. And the ability to speak and hear. And walking and running, although you can't do them right now. You can read and write. When you start adding up all the things you can do, you are a pretty amazing person."

"Pretty ordinary, you mean. Almost everyone can do all those things."

"That's true; however, you should never take those abilities for granted. You never know when you might lose them."

"Like I lost the ability to walk until my leg heals."

"Right. Fortunately, your leg will heal. Many people who have been in an accident like you were in wind up confined to a wheelchair."

"That would be terrible," Christine cried.

"Being unable to walk certainly makes life more challenging, but it doesn't diminish a person's value or the love their family or God has for them."

"I think this batch is done," Christine told Janet. "You and Mark talk a lot about God's love. You make it sound like He loves everyone."

"God does love everyone." Janet poured the apple pulp into the bowl and added sugar and spices.

"I don't understand how He can love bad people."

"God loves all people because He created them. He's not happy when we do bad things, but He still loves us. Just like the love of a father or a mother for their child doesn't depend on how the child behaves."

"My momma doesn't love me. And I don't even know my dad. He didn't care enough to even stick around and get to know me."

133

Janet was filling 8-ounce jars with the first batch of apple butter when Christine uttered that pronouncement. She completed the task before walking over to Christine and wrapping her arms around her.

"I don't know why your parents didn't love you as you deserved. I do know that God loves you. He created you, and He loves you just as you are."

Janet moved in front of Christine and knelt before her. She cupped Christine's chin in her hand and waited until Christine made eye contact.

"You are very special to God. He loves you, as He loves each person who has ever lived. He loves people without regard to their looks, their abilities, or their position in life. He loves them in spite of their behavior. He loves you, Christine, and He wants only the best for you."

Chapter 22

Kevin showed up at the Vinson's house on Monday morning of the following week to find Christine dressed and seated in her wheelchair in the kitchen. It was the first time he'd seen her since her shocking revelations ten days earlier. A nasty cold had kept him home and in bed for a few days. He felt much better by the week's end, but, as he was feeling a bit awkward about seeing Christine again, he had extended his absence by claiming to be worried about passing along germs to the patient.

Christine's confessions had been troubling, but her assertion regarding his fertility had filled him with self-doubt regarding his manhood. Although Kevin had no desire to reproduce, he would like to think that he could, should the desire ever awaken in him.

Kevin had spent more than one sleepless night trying to assess how Christine's belief might have spelled doom for their marriage. Did Christine see him as less of a man because he had never impregnated her? Did Christine strongly desire to have children and therefore sought out another partner who could provide her with that? He hoped the answer to the first question was no; it seemed unfair to penalize him for something that was not his fault and might not even be true. The answer to the second question was probably another no; even now, Christine showed no joy at the prospect of motherhood. In fact, Christine had not so much as mentioned her pregnancy except to offer it as evidence of her ability to procreate.

So how did Christine feel about this baby? Was she happy? Was she planning to keep it or put it up for adoption? Kevin felt certain, given her tearful confession, that she was planning to see this pregnancy through to the end. All these thoughts had run amok through Kevin's mind during the ride into town, and he had braced himself for another disquieting encounter with Christine.

Janet greeted Kevin at the door. He was surprised to see that she was not dressed for work. She was wearing a large apron over a pair of blue jeans and a sweatshirt.

"Come in, Kevin," she said, stepping back so that he could come through the door. "As you can see, I am not going to work. I took the day off to get some errands done and do some work around the house. I'm cooking up the last of my apples into applesauce, and then I need to go out for a while. Christine is in the kitchen."

Christine gave Kevin a big smile as he ambled into the large kitchen. For her part, Christine did not seem at all uncomfortable in his presence. The intervening week seemed to have been good for her.

"I like your hair," he managed to say as he perused her from head to toe. And there was much to take in.

The Saturday she spent with the church ladies had done wonders for her. Christine's hair was several inches shorter and fell flatteringly to her chin line. Light brown highlights brightened not only her hair but also her entire face. Someone, Janet he assumed, had assisted her in putting on makeup. Her fingernails were manicured and painted a lovely shade of rose. As he looked down, he noticed her toenails matched her fingernails. She looked like a million bucks.

Kevin's heart raced in his chest. What was this woman doing to him and why was he allowing it? He knew better than to let her in, yet that was exactly was he was doing. He needed to be rescued, and fast.

"Would you like a cookie?" Christine held out a tin of home-baked cookies. "I helped make them."

Kevin grabbed a handful and shoved one into his mouth. If he kept his mouth full of food, he would not have to speak.

"Janet's making applesauce," Christine explained. "I'm helping."

Christine beamed as she showed Kevin how she could use the food mill to pulverize the apples.

Kevin joined in by paring and coring apples for Janet. While he worked, Christine chatted incessantly, giving him a blow-by-blow narration on all that he had missed during the past week.

"Chris Jennings had surgery last Monday. He went home on Tuesday. He is doing fine. Robin went back to work today. Emily filled in for Robin at the orthodontic office while she was taking care of Chris. Oh, that reminds me, I didn't get to tell you that I met Oscar and Felix. You were right. I do love them. They are a strange pair. You know how much I love animals. Chris and Robin are going to take me to the dog show next Saturday. Chris should be well enough by then…"

Kevin only half-listened to Christine's recitation. He had met several of the members of Riverside Christian Fellowship and, while he liked them well enough, he was determined to avoid getting drawn into their lives. He had escaped religion for thirty-five years and he saw no reason to get caught now. He did note, however, the enthusiasm in Christine's voice and, inexplicably, his heart was warmed by the knowledge that Christine was surrounded by people who truly cared about her. A month ago, she had never met the Vinsons or their congregation, yet she spoke about them now as dear friends.

"Are you going to guess?" Kevin was brought back to the present by the questioning in Christine's voice.

"Sorry," he mumbled, as he felt his face redden. He had not meant for Christine to catch him not paying attention. "I guess I zoned out for a minute. What were you saying?"

"Guess what happened to me Saturday."

Kevin had no idea what she might be talking about. He only knew that Christine was clearly excited about her news and she seemed to waiting for him to guess. His mind drew a blank. He had to come up with something quickly, so he said the first thing that popped into his mind.

"You won the lottery."

"How did you guess?"

Kevin dropped the paring knife in his hand.

"What? You really won the lottery?"

"No, silly," Christine giggled. "I did win something, though. And it was almost as good as winning the lottery, wasn't it, Janet?"

"It was a very nice prize, dear," Janet agreed.

Kevin looked at Janet for some hint of what was going on. Janet merely smiled at him and went back to stirring the apples cooking on the stove. He turned his gaze to Christine. She seemed to be waiting for him to speak. He decided to oblige her.

"That's wonderful, Christine. What did you win?"

"Well," Christine began. "Karen came by in her van with her boys and picked me up. We met Greg and the twins at Old Mill Park for the...well, I forgot what it was called."

"The Great Rappahannock River Duck Race," Janet supplied.

Kevin retrieved the paring knife, rinsed it, and finished peeling the last apple in the bowl. With the apple peeling done, he pulled up a chair at the table. He was beginning to realize that Christine was going to milk this story for all it was worth. He was determined to pay attention to the end, for the retelling was giving her such obvious pleasure.

"Yes, that's it. They sell plastic ducks and race them down the river for charity. Greg had paid to adopt ducks for everyone, including me."

"Did your duck win the race?" Kevin asked, trying to help the story along.

"No interruptions allowed." Christine pretended to glare at him. She ruined it by smiling. "I want to tell you everything."

That's what I was afraid of, Kevin thought. But what he said was, "Go ahead. I'd love to hear it."

"Greg and the girls were waiting for us in the parking lot. Greg helped me into the wheelchair, and we checked in. There was a big banner over the table listing the sponsors. Marshall Orthodontics was one of them."

"Greg has sponsored the Duck Race for several years," Janet chimed in. "It's a great cause. The money from the race is used to buy Christmas presents and food for families in need. That's a pretty good reason, don't you think?"

"That's what Greg told Bethany when she asked him about it. I told them that my family might have been one of the families that was helped."

"Really?" Janet asked. "Would you mind sharing the story with us?"

Christine seemed a bit hesitant, but her voice was strong when she finally spoke. "When we were little, Momma never had enough money to buy us presents. She barely had money to pay the rent and buy food. But every year there were presents on Christmas morning. I would get a toy I really wanted and new clothes and a game or a video. So would my little sister. When I got older

Momma told me the presents came from churches and clubs that collected money to buy us stuff."

"That's great. Our church has participated in that program for years. It's nice to know that the gifts we provide are appreciated."

"When I told the children about receiving the gifts, they were concerned that I wouldn't get any presents this year since I live with you and Pastor Mark, and you aren't poor," Christine told Janet.

Janet and Kevin chuckled at the thought of the children worried about Christine's Christmas gifts.

"Austin was so cute," Christine continued; the animation in her voice kept Kevin engrossed in the conversation. "He put one hand on my shoulder and said, 'Don't worry. We'll all get you presents. And you can come to the Christmas dinner and see us in the Christmas play. It will be the best Christmas ever. You'll see.'"

Christine's eyes filled, and she blinked to keep the tears at bay as she shared that part of the story.

"I hugged him. It was so sweet. I felt like I'd been adopted. I didn't know what to say, but I didn't have to say anything. Greg changed the subject by announcing that he was starving."

"He's always starving," Janet interjected.

"That's what Brittany said. We ate lunch, and then it was time for the race to begin. Have you ever been to the duck race, Kevin?"

Kevin conceded that he had never been—probably because it was always held on a Saturday and he worked every Saturday, but he knew better than to mention his work schedule to Christine. It had been a frequent source of contention during their marriage.

"The ducks were released upriver and floated down to where we were. A net was stretched across the river to catch the ducks when they came down. The first one past the red ribbon was the winner. Each duck had a number written on it, so they knew whose duck won. Afterward, we got to keep the ducks. Bethany said they have a whole bunch of ducks in their bathroom."

"When the announcement was made over the public address system that the race would begin in five minutes, we all lined the riverbank to watch the ducks float down. Greg handed each of us a ticket with our duck's number on it. It wasn't long before the ducks started coming down the river. There must have been hundreds of them. They were so cute; they were all wearing tiny sunglasses."

"With so many ducks all looking alike, how did they keep track of the winner?"

"Volunteers stood in the water to snatch up the first four ducks to cross the finish line. The rest of the ducks were captured in the net and dragged to the shore. Then the real excitement started. An announcer began calling out the winners and their prizes. A teen-aged girl won fourth prize. She got two movie passes and gift certificates for concessions. Third prize was a Wal-Mart gift card. A Hispanic lady won. I don't think she had a clue what was happening. Her family had to shove her to the podium to get the prize. She started smiling when she saw what she won."

"I guess Wal-Mart means the same thing in any language," Janet commented.

"The second-place winner got a certificate for dinner for two at a local restaurant. An elderly man won that. Finally, they were ready to announce the first-place winner." Christine's face was beaming. Kevin was certain that she had won the grand prize, but he was careful not to ruin her moment by letting on.

"The announcer said, 'Our first-place winner will receive a $100 gift certificate good at any store in the mall and two tickets to the next play at Riverside Dinner Theater. And the winner is the owner of duck number 85.' Everyone got quiet as the announcement was made, then I heard people mumbling 'Maybe next year.' I kept waiting for someone to scream that they had won, but no one was. Finally, I looked down at the card in my hand. It was number 85. I started screaming and crying. Greg pushed me up to the front of the crowd to get my prize. I was so excited. I'd never won anything before, you know."

Kevin did know. Christine had considered it one of life's greatest tragedies that she had never won anything—at least not anything of enough importance to count. Kevin was happy for her. He knew she would never forget that day. He stood and walked over to her. Bending down, he enveloped her in a big hug.

"I'm happy for you." He genuinely meant it.

Christine returned the hug and thanked Kevin. As Kevin turned to walk back to his chair, Christine reached out and grabbed his hand. When he turned to look at her, he saw a look of uncertainty flash across her face. She smiled shyly at him, reminding him of the young girl who had won his heart so many years earlier.

"Would you like to go to the play with me?" she breathed so quietly that Kevin was sure he must have misunderstood her words. However, the anticipation on her face told him that he had heard her properly.

Kevin's emotions warred within him. In the past month, he had seen glimpses of the Christine he had loved and could easily love again, if he allowed himself to. However, he had no illusions that Christine was capable of loving him as he deserved to be loved. Of course, he could go as her friend and not as her date dat. He was not a big fan of the theater, but then again, maybe it would not kill him to go with her.

"What play is it?" he asked, stalling for time.

"Damn Yankees."

"As in the New York Yankees?" A play about a baseball team might be worth seeing.

"I don't know," Christine replied honestly. She had never actually seen a professional theatrical performance and knew even less about the theater than Kevin.

Janet, however, loved the theater. Mark bought season tickets to Riverside each year as a birthday present for her. "It is about the Yankees and their rivals, the Washington Senators. If you like baseball, you will undoubtedly enjoy the play." Janet wisely made no mention that the play was a musical.

Kevin hesitated another minute before agreeing to accompany Christine. He was rewarded with a huge smile. The tickets were for the opening weekend, still several weeks away. He made a mental note to rearrange his schedule so he would be off in time to escort Christine to the Friday night performance. Fortunately, she should have the cast off her leg and be walking again by then.

Chapter 23

Greg arrived at the office bright and early Monday morning. Catching sight of Robin's car in the parking lot, he grinned from ear-to-ear.

"It's great to have you back," Greg called out to Robin as he entered the building. She rose from her seat behind the check-in window and greeted him with a warm hug.

"Thank you. I'm glad Chris is doing well enough for me to be back." Her voice exuded cheerfulness, and she smiled at him warmly.

Even so, Greg had a disturbing feeling that all was not right. He took a step back and appraised her. Robin's eyes were missing their normal sparkle. She seemed weary, which was to be expected after spending the last ten days caring for her husband as he recuperated from surgery. No, Greg quickly decided, weary was not the correct word to describe her expression. Apprehensive. Yes, Robin looked apprehensive.

"What are you not telling me?" he asked gently, suddenly fearful that Chris's surgery may not have gone as well as he believed.

Robin hesitated for a moment. "There's something we need to discuss. Perhaps we could talk about it over lunch."

"I'd rather not spend all morning wondering what's on your mind," Greg told her. "It smells like the coffee's ready. It's still early. Let's discuss it over coffee…and doughnuts." Greg held up a box from Paul's Bakery.

Robin nodded her agreement.

Greg led the way to the break room. Robin poured two cups of coffee, while Greg grabbed a couple of napkins from the cupboard over the microwave. When they were settled, Greg offered up a prayer of thanks for their food and asked God's blessing on their workday.

Robin took a bite of doughnut and a couple of sips of coffee before speaking.

"Chris and I had a lot of time to talk while he was bedridden," she began.

She took another bite of doughnut, and Greg felt that she was stalling.

Greg reached for a second doughnut while he waited for her to continue.

"We talked a lot about our future—how we want to spend our retirement years, what are the really important things in our life, where we feel God is leading us." Robin hesitated, chewing on her lower lip. She seemed reluctant to continue.

Greg had a sinking feeling in his stomach. He was getting the distinct impression that this conversation was going to cost him a receptionist.

"Are you leaving us?" he asked gently.

Robin nodded her head affirmatively. Greg reached out and grasped her hand.

"It's fine. Really, it is fine," he reassured her. "As I recall, you were only filling in here for a few weeks until I found a permanent receptionist. You've been here nearly a year. If Chris wants his wife back, who am I to object?"

Greg smiled warmly at the gentle woman who was such an important part of his life and had been for much longer than the eleven months she had worked for him. Greg had first become acquainted with Robin and Chris when he moved to Fredericksburg eighteen years ago to open his practice. His late wife Cindy had known Robin since Cindy was in grade school. Although Robin was ten years younger than Cindy's mother Gretchen, Robin and Gretchen were best friends.

Greg has often heard the story of how the long and enduring friendship began. Robin had arrived in Fredericksburg in the fall of 1986 as an incoming freshman at Mary Washington College. Riverside's youth pastor visited the campus and extended an invitation to new and returning students to attend a special service and luncheon welcoming the students to Fredericksburg. He even offered to pick them up in the church van. Robin was one of seven students who took him up on the offer. During the service, the senior pastor called the students to stand at the front of the sanctuary facing the congregation. He asked for seven church families to "adopt" one of the students into their family for the year. Families that accepted the call went forward to stand by their student and pray for him or her.

Gretchen and Tom had not planned on participating in the program that year. They had their hands full with three precocious young children. However, Gretchen's heart stirred within her as she looked at the skinny African-American girl with the big Afro. It was not her skin color or her appearance that attracted Gretchen, however. It was the love of Jesus that shone through her sparkling eyes and her dazzling smile. Tom felt it too. Without saying a word, they both knew this beautiful young college student would become an important part of their lives.

Robin was adopted into the Sullivan family not only for her freshman year but for all four years she was enrolled at Mary Washington College. She ate dinner with them a couple of times a week, babysat their children, and even vacationed with them. Tom acted as a surrogate father at times, and Robin brought all potential boyfriends over for his approval. In fact, Tom introduced Robin to her future husband after he met Chris Jennings at a Christian Businessmen's Fellowship luncheon. When Robin graduated and married Chris, the new family decided to remain in Fredericksburg and bought a home in the same neighborhood as the Sullivans. A few years later, when Hannah was born, Cindy was the favorite babysitter for Robin's daughter. Hannah returned the favor by being the preferred babysitter for Cindy and Greg's twins until she left for college.

The bonds between the Jennings family and the Sullivan/Marshall family were strong. Greg wanted only the best for Robin and Chris, even if it meant he had to hire a new receptionist.

"There's more," Robin said expectantly.

When Greg looked into her dark eyes, he saw they were sparkling. Must be good news, Greg thought.

"Hannah and Michael are moving back to Fredericksburg. I'm going to take care of Nicole for them while Hannah works."

"So, that's it. I've been tossed aside by an infant." Greg laughed heartily.

Robin had been thrilled when she became a grandmother last spring. Most conversations with her since then had revolved around baby Nicole. Chris and Robin made the three-hour trip to see their precious grandchild at least once a month, and Robin's heart yearned for it to be more frequent.

"That little girl will have you both wrapped around her fingers in no time."

"She already does," Robin agreed.

Greg offered up a prayer of thanks for Robin's service to his practice, for her precious grandchild, and for the wonderful future that lay ahead of her and Chris. Then it was time to open the office.

At noontime, Greg made a point of joining Karen in the employee break room. Greg typically ate his lunch at his desk while doing paperwork and returning phone calls, but once or twice a week he set aside the lunch hour for some quiet time with Karen in an otherwise busy workday.

"I guess Robin told you she put in her notice," he began, as he joined Karen at the round lunch table.

"She did." Karen retrieved a dish from the microwave and put a second one in. She carried a plate of roasted chicken and broccoli casserole over to Greg. Since their engagement, Karen had begun packing a lunch for each of them.

"I'm going to miss seeing her every day in the office," Karen said.

Greg cast her a bemused look. "You won't be here, either."

"True, but I'll miss seeing her when I drop in to see you." Karen smirked.

Greg grinned back. It warmed his heart to know that Karen had grown close to Robin during the past several months. Robin had befriended, encouraged, and prayed for Karen, and in doing so had been instrumental in Karen's restored relationship with God.

"I'm going to miss you both," Greg countered. "Robin has been a great receptionist, and you…"

Greg stood and pulled Karen into his arms, "Well, hiring you was probably the best decision I ever made." He gave Karen a quick kiss.

The beeping of the microwave alerted Karen that her food was hot. When she was seated, Greg blessed their lunch.

"Do you have anyone in mind to replace her?" Karen asked between bites.

"I haven't even had a chance to think about it." Greg put down his fork and rubbed his eyes with both hands.

Karen noticed the strain on his face. She stretched out her left hand and gently stroked his right shoulder.

"Too many changes at one time, huh?"

Greg's nod told her she had properly interpreted his actions.

Thursday was Karen's last day. Despite her initial objections to Greg's suggestion to replace her, Karen had decided to give up her position as his business manager to devote more time to their soon-to-be blended family and to her growing furniture restoration business. Greg had advertised for a new business manager and found the right person on his second day of interviewing. Peter Ma, a recent graduate of Germanna Community College, had already begun working with Karen to learn her system. With an associate's degree in business management, Peter was more than qualified for the job. Peter would work three days a week and take classes toward a bachelor's degree on the other two.

As if all these changes were not enough, Katie's baby was due at Thanksgiving. She would work up until Greg and Karen's wedding, only four weeks away. Greg was already searching for her replacement. Katie had worked for Greg for six years, and they made a great team. Greg was delighted that she was going to be a mother and had made the decision to devote herself to raising her child, but his joy was bittersweet. She and Jenna, the other full-time hygienist, were almost like daughters to Greg. They had both started working for him while they were in their teens; he had watched them blossom into professional young women and wives, and now Katie would soon be a mother. Greg would miss having her assisting him.

"They say change is a good thing, and I'm not opposed to change, but…," Greg began.

"But replacing three of your four staff members in one month's time is really a lot," Karen finished for him.

"Yes." Karen heard the resignation in Greg's voice.

"I could do Robin's job for a while," Karen said brightly, all the while secretly hoping that Greg would not take her up on the offer.

Greg smiled, then leaned over and kissed her. "I do love you."

Greg kissed her again. "I want to be your husband, not your boss. I'll call the newspaper and run an ad this weekend."

"Maybe you don't need to do that," Karen said thoughtfully. "I think I know someone who would be perfect for the job. Let me make a call after lunch."

"Is there any more chicken?" Greg's stomach overrode his anxiety about his staffing challenges.

"Of course. I'm well acquainted with your appetite." For the umpteenth time, Karen marveled that her future husband could eat enough for two, or perhaps three, people without carrying any extra weight. Sometimes life just was not fair.

After lunch, Karen called Pastor Vinson at his office and discussed her idea with him. It took every ounce of self-restraint he could muster to listen patiently until she was finished.

"Why that's a marvelous idea," he gushed. "Bless God. I do believe it is a divinely inspired idea. Shall I speak to her for you?"

"Let me talk it over with Greg first. I'll call you back later."

Greg was so busy that it was nearly closing time before Karen was able to snag him for a few minutes. Despite Karen's enthusiasm, Greg balked at the idea initially.

"I'm not sure Christine is a good fit for the office. She certainly has wreaked havoc in the lives of a lot of people."

"I know that," Karen reasoned, "but people do change. Look at me. I wreaked some havoc of my own in the past."

He kissed her gently on the forehead. "God changed you because you allowed Him to. As far as I know, Christine has not allowed God into her life yet."

Greg had her there, Karen conceded. Yet, she felt certain that Christine was the right person for the job and that God had placed Christine in their lives for a reason. Since Greg was hesitant, Karen decided it was time to play the ace she had up her sleeve. "Mark thinks it is a good idea. He said it was an answer to prayer."

Greg knew he was outmanned and surrendered. He could not oppose his fiancé and his pastor. Karen phoned the church and was told that Mark had left for the day. She decided to call Christine herself.

~ ~ ~

Christine was in the den watching television from her wheelchair when Janet brought the phone to her. Kevin called occasionally to check in before coming over; other than those few calls, Christine had rarely received a telephone call during her month's stay at the Vinson's home.

"Hello," she said tentatively, half expecting to be told that the caller had dialed the wrong number.

"Christine, hi. It's Karen Harper."

"Oh, Karen. Hi." Christine's heart skipped a beat. Both times Karen had called previously, it had been to include Christine in a fun activity. Christine hoped another invitation was the purpose of this call.

"I hope I'm not interrupting anything important," Karen began.

"No, nothing at all." *Like I am ever doing anything important*, Christine thought.

"Good. Well, I wanted to talk to you about a job opening at Greg's office. We're looking for a receptionist to replace Robin, and I thought of you."

Christine was confused. As far as she was aware, Robin loved her job and did it quite well.

"Greg's replacing Robin?"

"I guess I should back up a bit. Robin put in her notice today. She has decided to be a full-time grandmother. So, Greg will need a new receptionist. Would you be interested in applying for the job?"

"Oh, I didn't know Robin was quitting. I need a job and being a receptionist is about the only job I'm any good at. So, sure, I'll apply. What do I have to do?"

"Can you come in tomorrow for an interview? At noon?"

"That should be fine."

"Great. I'll let Greg know. We'll see you tomorrow."

"Thanks," Christine added as she hung up the phone.

~ ~ ~

Christine rolled the wheelchair into the kitchen to share the news with Mark and Janet. Mark had just returned from leading a Bible study at the jail, and Janet was beginning dinner preparations. Christine shared her news with them. Since Mark had spoken with Karen earlier, the couple already knew what was coming, but they were careful not to ruin Christine's announcement.

"I can take you to your interview tomorrow," Mark told Christine. "We should think about getting a car for you soon, so you can get yourself to work when you are able. The doctor said your cast should come off in about two weeks and that you would be able to drive soon after."

Christine looked down at the floor. "I don't have any money to pay for a car," she began haltingly. "I don't think I can get a loan because I messed up my credit rating. I would pay it back, though, if you …"

"Whoa, hold on a minute there," Mark interrupted her. "I guess we forgot to tell you about the money."

"The money? What money?"

"The money from the insurance company and the money from Mr. Hardy. Together it's should be more than enough for you to buy a decent car and get insurance coverage."

Mark went on to explain the monetary settlement Mr. Hardy had agreed to pay in order for his son to avoid having to take responsibility for his mistreatment of Christine and for her unborn child.

Chapter 24

Kevin had left the Vinson's before Christine received the call from Karen. He was relieved that Christine had made no mention of their previous conversation and that this visit had gone smoothly and quickly. Janet invited him to stay for dinner, but he begged off, telling them he had other plans. What he neglected to say was that he had a date. His first real date since breaking up with Karen more than six months earlier.

Kevin had begun to think he was never going to meet another eligible, desirable woman when one showed up unexpectedly at his door, or more precisely, his bedside. He smiled as he realized his good fortune was a direct result of having been sick.

Wednesday morning Kevin had awoken to the same feverish chills and stuffy nose that had plagued him for two days. He had no desire to leave the comfort of his bed, but he needed fluids and medication. With no one to care for him, Kevin was left to fend for himself. As he lay in bed feeling sorry for himself, he imagined he heard the front door opening. Soft footsteps fell across his living room and made their way down the hall toward the bedroom.

"I must be sicker than I thought," Kevin muttered quietly as he stared at the door. The door opened and a beautiful woman appeared in the doorway.

Kevin rubbed his eyes. "I must be hallucinating." This time he spoke aloud.

The hallucination smiled at him. "Oh, good. You're awake. I'll get you something to drink."

Before Kevin could speak, the woman had disappeared back down the hallway, only to reappear moments later with a glass of orange Gatorade.

"Drink this," the lovely blond lady ordered him, as she reached behind him to raise his head.

Kevin took a sip. It tasted real. Maybe this was not a hallucination. She eased his head back onto the pillow.

"It's time for your cold medicine. Let's get you sitting up first." She placed the glass and the pills on the nightstand and helped Kevin to sit up. Then she handed him the pills and the Gatorade.

Kevin dutifully obeyed her simple commands. When the liquid had been swallowed, she propped an extra pillow behind his head so that he could recline comfortably. She flicked on the television using the remote control she found on the nightstand.

"You rest while I fix you some soup. You need nourishment."

"Wait," Kevin called out before she left him.

She turned and smiled at him. It was a brilliant smile that chased away every thought in his head.

"Yes?" she prompted when he remained mum.

"Yes," he answered. He knew he was acting like an idiot—it must be the fever—but he could not remember what he wanted to ask her. She turned to leave.

"Your name. That's it. I wanted to know your name."

"Felicia." She flashed him another dazzling smile.

"Felicia," Kevin murmured. He had a vague thought that he should be wary of an unknown woman having free access to his house, but she was too lovely and he was far too sick to be at all concerned about Felicia's presence. He laid his head back and closed his eyes. He drifted back to sleep with a lazy smile on his face and one word, Felicia, floating through his brain.

Kevin was dreaming about a beautiful nurse when he felt a hand on his arm. He jerked his arm away and rolled over on his left side. Why was someone trying to rouse him when he wanted to continue his pleasant dream? The hand shook his right shoulder a bit harder.

"Wake up, Sleepyhead." The voice was so pleasant that Kevin forced himself to open one eye and twist his head around to determine its owner. At the sight of the blond nurse from his dream, Kevin jolted back around.

"I thought I dreamed you," he said through a large yawn.

"I'm real alright."

The vision in the pink v-neck sweater chuckled, as she slipped one arm behind him. Kevin had a moment of deja vu. Hadn't Felicia done the same thing earlier? That's it, he remembered. The nurse was Felicia; she was here to take care of him.

"Let's get you in a better position."

Once Kevin was arranged properly, Felicia settled herself on the edge of the bed and spooned warm soup into his mouth. Kevin could not remember the last time someone had fed him. It was probably his mother. No, it was Christine. As much as Kevin tried to deny it, he had to admit that there was a time when Christine had cherished him and gone out of her way to care for him. When he was in the hospital with appendicitis, Christine had slept on a tiny loveseat three nights in a row so that she would be close by if he needed anything during the night. And when Kevin broke his leg, Christine had waited on him hand and foot for eight weeks while it healed. Christine had loved him passionately once. What had happened to them?

"Open wide." Felicia's voice drew Kevin back to the present.

Kevin scolded himself for thinking of Christine. Felicia was here now, and his life with Christine was in the distant past. He owed it to Felicia to give her his undivided attention. He did wish he knew who she was and how she happened to be in his bedroom. The effort of eating the bowl of soup tired Kevin, so that he fell back to sleep the moment Felicia left the bedroom.

On Thursday, Kevin awoke feeling much more like himself. His fever had broken during the night, leaving him feeling clammy and very much in want of a shower. Before he got a shower, however, he needed something to drink. His throat was parched.

As Kevin swung his legs over the side of the bed, he spied a glass of apple juice on the nightstand. He reached for it. It was cold and refreshing going down his throat. Kevin was baffled. He was even more puzzled as the smell of bacon sizzling on the stove reached his nose. The bacon mingled with the aroma of potatoes frying.

Kevin slipped on a pair of sweat pants over his boxers and pulled on a tee shirt. He made his way to the kitchen, praying that he was not hallucinating again. He had the strangest dreams yesterday—must have been the fever.

From the living room Kevin could see into the kitchen. There she was again, that same blond nurse from his dreams. What was her name? Oh, yes, Felicia.

Felicia looked up from the stove and smiled at Kevin. "I thought you might be hungry this morning. Come. Sit at the table. Would you like some coffee?"

Kevin blindly obeyed Felicia's commands and nodded his head "yes" to coffee. Felicia carried over a steaming mug, along with a carton of French vanilla half 'n half.

"I found this in your frig. Do you want some in your coffee?"

Kevin merely nodded. He was having difficulty finding his voice. The coffee tasted wonderful—much better than when he made it himself.

"Do you like scrambled eggs?" Felicia asked him. Again, Kevin nodded.

In a short time, Felicia placed before Kevin a plate piled high with steaming eggs, crisp bacon, and hash browns. Kevin smiled his appreciation. He picked up his fork to taste a bite before he remembered his manners. Felicia was dishing up a plate of breakfast for herself. He set the fork down and waited for her to join him at the small dinette table in the kitchen.

Only after Felicia took her first bite did Kevin attack his food. It was the best breakfast he'd had since, well, since Christine had left him. Christine was a wonderful cook and he had looked forward to sharing a hot breakfast with her before she left in the morning for work. Since he'd been on his own, Kevin had opted for cold cereal, or perhaps a bagel, for breakfast. Kevin shook off the memories of Christine.

"It's delicious. Thank you," Kevin told Felicia.

"You speak at last," Felicia teased. "You are very welcome." Felicia flashed him another of her brilliant smiles.

Kevin did not speak again until he had cleaned his plate. Felicia poured him a second cup of coffee. Kevin watched her and was struck by how natural it felt to be sharing a meal in his kitchen with a lovely woman. *I could get used to this*, he thought.

That thought frightened him a little as he realized he was fantasizing about a future with a woman he knew nothing about other than her first name.

"May I ask," Kevin ventured forth hesitantly, "who you are?"

"Felicia Hargrove. I live across the street."

"You do? Oh, right. You moved into the Simmons house. I saw you when I was raking leaves the other day."

Felicia smiled. "I noticed you, too."

"How is it that we've never been introduced before now?"

"I only moved in a couple of weeks ago. I've noticed you coming and going, but it's never seemed to be convenient to introduce myself."

"It's been a rather busy time for me." Kevin was not sure how much he wanted to reveal to this new neighbor, so he asked the next logical question instead. "Why are you here?"

"I separated from my husband a few months ago. He kept the house, and I moved in with a friend in a tiny apartment. That got old fast. I didn't like sharing a bathroom, and I missed having a yard. The place across the road was up for rent, so I took it."

"No," Kevin said, shaking his head. "Why are you here, in my house, taking care of me?"

"Oh," Felicia replied. "Well, the Newtons were leaving on a vacation Tuesday. They were concerned about you because your newspapers were on the front porch and you hadn't picked up your mail on Monday. They gave me your key and asked me to check on you. I popped in Tuesday evening and found you in need of some tender, loving care, so here I am."

"I see." Kevin reached out and clasped her hand. "And I am very grateful."

Felicia looked a bit uncomfortable. She pulled her hand away and began gathering up the dirty dishes.

"Why don't you get a shower while I clean up here?" she told Kevin.

When Kevin emerged from the bedroom, clean and feeling human again, he found Felicia had gone, leaving a spotless kitchen behind her. She had left a note on the kitchen counter with her phone number, directing Kevin to call her if he had a relapse or needed some company.

Kevin immediately picked up the phone and called Flowers by Rachel. He ordered a bouquet of fall flowers to be delivered to Felicia.

"What kind of card do you want to accompany the flowers?" the clerk asked him.

"A thank you card."

"What do you want it to say?"

Kevin frowned and ran one hand through his hair; he had not given any thought to what he wanted to say.

"Give me a second to think about it," he told the clerk. "Alright, I got it. 'Dinner Monday night at 6:30. Dress up.'" Kevin dictated.

~ ~ ~

Kevin eagerly anticipated his date as he drove home after his visit with Christine. He'd made a reservation at Chez Sophie, requesting a table by the window so they could look out on the Rappahannock River while they ate. Located in a restored Victorian manor built in 1827, Chez Sophie was widely considered the finest restaurant in Fredericksburg. Kevin felt a bit nervous, as Chez Sophie was the kind of place where he felt out of his element. However, he was certain it was not out of Felicia's league. Felicia deserved to be treated royally for all she had done for him.

Kevin dressed carefully in his best suit. He was glad he had when Felicia answered the door. Felicia looked stunning in a sleeveless black cocktail dress. She wore a simple strand of pearls around her neck and a matching bracelet on her right wrist. Her hair was swept back into a fashionable chignon. Kevin inhaled her delicate perfume as he helped her slip into a black satin trench coat. The lightweight coat was the perfect accessory for the cool autumn air.

Mr. Wilson had allowed Kevin to borrow a crystal red Corvette Coupe for the evening. Kevin walked Felicia around to the passenger side and opened the door for her. His stomach was doing flip-flops. Yes, sir, he was definitely out of his league. It was the same feeling he had his senior year in high school when he somehow convinced the homecoming queen to be his date to the Christmas dance. He found out later that she only went with him to make her ex-boyfriend jealous, but he was unaware of that at the time and they had enjoyed themselves immensely.

As Kevin walked around the car and climbed into the driver's seat, he willed himself to calm down.

Kevin managed to make small talk with Felicia on the drive to the restaurant without feeling like he was blabbering incoherently. For her part, Felicia seemed cool and collected. Kevin felt himself begin to relax.

The hostess took Felicia's coat and led them to a table for two. The sun had set and the city lights reflected off the river's surface. Kevin ordered his favorite meal—a New York strip steak, loaded baked potato, Caesar salad, and iced tea. Felicia chose broiled fish, steamed broccoli, a salad with fat-free Catalina on the side, and a glass of white wine.

"Could you bring some rolls right away?" Kevin asked the server after they had placed their orders.

Kevin was slathering his second roll with butter when it occurred to him that he was eating alone.

"Have a roll," he said, shoving the basket toward Felicia. "They're still warm, right from the oven."

"Thanks, but I'll pass."

The conversation never lulled while they ate, due primarily to the fact that Felicia talked almost non-stop. Over the salad course, she told him of her love of travel.

"I try to visit at least two new countries each year. Last year, we vacationed in southern Italy and on the island of Belize."

Kevin assumed the "we" was Felicia and her ex-husband, although she did not say.

"I went to Aruba in June," she continued, "with a couple of girlfriends. We had such a great time. I would love to spend Christmas in Paris one year. Of course, I would want to go to Paris with someone special. So, it probably won't be this year."

"Where have you traveled?" she asked, as the server cleared away the salad dishes.

"I've never been out of the country," Kevin confessed. From the look on her face, Kevin felt Felicia was either disappointed in him or felt sorry for him. "I spend most of my vacations in Florida, visiting my folks."

Their dinners arrived. Kevin dug into a perfectly cooked medium-rare steak, while Felicia picked at her fish and dove into a discourse on her frequent trips to New York City.

"Keeping up with the latest styles and fashions is a priority in my line of work."

"And what would that be?" Kevin asked in between bites of steak and potato.

"I'm an image consultant," Felicia told him breathlessly, as if there could be no better job in the entire world.

Kevin fought the urge to ask if image consulting was an actual job.

"What exactly does that mean?" he asked, hoping not to sound ignorant.

"I help my clients present themselves in a more positive light. I start by evaluating their wardrobes, personal appearance, and body language. We discuss what image they are projecting and what image they would like to project. Then I guide them in making changes that will give them a better self-image and allow them to be more confident. My favorite part of the job is taking clients to a stylist for a makeover. I also enjoy taking them shopping to pick out new wardrobes. It's amazing what a new hairstyle or the right make-up can do for a woman."

Felicia's face was aglow as she spoke. Clearly, she loved her job, and she loved talking about it. She was probably really good at it. The image she projected was of a woman who knew what she wanted and would let nothing stop her from getting it.

So why couldn't she keep her husband? Kevin quickly banished the unkind thought from his mind. He knew only too well that being a devoted, loving spouse did not guarantee a successful marriage.

Still, he could not help thinking that Felicia was helping people to present false images of themselves—images focused only on personal appearance and not on the substance of who they were. Felicia had continued talking while Kevin's mind wandered. He forced himself to give her his undivided attention.

"Of course, I believe in giving back to the community. I work with abused women to help them build up their self-confidence. It is criminal how some men abase the women they are supposed to love. Mental abuse should be a punishable offense, just like physical abuse. These women have been beaten down, physically and emotionally, for years, some for their entire lives. I love helping to build up their self-esteem so that they can see themselves as beautiful women with something positive to contribute to the world."

"Okay," Kevin thought, "maybe image consulting is not as shallow as it sounds." He was willing to give her credit for helping downtrodden women. Maybe she could help Christine.

Christine! How did she get back into my head? She is not my concern. Anyway, the church women seem to be helping her quite a lot. Kevin quickly dismissed the unbidden thought of his ex-wife from his head.

Kevin smiled. "It's wonderful that you are able to help hurting women."

"Sorry I prattled on so long," Felicia said demurely. "I do love what I do."

"And it shows. Everyone should have a job they feel that way about."

Kevin had cleaned his plate while Felicia talked. He noticed she had eaten only about half of hers when she pushed her plate away.

"I'm stuffed," she declared.

"How about some dessert? I hear they make the best key lime pie in town."

"I couldn't really, but don't let that stop you from having some."

Kevin ordered a slice of pie and decaf coffee. Felicia sipped on a second glass of wine while Kevin ate.

"What do you do?" she asked Kevin.

"I sell cars."

"Hence, the beautiful new Corvette," Felicia smiled.

"Don't get used to it. I borrowed it from the lot. It goes back in the morning."

"You're allowed to do that?"

"I am. It's a perk of the job. I don't know if Mr. Wilson lets everyone do it, but I can borrow any car I want for an evening."

"Nice perk."

"Yes, it is. It also helps me to sell more cars. I can honestly say I've driven the car and that it handles like a dream."

"Are you a good salesman?"

"I'm the best." Kevin could make the claim without being embarrassed or feeling as if he were boasting. He was simply stating a fact.

When Kevin walked Felicia to her door, he experienced all the uneasiness of a first date. Was this in fact a first date or just a thank you dinner? Would Felicia expect him to kiss her? If she invited him in, should he accept or decline?"

In the end, his worries were for naught. Felicia had her keys in hand and opened the door as soon as they reached the porch. She stretched up to place a friendly kiss on his cheek.

"Thanks for dinner. It was wonderful." She stepped inside the doorway as she spoke.

"My pleasure. Thanks for taking care of me last week."

"My pleasure," Felicia returned. She started to shut the door.

Kevin put out his hand to prevent the door from closing completely.

"Would you like to go out again sometime?" he asked hurriedly before losing his courage.

"That would be nice. Call me."

Chapter 25

Karen joined Robin in the break room of the orthodontic office.

"It's nice of Greg to take Christine to lunch on her first day of work," Robin commented to Karen as the two friends ate their lunches.

"I think so, too," Karen replied. "He wanted the opportunity to get to know her better in a setting where she might be a little more relaxed."

"She certainly is nervous, but she's catching on fast. Not that it's a demanding job. It doesn't take much skill to answer phones and schedule appointments."

"It may not be difficult," Karen admonished the older woman, "but it certainly is important. The receptionist is a new client's first contact with the office. If the receptionist isn't polite, professional, and organized, Greg could lose patients, and his business would suffer."

Robin smiled and nodded. She liked the way Karen put Greg's needs ahead of her own and how she was always thinking of ways to improve the running of the office.

"Speaking of business, how is your furniture restoration business coming along?"

"Quite well. Chad refers enough work to me to keep me busy. He's working on a couple houses on Princess Anne Street. The owners of both houses have some pieces to be restored."

"Are you still working out of your garage?"

"For the time being. We'll move into the new house in a few weeks. There's a large storage shed in the back that I'm planning to use as a workroom. Chad will have to give me a hand converting it into a workable space."

"It sounds like Chad's business has really taken off."

"Yes, it has. He hired two full-time employees, and he has a couple of part-timers, also. He's still working out of his apartment. I don't think that will last much longer. He needs to have an office."

The two women finished their lunches and cleaned up after themselves.

"I have some fabric samples I want to show you," Robin told Karen. "I'll get them and meet you in Greg's office in a minute."

"All this fuss seems unnecessary," Karen began as soon as Robin entered the office. "After all, I'm a thirty-seven-year-old bride with a son who's nearly sixteen. I keep telling Greg we should just have a simple ceremony in Mark's office. He won't hear of it."

"Of course, he won't." Robin held up a piece of celadon-colored silk to Karen's cheek. "A wedding is a joyous occasion that should be celebrated with those who love you."

Robin rejected the pale green fabric, saying it made Karen's complexion look washed out. The next sample was a soft cream satin.

"That's better, but not quite right. How about this one? It's ivory gold."

"I like it. It's not so close to white as the cream."

"The yellow undertones look good with your skin tone. Before you make up your mind, I have one more to show you."

Robin withdrew a length of shimmering silver satin.

"Oh, I love it," exclaimed Karen.

"I was hoping you would. It's my favorite. I think it will make a beautiful gown."

Robin set the fabric aside and grabbed a notebook off the chair. She flipped through the pages until she found what she was looking for.

"This is a sketch Lark drew of how she envisions your dress. What do you think?"

Karen gasped. "It's beautiful. I love it. Can Lark make it without a pattern?"

"Lark will create her own pattern. She has a flair for fashion design. She gets it from our mother. Mom is a fantastic seamstress."

"Do you sew?" Karen asked her.

"A little; nothing like Lark. I'm the organizer in the family. Lark is artistic and sensitive, but when it comes to planning.... Well, let's just say that Savanna's wedding would have been a total disaster if we'd left the planning up to Lark. Fortunately, she was wise enough to know she needed my help."

"You two certainly make a great team. I need both of you to pull off this wedding. Although I still think it's all really unnecessary. We would be just as married if we said our vows in Mark's office as we will be with a full-blown wedding."

"We're having a wedding!" Karen jumped at the sound of Greg's commanding voice. She turned to see her fiancé standing in her doorway.

"Since you *are* having a wedding," Robin added, as she stuffed fabric samples into a large shopping bag, "Karen might as well look stunning. And she will in a fabulous Lark Nelson original creation."

"Is that the dress?" Greg asked as Robin inched past him on her way out of the office.

"Never you mind." Robin scolded her boss. "You will see the wedding dress when your bride walks down the aisle and not one moment before. Is that clear?"

"Yes, ma'am."

Greg turned his attention back to Karen.

"Do you want to go to a movie tonight?"

"Sorry, I can't. Austin has a diorama to finish up for school tomorrow, Kyle has cub scouts, and Trevor has football practice. I haven't finished the homework assignment Mark gave us for our counseling session on Thursday. And I don't know when I'll have time to stain the coffee table for the Landry's. They want to pick it up Friday evening."

"I can help, you know. You don't have to try to do everything yourself."

"I know. I'm sorry. I'm still not used to having someone to depend on."

Greg kissed her softly.

"Here's my suggestion. You take care of getting Kyle to cub scouts and picking him up. Gretchen can bring the girls to your house after school. I'll swing by the high school to pick up Trevor, and we'll grab some Chinese take-out for dinner. After dinner, the girls can entertain Kyle, and I'll help Austin with his diorama.

You'll be free for a couple of hours to get some of your projects done. How's that sound?"

"It sounds like a plan."

Chapter 26

The ringing of the alarm woke Kevin from a sound sleep bright and early Sunday morning. He rolled to his side and looked outside through a slit in the curtain. The sky was a brilliant blue, and the sun was shining radiantly. If he had to get up early, it was nice to wake up to a beautiful day.

Kevin did not have the obligation of going to work, as the dealership was closed. Christine had begun attending church services with the Vinsons, so he no longer needed to sit with her on Sunday mornings. The fact that Christine was attending church, however, was a source of discomfort to Kevin and the reason he was rising from his bed earlier than he would have liked.

"A bet's a bet," he muttered, as he climbed from the comfortable bed and headed to the bathroom. He'd hung his navy sports coat and khaki Dockers on the front of the closet door before retiring last night. Mark had told him that he should not worry about what to wear to church and that casual attire was perfectly acceptable. Still, he had fretted as he tried to select clothing that would not peg him as a newcomer. He planned to get to church just before the service started and bolt out the door as soon as it ended.

As Kevin drove into town, he thought how strange it was that Christine was attending church voluntarily and seemed to be enjoying it. From what he could gather, Christine was there every time the church doors opened. Last Friday morning she called to tell him not to come over as she would be participating in the ladies' Bible study. He was unsure about what had come over Christine, but he was happy to not be spending all his free time sitting with her.

He was happy, wasn't he? If he were honest with himself, and he did try to be, he'd been a bit disappointed by Christine's call. It made no sense, he knew, yet that was what he had felt. He had actually been looking forward to spending time with Christine.

Their last few encounters had been pleasant, perhaps even enjoyable. That thought scared him. He did not want to enjoy being with Christine.

After her phone call on Friday, Kevin knew he had to get her out of his head. He had dialed Felicia's number and was relieved when she answered after only two rings. Regrettably, she was teaching a seminar all day Saturday and had to prepare on Friday. But she was free on Sunday evening and invited Kevin to her house for a home-cooked meal.

Kevin checked his watch as he walked up the sidewalk to the church entrance. It was ten minutes before eleven. He hoped he would be able to slip into a seat in the back unnoticed. But that was not to be.

Robin and Chris Jennings were standing in the entryway serving as greeters and welcomed him warmly. They even introduced him to a few people mingling in the foyer before the start of the service.

One lady grinned broadly at him and, ignoring his outstretched hand, enveloped him in a big bear hug. "I'm so glad to finally meet Christine's husband. She's told me so much about you. We are in a Bible study group that meets on Tuesday evenings. It's a support group for women who have …um, well, let's just say, for women who have had a rough time in life."

Kevin's face must have registered the shock he was feeling, because she stopped abruptly and laid her right hand on his forearm.

"Now, don't you worry any, honey. She told us you have always treated her like a queen. But, you know, of course, that she didn't have the easiest childhood. Well, I don't need to tell you any of this."

She embraced him again, as she added, "It is really, really good to finally meet you. I'm so glad you've decided to start coming to church at last."

Abruptly, she turned around and began a conversation with a middle-aged woman standing nearby. Kevin was never given an opportunity to inject a word into the conversation and therefore was not able to correct her misconceptions about his relationship with Christine.

"She talks more than any woman I know," Chris whispered conspiratorially to Kevin. "Maybe it's because she isn't married and doesn't have anyone at home to converse with."

Kevin had a witty comeback on the tip of his tongue; however, he restrained himself from saying anything so unkind while inside a church. Rather, he asked Chris if he was fully recovered from his recent surgery.

"I'm feeling well enough to be out in my garden," he told Kevin. "I'll have a nice batch of pumpkins for the Harvest festival in a few weeks. Robin took great care of me."

Chris smiled tenderly at his wife, who had just joined in the conversation, and caressed her cheek. "I think I'll keep her." He winked at Kevin.

Kevin felt a tug at his heart. He knew they had grown children. They must have been married close to thirty years, yet they looked at each other like a young couple in the bloom of love. He wished he had found a love like that.

"Christine is doing a great job at the office," Robin said, changing the subject.

Oh right, Kevin reminded himself. Christine had started training to take over Robin's position.

"I'm glad to hear that," Kevin replied, and he genuinely meant it.

"She's a great receptionist. She doesn't need my help in that regard. But I am going in next week to help her get to know the clients."

"Kevin!"

Kevin was startled to hear the familiar voice call out his name. Christine sounded glad to see him. She and Janet entered the foyer as Kevin had been about to take his leave of Robin and Chris.

"You're walking!" Kevin was astonished. He did not think it was quite time for the cast on Christine's leg to have come off. And when he looked down, he saw that it was, in fact, still on. She held a cane in her right hand.

"The doctor put me in a walking cast Thursday. I'll have it on for two more weeks. I have the cane in case I stumble. I'm still getting used to walking again."

"Congratulations. It's wonderful to see you up and about."

"You must sit with us," she told him.

Thinking of no graceful way to decline, Kevin followed Janet and Christine to a seat near the front of the church.

"There's a dinner after church," Janet told him as they settled into the pew. "I really hope you'll stay. There's always plenty of food."

"Yes, Kevin. Please say you'll stay."

Again, Kevin could think of no way to avoid staying for lunch without hurting their feelings, so he found himself agreeing.

The service started soon afterward. Attending a handful of funerals, and even fewer weddings, comprised the sum of Kevin's church experiences. He soon realized that he had entered into the service with many erroneous, preconceived expectations. Among the most strongly held was the notion that all religious music was solemn and sober. When the music minister indicated the congregation should rise, Kevin reluctantly reached for the hymnal in front of him and slowly stood to his feet. To his amazement the minister did not announce a hymn number; instead, the words of the song flashed onto a projection screen behind the choir. He was even more surprised when the song leader reached for a guitar and began to strum along with the other musicians. It took a moment for Kevin to register that the music was provided not only by a pianist and an organist, but also by a drummer, a trumpeter, and two additional guitarists. On second glance, Kevin decided that one guitar was actually a bass.

The music was considerably more contemporary than Kevin had expected. Even though he knew none of the songs, he found himself enjoying the upbeat tempos and made an attempt to sing along. After a couple of lively numbers, the music slowed down to be a bit more worshipful and ended with a quiet hymn.

Mark walked to the podium and made a few announcements, extending a warm invitation to everyone present to join in the after-service meal. Kevin was caught off guard when Mark asked for first-time visitors to raise their hands to be acknowledged. Kevin made a quick decision to ignore Mark's request and avoid drawing unwanted attention. Mark, however, did not give Kevin that option, but rather singled Kevin out and introduced him as a personal friend. Mark then encouraged the congregation to greet Kevin and the other visitors during the fellowship time.

Kevin found himself surrounded by many friendly faces welcoming him to their fellowship. The people he had not previously met naturally assumed that Kevin and Christine were married. And why not, Kevin told himself. The couple shared a last name and they were sitting together. More times than Kevin cared to keep track of, he heard someone tell Christine that they were so happy to meet her husband and they hoped that the couple would enjoy worshipping together at the church.

After the congregation was seated again, Mark made his way to the podium. Kevin willed himself to stay awake during the sermon that he anticipated would be dry and boring. Later he recognized that Mark's personality was far too engaging for him to deliver the sermon Kevin had fabricated in his mind. From the start Mark caught his attention and held it.,

"Today I want to talk to you about worship," Mark began. "Many people mistakenly use the word worship as a synonym for the music portion of a church service. Others think of worship as joining together with other believers to praise God and listen to his Word. We often speak of this time of fellowship as the "Sunday morning worship service," as opposed to Sunday school or the Wednesday Bible study."

"To be sure, singing, praising God, and studying the Word are components of worshiping God. But they are not the only aspects of worship. Webster's primary definition of worship is, "reverent honor and homage paid to God." Any act of ours that honors God and pays homage to God is an act of worship. In First Corinthians 10:31 Paul admonishes us with these words, "Therefore, whether you eat or drink, or whatever you do, do all to the glory of God." When our deeds bring glory to God, we are worshiping him. Sometimes our acts of worship are pleasurable to us, such as singing songs of praise, and seem to cost us little or nothing. At other times, our acts of worship may cost us time, energy, or money. David is recorded in Second Samuel 24:24 as saying, 'Nor will I offer burnt offerings to the LORD my God with that which costs me nothing.'"

"Praising God when we don't feel like it is one form of worship that costs us something. When we make a joyful noise to the Lord in spite of physical or emotional pain, the Lord honors our sacrifice. We take our eyes off ourselves and our problems, and we focus our attention on God. As we acknowledge God's greatness, our problems diminish. The Lord God, who is worthy of our praise, is able to deliver us from the stresses of this life. When I crawl out of my comfortable bed thirty minutes earlier than I would like in order to spend quiet time with God, He honors that sacrifice by meeting with me."

"Sacrificing our time to serve others in the name of Jesus is another way to worship God. Those of you deliver meals to the homeless are worshiping God through your sacrifice of time and by extending His hand to those in need. Others of you give financially to that ministry, worshiping God with your offerings."

"In closing, let me read Romans 12:1, 'I beseech you therefore, brethren, by the mercies of God, that you present your bodies a living sacrifice, holy, acceptable to God, which is your reasonable service.' I admonish each of you to make worship a regular part of your daily routine. And please remember, after the meal today, you will each have an opportunity to worship God by helping to clean up."

This was Kevin's first dinner-on-the-grounds, as he learned the after-church meal was called. As a first-time guest, he was sent to the front of the line, along with Christine. Kevin was not prepared for the vast array of food provided by the women, and men, of the church. Everything looked so good that he was tempted to try it all. He made a good effort and managed to get at least a bite of each entree on his plate before food threatened to spill over the sides. Christine was able to hold her plate in her one free hand; Kevin assisted her by filling her plate as she instructed him.

Christine pointed to an empty table under the shade of a large oak tree.

"Set your plate down," she told him, "and go back for your drink and dessert."

"You sit, and I'll get your drink," Kevin responded.

Kevin was back in a few moments carrying two plates of dessert. Christine looked at him askance.

"The coconut cake looked so good, I didn't want to risk it being gone before I got back," Kevin told her unapologetically. He set the plates down and went off to retrieve drinks for them both.

Christine took another look at the dessert plates. In addition to the cake, Kevin had brought a brownie, two chocolate chip cookies, and a slice of cherry pie. Cherry pie was Christine's favorite dessert; she was pleased that Kevin had remembered.

Kevin returned with two glasses of lemonade and found that Chris and Robin Jennings, their daughter Hannah, and her husband and daughter, had joined Christine.

"I see you're trying some of my scalloped okra and corn," Chris commented, as Kevin savored his first bite of the unusual dish.

"You made this?" Kevin asked, surprise evident in his voice. "It's wonderful. What did you call it?"

Chris smiled broadly at Kevin's compliment. "Scalloped okra and corn."

"This green stuff is okra, huh? I've never thought I would like okra, but this is delicious."

"You should try fried okra," Hannah interjected. "Homemade fried okra—not the fried okra you get in restaurants. That has too much batter. Mom shakes the sliced okra in flour and fries it in hot bacon grease with a little garlic salt. It's my favorite comfort food. I can make a meal of fried okra and slices of freshly picked homegrown tomatoes."

"Add in an ear or two of corn on the cob, and I'll have to agree with you," Michael, Hannah's husband, chimed in.

"Well, I prefer my fried okra with a side of Southern fried chicken." This came from Chris. "And no one fries chicken as tasty as my Robin."

Once again, Kevin was cognizant of the great affection Chris and Robin still shared after all these years. A glance around the church grounds verified that they were not unique. His gaze rested on many couples who had obviously spent more years together than Kevin had been alive—Mark and Janet Vinson, Tom and Gretchen Sullivan, Lark and Peter Nelson, and Donna and Bill Clark to name a few.

As they finished their meals, the members of the Jennings family dispersed to visit with other people, leaving Kevin and Christine alone at the table.

Kevin took advantage of the opportunity to ask Christine a question that had been gnawing at his mind. "So, I hear you joined a women's...."

Kevin searched for the right word.

"Support group," Christine supplied.

"Right. What's up with that?"

Christine looked a bit uncomfortable. "It's a group for women who have been abused either as children or in past relationships. They are helping me to forgive those who hurt me and to…"

"Build a better self-image," Kevin supplied. Conversations with Mark over the past few months, and with Felicia over the past couple of weeks, had given Kevin a new appreciation of how damaging Christine's past had been on her perceptions of her self-worth.

"Yes. Exactly." Christine seemed relieved that Kevin understood that much at least. "I didn't realize how much anger and bitterness I had inside me toward my mother and the men she brought into my life."

Kevin reached out and stroked Christine's hand. He was glad she was getting the help she needed.

"It feels so good to let go of the hurt and forgive them," Christine continued.

"I can understand that you can stop being angry with them, but how can you forgive them when they haven't apologized and probably are not the least bit sorry?" Kevin asked her.

"Pastor Mark told me that we have to forgive those who hurt us, whether they are sorry or not. He says that forgiving them is something we do for ourselves, not for them. It doesn't quite make sense to me either, but I can tell it's working. When I decided to forgive them, I felt a great sense of relief. Mark said it was because I let go of a big burden I'd been carrying around with me."

"Well," Kevin said, still a bit confused, "it seems to be working for you. Listen, this has been nice. Really. But I have to get going. It was good to see you."

Kevin rose from the table and took a step away before Christine grabbed his hand. Kevin stopped and looked down at their clasped hands, and then into Christine's eyes. The scared, vulnerable look was back.

Christine looked down at the ground and chewed on her lower lip. Kevin recognized that whatever she wanted to say was going to cost her. He took a step closer to her and knelt down so that he was on her eye-level.

"Just say it, Christine," he coaxed. "It will be alright."

"I also forgave you," she whispered.

Forgave me, Kevin raged silently, even as he looked away, so Christine would not see the hurt and anger in them. *Forgave me for what? For being a loving, supportive husband? For marrying you when no respectable man would have you? For always being faithful, even when you weren't?*

Kevin wanted to shout all these words at Christine. He did not, however. He had promised her she could tell him anything without fear of retribution, so he held his tongue and worked hard to prevent the rage that surged through him from showing in his eyes.

Kevin took a deep breath and exhaled slowly, deliberately. He turned back to Christine. She was chewing on her lip again. He did not trust himself to speak, and he honestly had no idea what he would say if he did speak. Kevin released Christine's hand, caressed her cheek, rose, and walked away.

On the drive home, he pondered Christine's comment. He did not know what to make of it. He knew that Christine was not referring to something as trivial as working on her birthday, which he had certainly done more than once, or not remembering her size when he bought her an article of clothing, something he had also done. She would never make a big deal out of forgiving him for such a small offense. No, she was telling him she had forgiven him for some big hurt he had caused her. Although Kevin racked his brain, he had no idea what he had done. He had always prided himself on the fact that he had not caused his wife the pain he had seen his friends and colleagues cause their wives.

So, why did Christine need to forgive me?

Chapter 27

Emily looked around her sparsely furnished guest room. "Christine was not exaggerating when she said she didn't have many belongings," she stated casually to Chad, who had just finished setting up Christine's bed.

"Kevin told me that when she left him, the living room suit he had given her as a gift were the only pieces of furniture she took. She took personal belongings, of course, but not much else. Someone bought her the bedroom furniture later."

"Her bedroom furniture is overwhelmed by this room. Maybe we should move the loveseat in here. There's plenty of room for it on that wall."

Chad followed Emily's finger. He agreed that there was room for the loveseat on the empty wall next to the bathroom. "One thing you can say about older houses is that they built nice, large bedrooms," Chad responded. "I'll get Mark to give me a hand with the loveseat."

Chad found Mark coming in the front door with the last box of Christine's things. In short order, the men had moved not only the loveseat, but also the matching chair and ottoman to the bedroom, and Emily had made up the bed.

Emily looked around the room. "It still looks a bit bare, but at least Christine will be able to sleep comfortably in her own bed tonight."

"She'll appreciate that, I'm sure," Mark concurred. "It's been a long time since she slept in her own bed or had any of her personal belongings unpacked. It will be a nice surprise for her to come to her new home after work and find her bed made up and her clothes hanging in the closet."

"I think that all our hard work has earned us a reward," Emily announced. "I made a blueberry cobbler this morning."

"Great idea," seconded Mark.

"Do you have any vanilla ice cream?" Chad smiled impishly at Emily, as he opened the freezer door and peered inside.

"This is delicious, Emily," Mark told her after downing his first bite. "It's still warm."

"I took it out of the oven just before you got here. I wanted to have a nice dinner and dessert to celebrate Christine's relocation."

"Emily, I can't thank you enough," Mark told her, "for what you are doing for Christine. She seemed to feel she was imposing on us and that it was time for her to leave. She didn't have any real options for moving out until you offered to rent her a room here."

"I am happy to do it. In the little bit of time I've spent with Christine, I've grown to like her. I think we will get along well."

"That's great. Janet and I have enjoyed her time with us. She's hard to get to know, though. Janet has spent more time with her than I have. Christine has shared a little bit about her past with Janet. She certainly grew up in less than ideal circumstances, and she's used to being taken advantage of."

"I'm glad she's working for Greg," Chad interjected. "She'll be surrounded by Christians at home, at work, and at church. Hopefully, she will begin to understand how much God loves and values her."

"I do hope so," Mark continued. "I am also hoping that she will show some interest in her child soon. She never mentions the baby."

"Is she seeing a doctor?" Emily voiced the concern they all felt for the child Christine was carrying.

"Yes, Janet has taken her twice to see an obstetrician. Everything seems to be progressing as it should, except for Christine's ambivalence."

"Maybe she's afraid," Emily said. "This is her first child, and there is a lot of uncertainty in her life right now."

"I'm sure that fear is a factor. Maybe her attitude will begin to change now that she has a job and a place to live," Mark said.

Emily realized that she needed to be sure the pastor understood her arrangement with Christine. "Christine is welcome to stay here until the baby is born. She will have to find a place of her own in the spring though. She's planning to save up money for a deposit on an apartment for herself and the baby."

Mark finished his last bite of cobbler before responding. "She did mention that. I guess I've been hoping that if you two hit it off, that she might stay a while longer."

Mark looked optimistically at Emily.

Emily looked down at her hands cupped together on the table, with the right one covering the left. "Oh, I'm sure we will get along fine. It's just that…"

Mark noticed the hint of a smile forming at the corners of Emily's mouth and wondered what was being left unsaid. He followed Emily's eyes as she cast a glance at Chad. Chad made no attempt to hide his big grin.

Chad reached out his large left hand and covered Emily's small ones, as his right arm slipped behind her back. "Emily will be getting a new roommate in the spring."

Understanding dawned on Mark. "I should have anticipated that. Congratulations to you both." He enveloped the happy couple in a group hug.

"I'm sure God has another plan in mind for Christine. For now, we will just have to be patient. I want to be certain that you are aware of Christine's background and spiritual condition. Christine was raised in circumstances that are a world apart from your upbringing."

Emily nodded. "I know I was blessed with a home life most children only dream of. It wasn't quite 'Leave It to Beaver' or 'Father Knows Best,' but it was close."

"Christine can't begin to identify with the happy, intact families portrayed in those shows. She had several stepfathers and more live-in 'uncles' than she can keep track of. Many of them took advantage of her and caused her a great deal of pain. Because of that she has a difficult time relating to God as a loving father."

"She mentioned," Emily inserted, "that she is going to the abused women's support group."

"The group has helped Christine tremendously. She is beginning to understand that the men who hurt her are responsible for their own actions and that she bears no guilt in the things that were done to her. Christine has shown great interest in studying the Bible and seems to enjoy attending church service. But she has not yet taken the step of faith required to accept Jesus Christ as her Savior. I'm afraid that Christine still sees herself as unworthy of

Christ's forgiveness. She has a very poor self-image. I believe that you, Emily, may be able to help her in that area."

~ ~ ~

After Mark and Chad took their leave, Emily brewed a cup of Earl Grey tea and took it and her Bible into the den for some alone time with God. The room was chilly, so she flipped on the gas fireplace and cuddled up in her favorite chair with an afghan covering her legs. She spent the next hour reading the Bible and asking God for wisdom in being the friend and witness Christine needed.

By the time Christine arrived home after work, Emily had arranged her hanging clothes in the closet and unpacked two of Christine's boxes. Emily had been hesitant to open the boxes until Chad reminded her of the circumstances under which they had been packed. Emily thought Christine would be more comfortable in her new home if she were surrounded by some familiar objects.

Emily set a Tiffany-style lamp on the nightstand, along with one of her own vases filled with purple Michaelmas daisies from her garden. She placed a jewelry box and two framed photos on the dresser. One photo was of Christine and Kevin on what Emily assumed was their wedding day and the other was of Kevin opening gifts in front of a Christmas tree. Emily thought it peculiar that these were the only pictures she found among Christine's belongings.

"Welcome home," Emily called out, as Christine walked unassisted and crutchless into her new home. The walking cast had come off Christine's left leg a little more than a week ago, and Christine had wasted little time in her efforts to become self-sufficient again.

"Thanks," Christine mumbled quietly.

Emily recognized that as a sign of Christine's nervousness and was not offended by her seeming lack of enthusiasm.

"Felix has taken a liking to your bed." Emily pointed the way to Christine's room. "You may have to share it with him."

Christine laughed, and Emily was glad that her light-hearted comment had the desired effect.

"I hung up your clothes and unpacked a few things. I hope you don't mind."

"No, not at all. Thank you."

Christine paused in the doorway and looked around her new room. She seemed startled by the photos on the dresser, and Emily worried that she had overstepped her boundaries. She breathed easier a moment later when Christine walked to the dresser and picked up the one of Kevin and herself.

"Wow. I haven't seen this picture in ages. I forgot I had it."

She turned to Emily. "Look how young I was—18 and barely out of high school."

Christine put the picture down and turned her attention to the other photo. "I took that picture on our second Christmas together. Kevin was just starting to golf and had managed to buy a second-hand set of clubs at a pawnshop. I found a pattern for crocheted golf covers, and I made them for him in the Redskins' colors. He was so surprised. I don't think he knew that I could crochet. It was a great Christmas."

"What a thoughtful gift. Maybe you could teach me to crochet," Emily said hopefully.

"I'd love to. I haven't made anything in a while, but I'm sure I still know how. It isn't hard. Of course, it can't be hard if I can do it."

Christine's words reminded Emily of how fragile Christine's self-esteem was.

"Well, I've never been able to do it. And I have tried a time or two. So, I'd be grateful for your tutelage. You've told me something I didn't know about you, so it's only fair I share some private information about me with you."

Emily held out her left hand and let Christine see the beautiful ring Chad had presented to her only two days ago.

"You're engaged. How wonderful!"

"Chad and I will be getting married in May. We don't want to detract from the attention Karen deserves on her wedding day, so we are keeping it quiet until after the wedding. You're the first person I've told outside of our family and Pastor Mark."

"Thank you for telling me. I won't tell a soul."

"I know. I had to tell you. That's what roomies do."

Chapter 28

Two weeks had passed since Christine had moved in, and Emily was pleased with how well things were working out. Emily could not ask for a better roommate. Christine made no demands as she did not want to be a bother. She was attending church regularly and seem to be enjoying getting to know the church members. Emily prayed daily that God would open doors for her to sprinkle seeds of faith and words of encouragement into Christine's life.

"Hi, Emily. I'm home," Christine's voice sang out as she came through the door.

"How was work?" Emily called out from the kitchen.

"Great. After such a busy weekend, it was almost relaxing to be back at work."

"You certainly did have a busy weekend. I know Chris and Robin appreciated all your help making pumpkin pies for the Harvest festival. How many did you all make?"

"Twelve! It was a lot of work, but I really enjoyed it. I had always bought canned pumpkin for my pies. It never even occurred to me that you could cook your own from fresh pumpkins."

"Robin and Chris have been doing that for years. Chris grows his own pumpkins for pies and decorations. If I know Chris, he's cooking the leftover pumpkins today and canning the pumpkin for pies at Thanksgiving and Christmas."

"He is. He dropped off a couple of cans for each of us in the office this afternoon." Christine held up two jars as evidence. "I love working at the orthodontist office. Everyone is so friendly. How was your day?"

"It was great. I spent the morning with Chad, and I gave two piano lessons this afternoon. Missy Page could hardly stop talking about the Harvest festival long enough to play her pieces. You impressed her with your face painting."

Christine beamed. "It was my first time. I didn't think I could do it, but Janet encouraged me to try. I'm so glad I did. It was great fun."

"It was amazing that you could do it so well with only one hand. When do you get the cast off your arm?"

"Tomorrow, I hope. I see the doctor in the morning. If it's healing like it should, the cast will come off. He said I'll have to wear a brace for a few weeks while I build my muscles back up. I will be so disappointed if it doesn't come off tomorrow."

"I'll be praying for you," Emily told Christine, as she checked the meatloaf in the oven.

"It still needs about half an hour. Everything else is about ready. Let's have a cup of tea while we wait, and you can tell me how your date went Friday night. We've been so busy I haven't had time to ask you about it."

Emily poured two cups of steaming water over chamomile tea bags and carried the cups to the table.

"It wasn't a date," Christine protested, although Emily noticed that the protest was half-hearted. Emily still did not have a good handle on the relationship between Christine and her ex-husband. They seemed to enjoy each other's company, yet Emily sensed an undercurrent of unresolved tensions.

"I made Kevin promise to go to the play with me weeks ago, back when I first won the tickets. He didn't know it was a musical or he never would have gone. He seemed to enjoy it, though. I loved it."

"It is a great play," Emily agreed. "But what I really want to know is, how did the two of you get along?"

"Fine, I guess. He hadn't seen me since that Sunday he came to church. I think he was shocked by my baby bump; I was barely showing a few weeks ago."

"Did you two talk about the baby?" Emily hoped she wasn't being too pushy.

"No, not at all. We've never talked about the baby. I think it upsets him that I'm pregnant."

Emily nodded understandingly. "I guess that makes sense, since it is not his child. Are you going to see him again?"

"He didn't ask me out, if that's what you mean." After a pause, Christine added. "I think he might be seeing someone."

Emily raised her eyebrows in question.

"He made a few comments about restaurants he had been to and a couple of movies he had seen. I got the impression that he was talking about dates. Of course, he is free to date anyone he wants."

Emily could tell that Christine was trying hard to be nonchalant, yet she got the impression that Christine still held deep feelings for Kevin. She decided it was time to change the subject.

"Can you keep a secret?" Emily asked Christine.

"Of course," Christine replied. "I don't have anyone but you to share secrets with anyway."

Emily got up and retrieved a long thin box from the hall closet. She carried it to the table and opened it up. Christine peered inside the box. It held an engraved wooden sign.

"Olde Towne Restorations," she read. "Houses and furniture restored by Chad Butler and Karen Marshall."

"What is it?" Christine asked Emily.

"A sign for Chad and Karen's new shop downtown. Only Karen doesn't know about it yet—the shop or the sign. It's a wedding gift from Greg. So, you can't tell anyone."

"No, I won't," Christine responded solemnly and with a hint of pride in her voice, Emily noted. "Thanks for telling me."

The oven timer buzzed, alerting Emily that the meatloaf was ready. She gave Christine a quick hug before hurrying to turn off the oven. She removed the meatloaf.

"I'll let it set while I mash the potatoes. Would you mind setting the table and dishing up the green beans?"

Within a few minutes the ladies were seated at the table. Emily blessed the meal. As they ate, she filled Christine in on the details of the wedding surprise.

"Chad has been operating his business from his apartment since he moved here last spring. Karen has been restoring furniture part-time from her house. Greg wanted Karen to have more space to work and also to be able to separate her work from their home life, so he decided to rent her a shop. When he asked Chad for assistance in locating the right spot, Chad decided he should have an office, too. Chad knew of the perfect place. It's right downtown on William Street, between Caroline and Sophia. Chad has remodeled it, so that there is a reception area, offices for him and Karen, and a work area for Karen. The work area has a large picture window. As shoppers pass by, they can watch Karen work through the window and see the furniture at different stages of restoration."

"What a great idea! I know Karen will love it."

"Yes, I think it is a wonderful plan. I will work for them, as the receptionist, bookkeeper, office manager, and salesman."

"About that..." Christine hesitated. "I know you worked at Greg's office whenever Robin needed to be off. Did you want...?"

"To work for Greg? Heavens, no. I mean, I enjoyed working there once in a while, but it wasn't..."

Emily's voice trailed off as she tried to come up with a tactful way to say that she found Christine's job to be too mundane.

"challenging enough for me. I need more variety in my work. I have a degree in business and working with Chad and Karen will allow me to use more of my skills." Emily stopped, hoping she had not insulted Christine.

"A business degree?" Christine sounded surprised, but not hurt. "I thought you were a music teacher."

"I studied music, also. I've played piano since I was seven. But my major was business. My parents talked me into it, as they said I would always be able to get a job. They were right. I got a great paying job right out of college. Unfortunately, it was for a large company in Richmond. I wasn't cut out for big companies or big cities. I worked there for two and a half years, though. Hated every minute."

"So, you quit and came back home?"

"When I came home last Christmas, it was apparent that my grandmother needed more care than my mother could give her. It was a great excuse for me to quit my job and move back here. This is her house. I moved in with her at the beginning of the year."

Christine seemed puzzled. "I haven't met your grandmother. Where is she now?"

"In a nursing home."

"Oh, now I remember. You mentioned that once when you visited with me at Janet's. What happened to her?"

"She fell and broke her hip. I was hoping she would recover enough to come home, but that doesn't seem likely. She's going downhill pretty fast. Her doctors don't expect her to live much longer."

"Oh, I'm sorry," Christine said quietly.

"Don't be. She's lived a long and happy life. I'm so glad I got to spend eight months living here with her. We spent hours upon hours looking at old family photos, reminiscing about her childhood and mine. When she's gone, I'll have those precious memories to comfort me. I wouldn't trade that time for anything in the world. Grandma is ready to go home. When the time comes, we'll be sad, but we'll let her go. I only pray that she doesn't suffer."

~ ~ ~

Christine had spent enough time in church and the ladies' Bible study to know that Emily believed her grandmother would go to Heaven. What Christine did not yet grasp was how Emily could be sure of that. Christine made a mental note to ask Emily about it one day soon.

Chapter 29

Christine came home after work the next day to find Emily on the couch surrounded by photo albums, scrapbooks, and a mountain of tissues.

"Is it your grandmother?" she asked gently, as she swiped dirty tissues from the couch and sat down beside Emily.

To Christine's amazement, Emily buried her head in Christine's neck and bawled like a baby. Christine wrapped her arms around Emily and patted her gently on the back. Emily cried harder. After several minutes, the sobs subsided. Christine released Emily and handed her a wad of tissues.

"I must look like such a mess," Emily sniffled, as she blew her nose. "I didn't expect it to hurt so bad; after all, we knew it was coming."

~ ~ ~

Funeral services for Martha Aileen Pannell Heflin were held on the first Thursday in November at 2 p.m. The members of Riverside Christian Fellowship had provided lunch for the family and friends in the fellowship hall before the funeral. The ladies had outdone themselves preparing food for the covered dish meal. Tables were laden with platters of fried chicken, pot roast, casseroles, salads, rolls, and more desserts than could be consumed by a small army. Enough tables and chairs had been set up to accommodate two hundred people, and there was hardly an empty seat to be found.

Christine had reluctantly agreed to attend the funeral. She'd only been to two funerals in her life, and they had both been highly traumatic affairs. Her grandmother had died at the age of 45 while Christine was still in elementary school, her fourth-grade year. Her mother was only 26 at the time and had been devastated by the loss. She had wept inconsolably at the funeral home when friends and family had come to express their condolences. Although Christine's mother sometimes sent her to church on a bus that picked up children in the trailer park, they did not have a church of their own or know any ministers. Her mother opted to not have a funeral. The funeral home found someone--Christine supposed he was a minister--to say a few words over the body at the gravesite. Christine had no idea what he said as her mother had wailed loudly the entire time he spoke.

The other funeral had been for her cousin Jerry. Jerry had been out drinking with friends and lost control of his car on one of the windy back roads near Thornburg. He was not wearing a seatbelt and had been ejected from a car, flown into the tree, and broken his neck. The doctor said he had died instantly and had not suffered. Christine was fifteen at the time; Jerry was only four years older. The funeral director had suggested that the casket be closed during the service, but Aunt Marlene would hear nothing of it. The funeral home was packed with friends and family members. Aunt Marlene stood beside the casket and rocked the body, weeping softly into his chest, throughout the service.

Those two experiences instilled Christine with a fear of funerals. It was only because Emily was her roommate and had shown her so much kindness that she felt compelled to be present for her grandmother's service. She was surprised to see Emily's mother eating as she held her grandson Andy. Christine's mother and aunt had been much too upset to eat for days after losing their family members. Far from hysterical, Donna actually seemed to be laughing at something Emily's brother Matthew was telling her. As she passed the table where the Clark family sat, she overheard Matthew saying, "Remember the time Grandpa took me fishing, and I hooked him in the ear. Grandma had to cut off the barb and push the hook through his ear." Everyone laughed, and Christine realized that the family members were sharing memories of their deceased loved one.

Christine found a seat beside Janet. She set down her plate and went back to get a drink.

"I'm sorry, dear, for not helping you with your plate," Janet told her when she returned. "You're getting along so well that I forget you only have use of one hand."

"At least it's my right hand. I managed just fine."

Christine nibbled at her food and pondered at how different this funeral was from those she had attended.

"Is something bothering you?" Janet asked gently.

"Not bothering me, really. But I am curious about something. Donna doesn't seem sad. When my grandmother died, my mom cried buckets."

"Donna is sad, but she is not letting her grief consume her," Janet explained gently. "She misses her mother and she will have some difficult days, but she can still take pleasure in the memories of her mother's life. She knows that death is really a beginning, not an end. Mrs. Heflin is in Heaven in the presence of our Lord and Savior. Donna looks forward to the day she will join her. That's our hope as Christians."

Christine wondered once again how they could be so certain about going to Heaven.

She started to question Janet on the subject; however, Janet was getting up from the table.

"I need to go back into the sanctuary. Mrs. Heflin's casket is going to be open for viewing until the funeral starts. I want to be close by in case Donna or her siblings need me. When you're finished eating, you should come on over."

Christine sat in the second pew from the back waiting for the service to begin. Karen Harper and Greg Marshall slid in beside her.

"She looks so peaceful," Karen whispered. "Don't you think so?"

"I didn't look," Christine confided.

"It is difficult," Karen reassured her. "But I find that it helps to see how peaceful the deceased looks."

Organ music filled the air, and Mark walked to the podium.

"We are here today to celebrate the life and homegoing of Martha Aileen Pannell Heflin. Martha was a loving wife to her late husband George, and a doting mother and grandmother. She was also a trusted friend to those close to her and a dedicated member of our church. She will be missed deeply. We mourn her passing, but it is for ourselves we mourn, not Martha. Her graduation to Heaven is our loss, but it is her gain. She is in the presence of Jesus Christ. Paul said in Second Corinthians 5:8, 'We are confident, yes, well pleased rather to be absent from the body and to be present with the

Lord.' As Christians, we all look forward to the day we escape these frail earthly bodies and are transported to our Heavenly home."

After Mark's introductory remarks, the congregation joined the choir in singing, "In the Garden." Christine was shocked when Donna Clark walked to the podium. There were tears in her eyes, yet she radiated joy and serenity.

"Many of you know that mother broke her hip a few months ago and spent her last days in a nursing home. Her body was failing her, but her mind was sharp. She so appreciated that many of you took the time to visit her and send her cards. Your thoughtfulness brightened her days. Every time I visited her, she asked me to thank you all for your kindness. She also made it very clear that she was ready to go home and be free of her frail body. My siblings and I thank God daily for the role models our parents were and for the Godly training they instilled in our lives."

Christine found tears flowing down her cheeks when Donna was finished. This was so very different from the other funerals she had attended. Even in their sadness, Mrs. Heflin's family had peace and joy.

Mark returned to the podium, "I would like to speak to you for a few moments about the things Martha would want each of you to know if she were here today. First, she would want you to know that Heaven is a very real place, and so is hell. We all have pictures in our minds of the beauty and wonder of Heaven. Heaven will be incredible beyond our most vivid imaginings. The best part of Heaven, however, will be to be in the presence of Jesus Christ. Those who have not accepted God's free gift of salvation will not have this wonderful experience. They will face an entirely different eternity. Jesus himself described hell as a 'furnace of fire' where there will 'weeping and gnashing of teeth.' He told us that hell was prepared as punishment for the devil and his angels. Jesus does not want any of us to go to hell. There is only one way to escape that fate, and it is to repent of our sins and confess Jesus Christ as Lord of our lives."

"Secondly, Martha would want you to know that Jesus is the only way. Jesus himself told his disciples, as recorded in John 14:6, 'I am the way and the truth and the life. No one comes to the Father except through me.' Peter said in Acts 4:12, 'there is no other name under heaven given among men by which we must be saved.'" Jesus is the only perfect person who ever lived. He is the only one who could pay the price for our sins. He went to the cross for our sins—yours and mine. And He's the only one who defeated death."

"Finally, Martha would want you to know that your life here on Earth will be so much better, so much happier, if you make Jesus your Lord. Many people have the misguided belief that Christianity is a religion of 'don'ts'. They think Christians cannot have fun. Let me assure you how false that thinking is. Without a doubt, as a Christian, I have missed out on plenty. I've missed out on hangovers, drug addictions, bad relationships, and a whole host of other things. And I'm thankful I've missed out on them. The Christian life is more wonderful than I can possibly describe. Which isn't to say that Christians live in a bubble where we're sheltered from the world's problems. We experience the same types of problems as those who don't know Christ. The difference is that we have Christ to walk with us as we deal with them. Every day I wake up and have peace. I have joy. I have the Holy Spirit walking by my side and guiding me through difficult decisions. Jesus said He would never leave us or forsake us. I am puzzled by the number of people who hear the gospel and don't accept it. Not only would they gain Heaven; their everyday life would be so much better."

"Please do not leave this place today without making Jesus your savior. Martha made that decision years ago, and she is enjoying her reward. She wants the same for each of you."

"Let us pray, 'Lord, we thank You for allowing us to know Martha Heflin and for the assurance that Martha is in your presence today. But, Father, our hearts are heavy because we miss her. You promised to send the Comforter to be with us. You know the sorrow we are experiencing, because You sacrificed your Son for us. We ask You to wrap your arms around us, and particularly Martha's children and grandchildren, and let us feel your strength supporting us. We pray that every person here today would invite Jesus into their hearts as their Lord and Savior. We ask these things in the precious name of Jesus. Amen.'"

The choir sang a closing hymn, and the service was over. Donna and her family stood at the back of the church with Mark and Janet Vinson at their sides and greeted each person who had come to pay their last respects to their mother and grandmother.

There had been tears aplenty and more than a few sobs, yet the service had been dignified and serene. There had been none of the hysterics Christine had expected. The pastor's message had been an eye-opener for Christine as well. She had never entertained any notion that she was headed to Heaven when she died, but she certainly had never considered that she might spend eternity in hell. She had not truly believed that either place existed. She always thought that some parents used the promise of Heaven and the threat of hell to manipulate their children's behavior, in much the same way other parents used Santa Claus. God, like Santa, was keeping a list; He knows who's naughty and who's nice, so you better be nice. Pastor Mark's words challenged these beliefs. Maybe Heaven and hell were not myths, like Santa and the North Pole, but rather were the very real places Mark believed them to be. If so, Christine knew where she was headed. She had no illusions that she would make anyone's "good" list.

Chapter 30

In the sanctuary of Riverside Christian Fellowship, Mark was bringing the Sunday morning service to a close. From her vantage point in the dressing room on the second floor, Karen peeked through the curtains covering the small window. The church was packed. In addition to the regular attendees, there were many well-wishers here to witness the happy couple begin their new life together. As she looked down at her family and dear friends, Karen was thankful that Greg had insisted they have a church wedding.

In another moment of genius, her soon-to-be husband had requested that the ceremony be held immediately following the morning worship service. That arrangement allowed the entire congregation to witness their nuptials without sacrificing a Saturday afternoon. Most of the out-of-town guests were in attendance for the service and had the opportunity to worship with the congregation. Greg and Karen prayed that God would get the attention of at least one person today through Mark's sermon.

Karen peered through the window again. The service was over, and Mark was extending an invitation to everyone present to remain for the wedding ceremony and the lunch reception to follow.

Karen did not see her groom anywhere. She assumed he was stationed in the choir room out of sight. Gretchen Sullivan was seated in the place of honor reserved for the mother of the groom, and Chad was escorting their mother Jean to her seat across the aisle from Gretchen. Carl and Marsha Harper, Karen's in-laws and grandparents to her sons, were seated directly behind Mrs. Butler. Karen was thrilled that the Harpers had warmly accepted Greg and his daughters into their family. They were delighted to finally have granddaughters to spoil, a sentiment they had repeatedly expressed to Karen over the past couple of months.

"Karen, you look gorgeous. It's time to start."

Karen turned to Kim, her life-long friend. She was thrilled that Kim had agreed to be her matron of honor. Although Kim lived in Chester and the two friends saw each other only a couple of times a year, Kim had played an important role in Karen's restored relationship with God and in Karen and Greg's romance. It was Kim who first introduced Karen to furniture restoration; God had used Karen's hobby to demonstrate to her the restoration that was needed in her own heart. And it was Kim who made the aprons that Karen presented to Bethany and Brittany on their ninth birthday; Karen's insightful gift opened Greg's eyes to the reality that she was the woman God had set apart for him.

Karen followed Kim out of the room into the wide hallway where Karen's father awaited her. He opened his arms to envelope her in a gentle hug and kissed her softly on the cheek.

"I've never seen you look more beautiful, honey," he told her.

Karen's eyes misted over. She had certainly never felt more beautiful than when she slipped on the shimmering silver dress that Lark had created for her. The full-length satin gown boasted an empire waist and a flowing skirt. The modest v-neckline was accented with scalloped lace trim. It was the perfect combination of elegance and modesty—just right for an "older" bride, as more than one store clerk had referred to Karen as she shopped for accessories.

Stewart Butler offered his arm. Karen placed her hand in the crook of his elbow, and they made their way down the staircase to the foyer of the church. Together they stood at the back of the church awaiting their cue to walk down the aisle. Karen peeked through a crack where the double doors did not quite meet. She saw Greg standing at the front with Tom Sullivan, Trevor, Austin, and Kyle. She breathed a silent prayer of thanks to God for blessing her life with these wonderful men.

The music began. Kim waited with Bethany and Brittany. Brittany was the first down the aisle, followed by Bethany and then Kim. As she watched them Karen took advantage of the moment to reflect back on all the changes in her life since she had moved her family to Fredericksburg fifteen months earlier. God had blessed them greatly in those months.

The wedding ceremony went off without a hitch. Karen and Greg spoke their vows with love and conviction. After the ceremony, a catered lunch was served in the fellowship hall. Toasts were made, and the cake was cut. Then it was time for Greg's gift to his bride.

Christine recognized the long, narrow box that had been stored at Emily's house. Today it was beautifully wrapped in white and silver wedding paper and tied with a large silver bow.

"Is that a shot gun, Greg?" one of the men called out.

"Either that or a ball and chain," someone else teased.

"Well, it's certainly not jewelry," Gretchen pronounced loudly. "I told Greg to buy her jewelry."

"He did," Karen assured her. She pointed to the gorgeous diamond necklace and matching earrings. "He gave them to me early so I could wear them today."

"Hurry up and open it," Chad demanded. He seemed particularly anxious for Karen to reveal what the box held.

Karen unwrapped the gift and lifted the lid of the sturdy cardboard box. Her breath caught in her throat and a tiny gasp escaped. When she looked up at Greg, tears glistened in her eyes.

"Oh, my," she whispered. Her hand covered her mouth as she struggled to regain her composure. She offered Greg a soft "thank you" and a quick kiss before holding up the sign for all to see.

The murmurs that went through the crowd signaled that many of the guests understood the significance of Greg's gift. Even Kevin was touched by Greg's insight into his new bride's deepest desires.

"I'll hang the sign while you're in St. Thomas, Sis," Chad told her. "We officially open for business right after Thanksgiving."

~ ~ ~

Kevin paced restlessly around his living room as he waited for his poker buddies to arrive. Usually, the Monday poker game was the highlight of his week. Today, however, Kevin just was not in the mood.

He had awakened in foul humor this morning. He recognized that the cause of his tension was Karen's wedding yesterday. Kevin had been flattered when he received the invitation from Karen and immediately, almost without thinking about it, returned the response card indicating that he would be attending. At the time he thought that Felicia would attend with him. Sharing in Karen and Greg's happiness would not be difficult now that he was seeing Felicia. He was not envisioning a future with Felicia, but he was enjoying spending time with her.

Kevin had assumed that Felicia would be available without asking her. By the time he got around to it, several days before the wedding, Felicia had made plans to spend the day with an unnamed friend. No amount of coaxing had persuaded her to change her plans and accompany Kevin to the wedding. Thus, Kevin had found himself entering Riverside church alone. He had timed his arrival to coincide with what he hoped was the conclusion of the church service. As much as he liked Mark, Kevin had no intention of sitting through a sermon before Karen's wedding.

An usher Kevin did not recognize showed him to a pew near the back of the church. Mark was no longer preaching; however, the service was still in progress. Kevin could see Mark and some men praying at the front of the church with an elderly woman. Several people were kneeling at the altar, apparently in prayer. Kevin looked around the church for familiar faces and nodded in greeting to those who caught his eye.

Kevin had not noticed Christine returning to her seat until she slid into the pew and sat beside him. When he did look at her, he was caught off guard by her growing belly; it seemed to have doubled in size since he had last seen her, even though only a few weeks had passed. That observation put a damper on his mood.

"Hi, Kevin. Will you hand me my purse?"

Kevin looked down to find Christine's purse beside him on the pew. He was frowning when he handed it to her.

"It appears that you haven't told people I'm not your husband." The words came out more harshly than Kevin had planned.

Christine looked down at the pew. After a moment, she answered simply, "I didn't see the point. I actually didn't expect you to come back to the church."

Kevin could not argue with her logic. "I didn't expect to come again either. Karen invited me to the wedding, so here I am."

"Of course. I can move, if it would make you more comfortable."

"No, you better stay here."

In response to Christine's questioning look, he added, "If you move, everyone will think we've had an argument and don't want to sit together."

Christine chuckled. "You're right. It's best to appear to be a happy couple. It's good to see you. I've kinda missed you lately."

It felt good to be missed, Kevin thought, and he acknowledged to himself that he had missed her a bit, too. Not that he would admit that to Christine. "You look happy," he said instead.

"Thanks. Janet says I have the expectant mother glow."

Kevin turned away and pretended to get engrossed in the wedding program he was handed as he came in the door. He did not want Christine to see how much it pained him that she was carrying Larry's baby. The wedding started, and Kevin was spared any further conversation.

Kevin found the ceremony to be quite moving. Karen looked stunning, as a bride should on her special day, he thought. He experienced pangs of guilt as memories of his own wedding flashed before him, and he found himself regretting that Christine had been denied the experience of walking down the aisle in a gorgeous gown with all eyes fixed upon her. The feeling stayed with him so strongly that he felt prevailed upon to question her about it during the reception.

"It was a lovely ceremony, wasn't it?" Christine asked him, as they made their way from the sanctuary to the reception hall.

"Is this what you wanted, Christine? Do you feel cheated because we didn't get married in a church with lots of guests?"

"Are you kidding? No, of course not. I would have been petrified. There is no way I could have stood up there like Karen in front of all those people."

"Me neither." Kevin smiled at her, relieved. "A quiet ceremony at the river was the right choice for us."

The caterers had done an excellent job on the food. Kevin and Christine shared a table with Kim and Hector Perez and Savanna and Scott McAfee. The couples had daughters born within a few weeks of each other the previous spring. Naturally, much of the conversation centered on babies.

"Do you know what you're having?" Scott asked Kevin.

Kevin was caught off-guard by the question.

Christine saved him. "No, we want to be surprised."

"We had an ultrasound and were still surprised," Hector said. "The doctor was positive Josely was going to be a boy."

Karen and Greg circulated through the crowd, thanking their guests for sharing this day with them. Their arrival at the table provided an opportunity to change the subject. Kevin found himself relaxing and starting to enjoy himself. He applauded as the happy couple graciously fed each other bites of cake, raised his glass of sparkling cider in a toast, and was moved by Greg's thoughtful gift to his bride.

The celebration ended, and Greg and Karen took their leave. Kevin was preparing to follow the happy couple's lead when Emily stopped by their table. She spoke quietly to Christine before leaving with Chad and his parents. Christine leaned over and whispered in his ear.

"Will you give me a ride home? I came with Emily. She is going with Chad to watch Greg and Karen open their gifts."

As he assisted Christine into the car, he was certain that they appeared to all observers to be happily married, expectant parents. *Oh, well. Let them think what they want.* Eventually, the truth would come out.

Emily's cottage was a short five-minute drive from the church. Kevin would drop her off and it would be over. He would have survived another encounter with Christine relatively unscathed.

"Turn left at the next light," Christine instructed him. "Emily's house is two blocks down on the left."

The light was red. *Almost home free*, Kevin thought.

"It moved!" Christine exclaimed. "I felt the baby move, Kevin."

Christine instinctively grabbed his hand and put it on her belly. Kevin felt the baby move under his hand. Kevin had never experienced anything like it. Emotions raged within him. For the first time in his life, and only for a fleeting moment, he wished the child were his and that he was going to be a father.

All night Kevin had tossed and turned, nightmares of fatherhood robbing him of any chance of getting a good night's rest.

In one dream, he was watching Christine give birth. He'd never witnessed a birth, but he knew something was terribly wrong—Christine was bleeding profusely—and there was nothing he could do as he watched helplessly. In another nightmare, Christine had asked him to watch the baby, and he had somehow managed to lose the child. He raced through the streets of downtown Fredericksburg, looking everywhere, to no avail.

Kevin woke up drenched in sweat. He was terrified by the thought of being a father and, at the same time, filled with despair that he never would be one. His morning got off to a miserable start. To make matters worse, Felicia's car was still gone. It appeared she had stayed out all night. With nothing to take his mind off of his nightmares, Kevin had been in a stew all day.

~ ~ ~

"Why did I go to that stupid wedding yesterday?" Kevin shouted at himself through clenched teeth.

"I don't know. Why did you?"

Kevin was so startled by the unexpected reply that he dropped the poker chips he was carrying. The clasp on the aluminum case sprang open, sending poker chips flying across the room in all directions.

"Josh, you nearly gave me a heart attack," Kevin exclaimed, grabbing his chest and collapsing into the nearby recliner.

Josh was doubled over in laughter. He tried to speak, but the words kept getting cut off.

"I've....never....seen anyone...jump so high," Josh managed to choke out.

"What do you mean by sneaking in here and scaring me like that?" Kevin bellowed.

"Sneaking in here? The door was open." Josh stopped to wipe away the tears of merriment that were forming in his eyes. "Oh my, that was the funniest thing I've seen in a month of Sundays."

"It wasn't that funny," Kevin said dryly.

"Yes, it was."

Kevin glared at him before looking around the room. "What a mess. Help me pick up the chips."

195

"I don't think so. Clean up your own mess. I'm gonna have a cold one."

Josh headed to the kitchen with a six-pack in each hand. Kevin heard the refrigerator door open.

"Want one?" Josh called to him.

"Maybe later," Kevin called back.

Josh returned to the living room to find Kevin peering under the couch, one arm extended under it as far as he could reach.

"Get up," Josh told him. "I'll help you move the couch."

Josh was smirking as Kevin righted himself. "You are enjoying this, aren't you?" he asked his friend.

"Of course. What are friends for if not to laugh at us in our misery?"

Kevin crawled around the room on his knees picking up the 500 scattered chips, while Josh watched the show.

"I'm not miserable," Kevin muttered.

"You could have fooled me. You've been miserable for months--since the day of Christine's accident to be precise. And do you know why you're miserable?"

"I'm sure you're going to tell me."

"You are miserable because you are spending time with your no-good, two-timing ex-wife."

"Don't talk about Christine like that." Kevin's voice was tinged with anger.

"You've changed, Kevin. Two months ago, you would have gotten angry if I had said anything nice about her. Now, you defend her. You spend your free time taking her to plays and attending weddings with her. She's like a black widow spider enticing you into her web. You managed to escape from her before, but she's going for the kill this time."

"I didn't go to the wedding with her. We just both happened to be there."

"You both happened to be there? C'mon, Kevin. Who are you kidding other than yourself? You both happened to be at the wedding because you are a sap. Who goes to his ex-girlfriend's wedding? And with his ex-wife, no less?"

"I didn't go with Christine. I went by myself. I'm dating Felicia now. Remember?"

"Right. Felicia. The mysterious new girlfriend. If you're so into Felicia, how come she wasn't your date to the wedding?"

"Felicia was busy. She had plans. With a friend."

Josh seemed to accept that. "So, how was the wedding? Did you dance with your ex?"

"The wedding was very nice. They didn't have dancing."

"No dancing? What did you do at the reception?"

"We ate and talked. The food was excellent."

"It sounds boring to me." Josh changed to subject to his favorite one. "Can't wait until Sunday's game. Only six more days."

The ringing of the doorbell alerted the men that another member of the poker group had arrived. Josh took great delight in explaining to each of their poker buddies in some detail why Kevin was still crawling around the room picking up poker chips.

Chapter 31

At long last the day of the Dallas-Washington football game had arrived. Since Kevin was providing the much-coveted tickets, Josh had agreed to cover the rest of the expenses for the day. Josh picked up Kevin at his house at 9 a.m., a full four hours before kick-off, on what promised to be a very pleasant fall Sunday.

Kevin came out the front door as soon as Josh pulled into the driveway. He was wearing the John Riggins jersey his father had bought him for Christmas several years earlier. The autographed jersey was one of Kevin's most treasured belongings; he had worn it on every trip to FedEx Field since he received it, and the home team had won each of those games.

"Go Washington," Kevin shouted, as he opened the passenger door. He tossed his stadium cushion and a blanket into the back seat. A large thermos of coffee and a couple of toaster pastries stayed with him in the front.

"Kill Dallas," Josh returned. "I'm glad to see you are wearing your lucky jersey."

Josh was also wearing a Washington jersey; his was an Art Monk jersey he bought on eBay in honor of the former player's induction into the National Football Hall of Fame.

"I brought breakfast." Kevin offered a toaster pastry to Josh. "Are you ready for coffee?"

"Sure." Josh held the pastry with his teeth as he backed out of the driveway. Kevin managed to fill two travel mugs without spilling any coffee.

Even though the hour was early, traffic was heavy heading north on I-95. It seemed that everyone was trying to get to FedEx Field early enough to tailgate for a few hours before kick-off. There were no accidents, however, so Kevin and Josh made good time. They were parked and ready to begin cooking before 11.

Josh pulled a small charcoal grill from the back of his Uplander. Kevin grabbed the charcoal and lighter fluid, followed by two chairs.

"What are we cooking?" Kevin asked.

"Bratwursts and Italian sausages. There's potato salad in the cooler, if you're hungry."

"I'll wait to eat, but I will take a soda." Kevin grabbed a couple of colas from the cooler and handed one to Josh.

"How are things going with your new lady?" Josh asked, pulling up a chair alongside Kevin's.

"Pretty good. She cooked me a homemade dinner the other night. I think she was trying to make up for not going to the wedding with me. She's a great cook, even if everything she makes is healthy and good for me."

"You've always been a softie for a good cook," Josh joked.

"We had an interesting conversation after dinner. She made sure that I knew she was ready, willing, and anxious to take our relationship to the next level."

Kevin tried to sneak the comment in nonchalantly but knew he failed miserably.

"Way to go, Kev. I hope you took her up on her offer."

"Well, it wasn't an offer, exactly. She requested that I get tested first."

"Tested? Oh, right. You have to get the Good Housekeeping seal of approval before you can play with girls these days."

Josh placed two brats and two sausages on the grill. "So, when is the test?"

"First thing tomorrow morning."

Josh gave him a thumbs up.

"I am a bit nervous. I haven't had a "first-time" with a woman since Christine."

"I get that," Josh said. "I would feel that way if I were in your situation."

The game proved to be a real nail-biter. Washington was up by 7 after the first quarter, but Dallas scored two touchdowns in the second. Washington got a field goal as the half wound down, bringing them to within four points of the Cowboys.

Washington got the ball to start the second half. They executed a beautiful drive and scored a touchdown on their first possession to regain the lead. The teams traded punts until late in the fourth quarter when the Dallas punt receiver broke free up the middle to set up a field goal and tie the game. It looked like the game was headed into overtime when a Washington defensive end picked off a pass and raced into the end zone.

Ninety thousand fans, along with Josh and Kevin, went crazy in the stands. They took their time leaving, wanting to bask in the glory of a great win over their most hated enemy for as long as possible.

"Football doesn't get any better than this," Kevin shouted to Josh as they slowly made the way out of the stadium and back to the car.

"Be sure to thank your dad for me. This is the best birthday present ever."

For most of the drive home, the guys recapped the game for each other. As they were nearing the Fredericksburg exit, Josh returned to their earlier conversation.

"Kev, earlier, when we were talking about Felicia's…offer, you said your last first time with a new woman was Christine."

"You know I haven't been with a woman since Christine. You don't need to rub it in."

"No, I'm not. It's just that…um…there's something you need to know. I should have told you this a long time ago, but…well…I didn't and I'm sorry."

"You sound serious. What gives?"

"Christine cheated to get back at you…because…she thought you cheated on her."

"What!" Kevin nearly shouted. "I never even looked at another woman while we were married."

"I know, Kevin. I know."

"I took my marriage vows seriously."

"I know."

"Christine's the one who broke her vows and destroyed our marriage."

"I know, but…well, it's just…Kevin, this is so messed up." Josh was glad the heavy traffic volume forced him to keep his eyes on the road.

"I think you had better explain." Kevin's words were deliberate and strained.

"Christine saw you with another woman. You were going into a hotel room."

"I've never done any such thing."

"Well, Christine thinks you did. Christine came to the showroom one day very upset and crying. Richie, Bobby, and I were in the lobby when she came in; we calmed her down and asked her what had happened to upset her. She told us she had seen you going into a hotel room with some woman. She couldn't see the woman's face, but she saw yours plainly. She was certain you were having an affair."

Kevin felt all the air go out of his lungs. He would not have been more stunned if Josh had punched him in the stomach. None of this made any sense. His mind ran amok as he tried to comprehend what Josh had just told him.

"Josh, I never cheated on my wife." Kevin punctuated each word for emphasis.

Josh took the exit for Rt. 3. He did not speak until he stopped at the next red light. Then he turned to face Kevin. "I believe you. But what I believe doesn't matter. Christine believes you did. Richie and Bobby convinced her that she was right. They told Christine that you'd been taking long lunches and that they'd seen you pulling into the Twilight Motel a couple of times. I didn't believe a word of it, but I couldn't convince Christine otherwise, especially with Richie and Bobby egging her on."

"Wow. I'm stunned. This does help to explain something Christine said that's been bothering me. She told me she had forgiven me. I had no idea what she was talking about. I guess this is it."

"Yeah, probably."

"Who was this imaginary affair with?" Kevin asked, his voice tinged with resignation.

"Christine didn't know who the woman was. From the timing, we deduced the woman had to be Amy Adler."

"Amy Adler!" Kevin shouted. "You think I had an affair with Amy Adler?"

"No, I don't think you had an affair with anyone. Christine thinks you had an affair."

"With Amy Adler?"

"Yes."

"Amy Adler is my cousin," Kevin said as firmly as he could without shouting.

"Your cousin," Josh shouted. "Your cousin! Are you serious?"

"Absolutely. You knew that. You did. Didn't you?"

"No. I didn't know that and apparently, neither did Christine."

"Of course, she knew that. She had to have known." Kevin searched his memory bank. "She was at Aunt Marjorie's third wedding. I am sure that I introduced them. And I must have mentioned it to you when Amy came to work at the dealership," Kevin ventured.

"No, I would have remembered that."

"Oh, right. Amy asked me not to tell anyone. She figured either everyone would expect her to be a super salesman like me or else she would get special treatment. She got the job without my help, and she wanted to succeed without it."

"Okay, Amy's your cousin, and, of course, you didn't have an affair with your cousin. So, what were you and Amy doing in a hotel room together?"

Kevin thought for just a moment before he remembered. "We were visiting Uncle Henry."

"Who's Uncle Henry?"

"He's our uncle—our great uncle actually. My grandmother and Amy's grandmother are sisters. Henry's their younger brother. He owns a couple of furniture stores in Raleigh. Henry was passing through town, and he wanted to meet us for lunch. We picked him up at the hotel."

"Wow. You should have said something to someone."

"It didn't seem important," Kevin rejoined.

"Yeah, but it was. Christine saw the two of you and assumed the worst. She told me later that she came to the store to wait for you. She wanted to see the look on your face when you came back and found her there. After her talk with Richie and Bobby, she decided you were guilty and didn't wait around for you to come back."

Josh pulled into Kevin's driveway.

"I need to come in, Kevin," he told him. "There's more that you need to hear. I've carried this around with me for a long time, and I really want to get it off my chest."

Kevin grabbed his stuff, and they went inside.

"Does the rest of it involve Richie?"

Josh nodded. "I'm sorry."

"So, it was Richie." Kevin's voice was heavy with sorrow.

After Kevin had caught Christine in bed with Mike Sloan, she had admitted that Mike was the third guy she had cheated with during the marriage. Kevin had later learned that the second man was someone she let pick her up during a drinking binge in a bar. But, until tonight, Kevin had not known who had actually wrecked his marriage.

Kevin would never have imagined that Richie would betray him like that. He'd worked with Richie for years at the dealership, and they had stayed friends after Richie left to sell real estate.

"How could he do that? How could he sleep with my wife and still play poker with me every Monday night? How can he sit at the table and look me in the eye, knowing he destroyed my marriage?" Kevin paced around the den as he shouted out the rhetorical questions.

"He doesn't think of it like that."

Kevin glared at Josh.

"Richie isn't a big believer in monogamy, and I guess he figured you weren't either. Christine thought you were sleeping with Amy, and Richie took advantage of the situation. He can play poker with you because, in his mind, he was just being a guy."

Kevin took a seat on the couch, facing Josh. "Did you think I was cheating on Christine?"

"I guess I did at first. I'm sorry about that. When Amy quit the dealership and moved away, I figured you had broken up with her to save your marriage."

"Uncle Henry offered Amy a job as manager and part-owner of one of his stores. She jumped at the chance and moved to Raleigh. I guess I never mentioned that to Christine, either."

Josh's heart broke for his friend's pain. "After Christine moved out and you were so broken up about it, I realized that it didn't make any sense. But, by then, it was too late to fix it. I could only hope that you would meet someone else and move on."

Kevin and Josh sat in silence for a long while.

When Kevin finally spoke, his voice revealed how defeated he felt. "Thanks for telling me, Josh. It really hurts and I don't know how to handle it, but I'm still glad to finally know the truth."

"There's more, Kevin." Josh's face was as solemn as Kevin had ever seen it.

"I'm not sure I can handle more," he said truthfully. "But I guess it's best to get it over with."

"It's worse."

"How could it possibly be worse?"

"The baby was Richie's."

Josh was right; it was worse. Kevin closed his eyes and fought back the bile rising from his stomach.

"Baby? Christine was pregnant? What happened to the baby?" That sinking feeling in Kevin's stomach was back. He was certain that he did not want to know the answers, but he had to ask.

"You didn't know! You said…she told you… she told you she had an abortion."

Kevin cradled his face in his hands, as he struggled to gain his composure.

"Christine told me about an abortion she had in high school." His voice was tinged with the pain he was feeling.

"Oh."

Another uncomfortable silence ensued.

"Lisa and I tried to talk her out of it. Lisa pleaded with her to not kill the baby. We told her that maybe it was yours."

"It might have been mine."

"I thought you couldn't father children."

Kevin flinched. He took a deep breath. "That's what Christine says. I don't know. But, even if it's true, she didn't know that for sure back then."

"You need to see a doctor and find out."

"I suppose. It's not the kind of thing a guy wants to know about himself."

"No, of course not. Still, you should do it."

"How do you know so much about all this?" Kevin's questions were not accusatory. The anger had drained from him; he simply wanted answers.

"Christine and Lisa were pretty good friends back then. She wanted Lisa to go with her to the clinic, but Lisa refused. Christine was so angry that she declared she wouldn't speak to either of us, ever again. And she didn't until that day we saw her with Larry."

"Who took her?"

"Bobby's wife. She said Christine cried all the way home. A week or so later, she went out to a bar and got drunk. She told you about that, didn't she?"

Kevin nodded, but he made no effort to speak.

"Everything that happened after that you already know."

Josh stayed a little while longer to be certain that Kevin would be all right. When he left, Kevin reached for the phone and dialed Mark's number. It rang several times without being answered before Kevin realized that Mark was probably at church.

"Just as well," Kevin thought. "I don't want Mark to talk me out of what I've decided to do."

Chapter 32

Sunlight filtering through the sheer bedroom curtains and across his face nudged Kevin awake. He stretched and rolled onto his side, bunching up his pillow beneath his head.

"It feels so good to sleep in my own bed," he murmured.

Three uncomfortable nights on his mother's lumpy guest room mattress were more than enough. Kevin was delighted by the sunshine. He'd spent a dreary, rainy Thanksgiving with his parents in Sarasota. He had to leave the Sunshine State to find the sun.

With some reluctance, Kevin pulled himself from his plush bed. He started a pot of coffee and jumped in the shower while it brewed. He downed a bowl of cereal and was pouring a second cup of coffee when he remembered the mail. He'd been too worn out from the flight last night to think to check the mailbox.

Flipping through the mail as he walked back into the house, Kevin spied "Spotsylvania Health Department" in the upper left corner of one envelope. He quickly scanned the enclosed letter.

Kevin folded the single sheet into fourths and stuffed it into his shirt pocket. He was anxious to share the results with Felicia, yet he thought waving them in her face when she answered the door might be overdoing it a bit. Kevin had yet to inform Felicia that he had been tested; he hoped she would be pleasantly surprised by his news.

Kevin cut across his lawn, crossed the street, and strode up her driveway. He was so intent on his mission that he failed to notice the Land Rover parked next to Felicia's black Mercedes in the driveway. Kevin knocked confidently on her door.

From inside the house, Kevin heard a man's voice call out "I'll get it, Felicia."

The door opened and Kevin was face-to-face with a buff, thirty-something man clad only in sleep pants. He appeared to have spent the night.

"Yes?" the man asked.

Kevin realized that he had been staring at the man like a complete idiot.

"Oh, um, hi. I'm Kevin from across the street." Kevin pointed to his house.

"Nice to meet you. I'm Jackson Hargrove. Do you want to come in?"

"Sure, I guess."

Jackson stepped back and let Kevin come in.

"Is Felicia here?" Kevin asked as he followed Jackson into the kitchen.

"She's in the shower. Is there something I can do for you?"

"No, I wanted to talk to Felicia…Who did you say you are?"

"Jackson. Felicia's husband."

"Husband? Don't you mean ex-husband?"

"Nope. Not yet anyway. I'm still her husband, at least for another six months. Isn't that right, Felicia?"

Kevin turned and saw that Felicia had entered the kitchen from the bedroom. She was wearing a short, silk bathrobe and toweling her wet hair. Felicia stopped abruptly as she spotted Kevin, clearly unnerved by finding him with her estranged husband in her kitchen. Her eyes flitted from one man to the other as she struggled for something coherent to say.

"Kevin…I didn't expect you…to be back yet… I thought you…were…still in Florida."

This was not the welcome Kevin had envisioned. "I got in last night," he managed to say.

"Welcome home…I see you've met Jackson." Felicia nodded uncomfortably toward her husband.

For his part, Jackson did not appear to be the least bit bothered by the encounter. He smiled suggestively at Felicia. "I was just explaining to Kevin that you and I are still married and will be for some time. After last night, the separation period will have to begin again. Isn't that right, Sweetheart?"

Felicia looked embarrassed by Jackson's comments but made no reply.

Kevin could think of no place he wanted to be less. "I didn't mean to barge in like this. I didn't realize you had a guest. I should be going."

207

He turned and beat a path for the door. Felicia caught his arm as he was about to make his escape.

"This isn't what you think, Kevin," she said softly.

"So…he didn't spend the night with you?" he asked accusingly.

"Well, okay, then. It is what you think. He is my husband, after all."

"I thought you were divorced. Why have you been going out with me if you are still married to Jackson?"

"I never said I was divorced. I said I had left my husband. Last night doesn't change that. We are still planning to divorce."

"You have a strange way of getting divorced," Kevin spat out at her as he headed for the door.

Kevin stormed home so angry he was itching to hit someone. Not just any someone, though. He wanted to hit Mike Sloan. Well, maybe not Mike. Mike was too far away. He had moved down toward Richmond. Besides, Kevin knew that Mike was not the one who had ruined his marriage. Richie was. Yes, he wanted to hit Richie. Even better. He knew where Richie lived, and it was not all that far away.

His tires peeled as he sped out of the driveway. By the time he got to Richie's house, Kevin was primed for a fight. He pounded his fist on the front door, rang the doorbell five or six times in quick succession, and pounded some more.

"Alright. Alright, I'm coming," he heard Richie shout.

Kevin stepped back from the door and onto the grass.

"Oh, it's you. Come on in, Kevin." Richie held the door open. Obviously, he had no clue as to Kevin's intentions. Josh must not have told him about their conversation.

"No, you come out here," Kevin demanded.

Richie shrugged. "Whatever."

Kevin's fist hit Richie's jaw without warning. Unfortunately for Kevin, he had been so anxious for a fight that he swung when Richie was rather far away and his blow glanced off without doing Richie any real harm.

"What the…" Richie began, rubbing his chin. "What's gotten into you, Kevin?"

He kept a safe distance from Kevin while preparing himself in case Kevin hit him again.

"I know that you slept with Christine." Kevin had his fists balled in front of his chest. He wanted to hit Richie again, but first, he wanted to hear Richie admit what he had done.

"You're crazy."

"Josh told me everything—how you lied to Christine so she would think I was having an affair and how you pretended to comfort her so you could worm your way into bed with her."

Richie had the gall to look smug. "Okay, I admit it. So what? You were sleeping with that sales girl. What was her name? Amy?"

"I never slept with Amy. She's my cousin."

"Cousin, eh? Too bad I didn't know that at the time. I would've made a move on her. She was pretty cute."

Kevin swung wildly at Richie. "Leave Amy out of this."

"Listen, Kevin. I don't know why you are so upset. I did you a favor. Christine is a tramp—always has been and always will be."

A shoe whizzing past Richie's head distracted him, so that Kevin was able to get in close and connect with a second punch. This one found its mark, landing hard on Richie's nose. Kevin heard a sickening crunch upon impact and saw blood spurting. He did not need a doctor to tell him he had broken Richie's nose. The sounds of Richie moaning on the ground, combined with a copious amount of blood, were enough to cool Kevin's rage.

"That's for ruining my life," he screamed at Richie.

As Kevin turned and headed for his car, he spotted Richie's wife watching the men from the front porch. She was barefoot and held a shoe in her hand. One look at her face and Kevin knew that she believed Richie had gotten what he deserved. She confirmed it as she walked over to Richie and began hitting him with the shoe. Kevin's last view as he drove away was of Richie curled up on the ground trying to deflect blows from his wife while protecting his nose from further damage.

Kevin did not know where he was headed when he left Richie's house. He knew that he did not want to go home. He drove around mindlessly for a while, finally deciding he needed a friendly ear to bend. His first thought was of Mark. A glance at the clock on the dash told him that Mark would still be conducting the morning church service. It seemed odd that after being acquainted with Mark for only a few months, the pastor was the first person who came to mind when Kevin was hurting and needed a friend. It used to be that he went to Josh with all his problems.

"I wonder if Josh is back," Kevin mused.

He knew that Josh had taken the family to South Carolina to visit his in-laws over the Thanksgiving holiday. They were due back sometime today. Kevin decided to take a chance and headed over to Josh's house on Smith Station Road.

Kevin was surprised to find that not only was he home, but Josh was outside putting up Christmas lights on the front of the house.

"When did you get home?" Kevin called out, as he strode across the lawn to where Josh was perched on a ladder.

"Late Friday night," Josh replied. "Hand me another string of lights from over there. When did you get back?"

Josh pointed to a box of decorations on the stoop. Kevin walked over and grabbed a paper towel tube with lights wrapped around it. He held it up for Josh to see.

"Last night. You certainly are organized." Kevin handed the lights to Josh.

"We have to be organized or we would never survive with so many kids." Josh took the lights, stretched as far as he could to his left, and began clipping the lights to the gutters.

Josh worked from left to right and continued attaching the lights until he could reach no further to his right. Then he handed the tube of lights back to Kevin, moved the ladder about eight feet, and began the process again.

"Don't just stand there," he told Kevin. "As long as you're here, you might as well help."

Kevin shrugged. "What do you want me to do?"

"Start setting up the manger scene on the front lawn." Josh pointed to a couple of large boxes in front of the garage door.

Kevin grabbed the first box and dragged it to the middle of the yard. He pulled out Mary and baby Jesus first.

"I thought you were still in South Carolina."

"If you thought I was away, why did you come by?" Josh ragged him.

"I hoped you'd come home early. I need someone to talk to and who better than my best friend."

Josh looked rather concerned. He was not concerned enough however to cease his work. He moved the ladder once again and walked over to the porch to retrieve another string of lights.

"What's on your mind, my friend?"

"For starters, it turns out that Felicia is not divorced. She and her ex, I mean her husband, are separated. And they are quite friendly with each other."

"How friendly?"

"Friendly enough to occasionally spend the night together."

Josh raised one eyebrow questioningly. "Really? That's pretty friendly."

"A bit too friendly for my taste."

"I'm sorry, Kev. I thought she was really into you."

"So did I. I even got tested. Went over to her house this morning to share the good news with her, and there he was. They made no attempt to hide what happened."

"What did you do?"

"I drove over to Richie's and broke his nose."

"You didn't!" Josh stopped hanging lights, climbed down the ladder, and walked over to Kevin.

Kevin placed a wise man beside the manger before answering. "Yeah, I did."

"Wow." Josh's voice held traces of admiration. "He deserved it. Good for you, Kevin."

"He did deserve it." Kevin slid Baby Jesus closer to Mary and stood Joseph to Mary's right. "Somehow I don't feel good about it though. I thought I would, but I don't."

Josh gave Kevin a pat on the shoulder. "Well, I hope you don't feel bad about it. He had it coming. Richie is a snake. He's been cheating on Emma for years and getting away with it. Was she there? Does she know he slept with Christine?"

"She watched from the porch, and she heard everything. She was beating Richie with a shoe when I left."

Josh chuckled as he arranged the animals to face the manger. "Good for her, and good for you. I mean it, Kevin. I'm proud of you. You stood up for yourself and gave Richie what he deserved."

Josh climbed back up the ladder and finished hanging the lights.

"Why are you decorating already?" Kevin asked him. "It's a month until Christmas." Kevin had a sneaking suspicion that something was not quite right.

"The yard looks good enough for now. Let's go inside and talk," Josh suggested.

Kevin followed Josh inside to the kitchen. Josh pulled a jug of apple cider out of the refrigerator, poured some into two mugs, and placed the mugs in the microwave.

"Have you had lunch?" he asked Kevin.

"No. I guess it is lunchtime."

Josh flipped the oven on and grabbed a pizza from the freezer. "We can talk while the pizza cooks."

The house was quiet, except for the sounds of Josh opening the pizza box and the microwave humming.

That's odd, Kevin thought, a bit alarmed. Josh's house was never quiet. Not with all those young children.

"Where's Lisa?" he asked, almost afraid to hear the answer. "And the kids?"

The microwave buzzed. Josh brought the hot apple cider to the table and put the pizza into the oven before sitting down. Kevin felt a knot tightening in the pit of his stomach.

"They're in South Carolina with Lisa's folks."

"You came home without your family?" *This cannot be good.* The knot got a bit tighter.

"It's not what you think," Josh said quickly. A little too quickly to Kevin's way of thinking.

"Should I be worried about your marriage?" Kevin eyed Josh suspiciously, wondering what offense Josh had committed to make Lisa send him home alone. He hoped Josh had not done something really stupid, something irreparable.

"No. Of course not. I knew that's what you were thinking. Lisa hasn't left me or moved back in with her parents. It's nothing like that at all."

Kevin breathed a sigh of relief. He was glad that Josh had not strayed. Of all his long-term friends, Josh and Lisa were the only ones who seemed capable of going the distance. Their marriage gave Kevin hope for the institution of marriage. Still, Josh had failed to answer the question. Why was Josh here and his family in South Carolina?

Kevin stared hard at Josh, waiting for Josh to continue. Josh seemed reluctant to go on. Kevin waited him out.

"I'm doing some work around the house, fixing the place up. Lisa stayed at her parents so I could work without the kids being underfoot." Josh got up and checked on the pizza, even though it had only been in the oven a few minutes.

"So...while you were eating Thanksgiving dinner, you got a sudden urge to fix the dripping faucet Lisa's been bugging you about for three months. And decorate for Christmas. Is that it?"

"No." Josh exhaled loudly. "I don't know how to tell you this, Kevin."

"Just say it."

"I'm getting the house ready to go on the market. We're selling the house."

Kevin nodded amicably. "Makes sense. You need a bigger house with another baby on the way. What's the big deal? Have you found another house?"

"Yes. We found a great house. One with enough room for a family of eight." Josh actually smiled. He seemed to be waiting for his words to sink into Kevin's brain.

It took a while. "Eight? How many kids do you have now? Three?"

"Four."

"Four, plus you and Lisa and a new one. That's only seven. Well, I shouldn't say 'only'. Seven is a lot. But, it's not eight." Kevin pointed his finger and smirked—he had Josh there.

"It's eight when the new one is twins."

"Twins. Twins!! Are you crazy? You're going to have *two* more kids! You're going to have six kids!"

"I know. It staggers the mind. Of course, we didn't plan on twins."

"How will you handle having six kids? You're way outnumbered already."

"You're right. We're going to need a lot of help. That's why we're moving."

That got Kevin's attention. "Where is this new house?"

"In Manning."

"I never heard of Manning. What's it close to?"

"Lisa's parents."

The oven timer rang. Josh got up and took the pizza from the oven.

"Oh." The light finally dawned on Kevin. Josh was moving *away*.

"When?" he asked Josh, as Josh returned to the table with two plates of pizza.

"Right away. As soon as we can sell this house. Actually, we won't wait for the house to sell. We found a house we love and made an offer on it. They accepted. We close the deal in three weeks. We hope to be settled in for Christmas."

"Whoa. Too much information too fast. It's only been five days since I last saw you. In five days, you decided to move, found a house, and made a deal."

"Yes. Before we left on Tuesday, Lisa had an ultrasound, and we learned she is carrying twins. On the way to South Carolina, we discussed our options. We decided we need to be close to Lisa's parents. We looked at houses Wednesday, and all the pieces fell into place. Lisa's father has the cash to pay for the house, and we'll make mortgage payments to him. Everything worked out like it was meant to be—like it was destined."

Josh seemed to be very happy about the decision. Kevin, however, was anything but happy.

"What about a job?"

"I'm going to work for Lisa's dad in his insurance office. He'll train me in the business. When he retires in a couple of years, I can take over. Lisa's mother retired a few months ago. She will help Lisa with the kids. I'll have a future as a business owner. It's going to be great. I can hardly wait."

Kevin could not imagine a more boring job than selling insurance or a worst situation than working for one's father-in-law. Of course, Lisa's family was nothing like Christine's. They were loving and supportive and had embraced Josh as their own son when he married Lisa. Maybe it was because they only had daughters—

Lisa and her sister, Rachel—or maybe it was the kind of people they were. Josh would probably love working for his father-in-law, and Lisa would be thrilled to live near her parents again. She had missed them terribly since they had purchased the insurance agency in Santee, South Carolina, and moved four hundred miles away.

The move seemed to be perfect for just about everyone except Kevin. He was losing his best friend on the same day he realized his new potential love interest was not the woman he hoped she was. He suddenly felt very lonely.

"Since you have nothing better to do, you might as well help me paint." Josh's comments drew Kevin from his moment of self-pity. Josh looked at him hopefully.

"Might as well."

"Hey, Kevin. When you had your 'test,' did you have them check out your..?"

"Yes," Kevin answered, none too cheerfully. "It completely slipped my mind. I didn't even read that part."

Kevin pulled the test results from his pocket, unfolded the sheet, and read it before handing it to Josh.

"Sorry, pal. You would have made a great father someday."

When Kevin headed home several hours later, he was completely spent. He and Josh had painted both of the children's rooms, the two bathrooms, the hallway, and the living room. The task was made easier because Josh had spent most of Saturday packing many of the belongings the family would need in South Carolina. He was impressed with how much Josh had accomplished in only two days.

"Josh must really be excited about the move," he thought glumly.

Kevin arrived home long after dark.

"I wish I had thought to leave the porch light on," he muttered as he fumbled for the keyhole."

He finally managed to unlock the door and step into the house. Light from the kitchen illuminated the foyer.

"I don't remember leaving the kitchen light on."

Kevin had the feeling that someone had been in his house. He listened carefully—no sound except his own nervous breathing. He took a quick look around; nothing seemed to be out of place. He picked up a brass candlestick from the entry table before slowly inching his way down the hall to the kitchen.

What he found both surprised and relieved him. A large German chocolate cake sat in the middle of the island counter, a handwritten note sticking out from under the crystal cake plate.

"I'm sorry. Can we talk? Call me. Please! FH"

Kevin's first inclination was to ignore the note. He would not however allow any bad feelings toward Felicia to interfere with his enjoyment of the delicious-looking cake. He planned to enjoy every luscious bite.

Kevin had the knife poised above the cake to cut the first slice when his conscience got the better of him. Felicia deserved a hearing. Nothing she said would convince Kevin that the two of them should continue dating, yet he wanted to be on good terms with her. She was his neighbor, after all, and it would not do for neighbors to have unresolved issues between them.

Kevin started a pot of decaf before picking up the phone and dialing Felicia's number. On the fourth ring, it went to voice mail. While leaving a message, he was interrupted by someone knocking on his front door. Kevin was still cradling the phone to his ear as he opened the door.

Felicia stood on the other side. Kevin ended the call.

"I was just leaving you a message." He held the door open for Felicia to enter.

"I saw your lights were on, so I came on over," she told him. "Did you find the cake?"

"Yeah. I forgot you still had a key to my house."

"Do you want it back? I guess I should have given it back to the Newtons, but I never got around to it."

"Why don't you keep it? I might need someone to look in on me the next time I'm sick. I'd much rather wake up to your pretty face than to Bob Newton's ugly mug."

A beep alerted Kevin that the coffee was brewed. He led the way to the kitchen.

"Does that mean we can still be friends?" Felicia asked, her voice full of hope.

"Friends, but nothing more. I'm not going be involved in breaking up a marriage that may not be over." Kevin's voice left no doubt that he was committed to this decision.

He reached into the cupboard for two mugs and plates.

"Cake?" Kevin asked.

Felicia nodded.

Kevin handed her a piece of cake, then poured them each a cup of coffee.

"This is delicious, Felicia, and terribly, terribly decadent. Thank you from the bottom of my heart."

"You're welcome. Just so you know, Jackson and I have a complicated relationship. We love each other. We just can't live with each other without fighting. So, we're living apart. I don't think either one of us actually wants a divorce. However, since we are separated, Jackson and I are free to see other people. It's the best of both worlds."

Felicia's words seemed to make sense to her, but Kevin was confused.

"And seeing other people includes sleeping with them?"

Felicia picked up her empty plate and set it in the sink. "Sure. Why not?"

"So, if the tables had been reversed this morning, Jackson would not have been upset to knock on your door and find me there?"

"Not at all. He's very open-minded. Does that change your earlier declaration about just being friends?" Felicia's tone was cautiously optimistic.

"No. It doesn't change anything. I am just trying to understand your relationship with Jackson."

"Like I said—it's complicated. If anyone could understand it, though, I would think it would be you."

"Really? Why me?"

"Because of your relationship with Christine. You two have a seriously complicated relationship."

"I don't think it's so complicated. I mean, sure, I helped take care of her when she was laid up, but that's over. I avoided her for years before the accident, and I'll do my best to avoid her in the future."

"Don't be so naïve, Kevin. You go out of your way to see her. You took her to a play, and you see her at church. Speaking of church, you've let everyone there think the two of you are still married and that you are the father of her baby. That is a complicated relationship if there ever were one."

"I didn't want to embarrass her." Kevin was confused. "How do you know all this?"

"*You* told me. You may not realize it, but you talk about Christine all the time."

Kevin was vigorously shaking his head from side to side. "I do not. I promised myself I would never bring up Christine's name when I was with you."

Felicia laughed. "Well, then, you failed miserably. I feel like I know everything there is to know about Christine, and I've never met the woman."

Kevin was sure Felicia was mistaken. He had made a concerted effort to not talk about Christine to Felicia. "If I do talk about her, it's only because she is so annoying."

"She gets under your skin, Kevin, because you are still in love with her."

Kevin started to protest, but no words came.

"Open your eyes, Kevin. Christine is the woman you want. You don't want to want her, but you do. I understand. Believe me, I understand. I'm happier when I don't live with Jackson, but I don't want to cut him out of my life. I still love him, and I probably always will. And you will always love Christine. The real question that needs to be answered is 'Does Christine still love you?'"

Chapter 33

Kevin looked at the calendar. Christmas was still two weeks away. He wished it would hurry up and get here, so it could hurry up and be over. He could not remember a time when he had dreaded the holidays more. He had nothing to look forward to this year—no one with whom to open gifts, no invitations to Christmas dinner, and no Christmas parties to attend. Even the Christmas of his divorce was cheerful compared to what he was feeling this holiday season. That year his family had gone out of their way to keep his spirits up. This year his family had abandoned him.

Kevin's parents had announced over the Thanksgiving feast that they would celebrate Christmas by taking a Caribbean cruise. Then his sister Cindy informed him that she would be spending the holidays with her in-laws at their time-share condo in Aspen. That left his brother Troy. Kevin had hinted to Troy that he would welcome an invitation to spend the holidays with Troy's family in Charlotte. Troy had other plans, however. He and his wife were taking their three offspring to Disney World for a magical Christmas.

As if all that were not enough, Kevin had said goodbye to Josh last night. If Josh were here, he would certainly have included Kevin in his family's holiday celebration. Instead, Josh and Lisa would spend Christmas in their new home in South Carolina. Josh's departure and Kevin's right hook to Richie's nose had put an end to the Monday night poker games. Kevin had not heard from the other members of the group, so he assumed those friendships had gone the way of the game. Now that Felicia was out of the picture and his obligations to Christine were in the past, Kevin felt totally alone.

With so much time on his hands, Kevin found his thoughts returning again and again to Felicia's assertion that he was still in love with Christine. He had tried in vain to convince himself that Felicia was wrong, but it was no use. The truth was that he had never stopped loving Christine, not even in the darkest days right after he learned of her infidelity. Kevin was also painfully aware that loving Christine and trusting Christine were two very different things.

Kevin had avoided speaking to Christine since the day of Karen and Greg's wedding. Since Josh had filled him in on the missing pieces of the puzzle, he had not trusted himself to speak with her. He had called Mark a few days ago and asked him to pass along a message to Christine. Her response had been the reason for Mark's telephone call this morning. Mark wanted to meet with Kevin face-to-face to discuss Christine's reaction.

The second Monday in December had dawned sunny and unseasonably warm. Wanting to fully enjoy the rare pleasant late fall day, Kevin had suggested he and Mark talk while hitting a bucket of golf balls at the Lake of the Woods driving range. To Kevin's utter surprise Mark had agreed to meet him at the range.

"It's good to see you, Kevin." Mark shook hands with Kevin in the parking lot. "I haven't seen much of you lately."

"I've been busy," Kevin responded, "helping a friend move." He told Mark about Josh's relocation as they paid for a bucket of balls and made their way to the driving lanes.

"I gave Christine your message," Mark began. "She was quite upset--traumatized."

"Good," Kevin countered flatly. "I imagine her feelings were similar to mine when I learned what she believed I had done with Amy."

"That must have been a terrible shock." The genuine sympathy in Mark's voice penetrated the shield Kevin had erected.

Kevin soon learned that Mark was not exaggerating when he told Kevin that golf was not his game. He was thankful they had not committed to a round of golf. Mark's first tee shot hooked badly and nearly hit a cart driver retrieving balls far off to their left.

"Christine shared the whole story with me. I only got her perspective, of course. However, I believe it was fairly accurate. She painted a very unflattering picture of herself. She was quite upset to realize that she destroyed your marriage on a false assumption."

Kevin gave Mark a pointer on how to correct his hook. Mark overcorrected and sliced his next tee shot.

"I hope she realizes I was totally committed to our marriage and completely faithful to her." Kevin smacked the ball with a vengeance.

"Nice shot, Kevin," Mark told him.

"It had the distance I was looking for. Unfortunately, I was aiming for that flag to the left--sliced it a bit."

"She does now. She's always known her infidelity was wrong, but she justified it as an impulsive reaction to your behavior. Now, she doesn't even have that to soothe her guilt."

Kevin found that news was not as pleasing to him as he had expected it to be. He showed Mark how to correct his stance. Mark missed the ball entirely on his next swing. Kevin decided to leave Mark to his own devices and concentrate on improving his own accuracy.

"May I ask you a delicate question, Kevin?" Mark set aside the golf club and looked intently at Kevin.

"Sure. Fire away."

"What was your intent in passing that news on to Christine? Were you trying to get back at her for hurting you?"

Kevin straightened up and took a deep breath before answering. "I honestly don't know. I do know that I wanted vindication. She told me a while back that she had forgiven me, and I wanted her to know that I don't need forgiveness. I didn't do anything wrong. It was all her doing."

"Kevin, you know that is not true. Yes, she was the one who was unfaithful. She made a big mistake in judging you without asking you about your relationship with Amy. But you made mistakes, too."

Kevin went back to hitting balls. He did not respond to Mark's statements.

"Kevin, you shut Christine out. How is it that your wife was unaware that your cousin had moved to Fredericksburg and was working with you at the dealership? Did you talk to her at all? Christine was vulnerable because you weren't treating her with the love and respect due to your wife."

"So, it's my fault that we're divorced. Is that what you're saying?" Kevin's voice was tinged with indignation.

"No. I'm saying that you are not blameless. None of us are. Everyone needs forgiveness."

Kevin stopped hitting and looked at Mark. "You're not just talking about Christine and me forgiving each other, are you?"

"You're right. I'm talking about asking God's forgiveness for your sins. It's something everyone needs to do. When we confess our sins and ask his forgiveness, we become one of God's children. Christine took that step recently. You need to do, too."

Kevin thought about Mark's words as he finished off the bucket of balls. Mark seemed content to wait quietly until Kevin was ready to talk more about the subject. They were approaching the parking lot when Kevin finally replied.

"I'm glad for Christine. She had a lot of sins to be forgiven. I hope that religion will help her to be a better person. But I'm not like Christine. I'm a good person. I don't lie or steal. I love my parents. I'm an upstanding citizen. I don't even cheat on my taxes. I don't need religion to help me be a better person."

Mark had anticipated Kevin's response, and he had a ready answer.

"I'm not talking about religion, Kevin. I'm talking about having a relationship with God. God created you to have a personal relationship with him. Sin separates you from God and prevents you from having a relationship with him. No one is perfect; we have all sinned. You may be a good person, based on the world's standards, but you cannot live up to God's standards. Have you ever been jealous? Unkind? Rude? God defines those behaviors as sin."

"Okay. I'm not perfect. I get it. But I'm not in the same category as Christine."

"No, you're not. Christine has been saved from her sins. She knows she is going to Heaven when she dies. Do you want to have that assurance, Kevin?"

Kevin did not like the implication of what Mark was saying.

"Let me get this straight. Christine just said, 'I'm sorry, God'? That's all she had to do? And it's all 'water under the bridge?' All the hurt, the lies, the immorality. None of that matters. Is that what you're telling me?"

"Basically, yes. She still has to live with the consequences of her sins, but God no longer holds them against her. She's been given a clean slate. With God's help, she will try to live a sin-free life from here on out. Of course, she will fail—we all do—but when she does, she can come back to God, confess those sins, and be forgiven again."

"How many times," Kevin asked, "will God let Christine come back and ask for forgiveness?"

"Infinitely. As many times as she fails, she can receive forgiveness." Mark let that sink in before continuing. "Kevin, you need God's forgiveness, too. Everyone does. I know this is all new to you, and you don't seem ready to take that step today. I'd like you to think about what I've told you. Don't just take my word for it, though. You need to read the Bible and discover what God says for yourself. Do you have a Bible?"

Kevin shook his head. "No.'

Mark opened the door of his car and retrieved a book from the passenger's seat.

"I'd like to give you this one. The Bible is God's word to us. It teaches us how to live a life pleasing to God."

Mark flipped the Bible open to the book of Mark.

"You should read the New Testament first. Mark is a good place to start. It is one of four books, called gospels, that record the life, death, and resurrection of Jesus Christ."

Mark inserted a pamphlet into the Bible as a bookmark and handed the Bible to Kevin. Kevin accepted the Bible, and Mark drove away.

Chapter 34

Christmas Eve fell on a Sunday, and Mr. Wilson honored his commitment by not opening for business on the last shopping day of the Christmas season. Saturday was very busy at the dealership as buyers took possession of cars purchased as gifts for loved ones and a few last-minute shoppers haggled for the best possible deals on showroom models. Kevin was tired, but satisfied, as he headed home well past ten in the evening. He had exceeded his personal sales goal for the month with two sales today.

Once Kevin was home, his mood changed. He was struck by a heaviness of heart as he faced the prospect of spending Christmas Eve and Christmas Day alone. He planned to spend a few hours Sunday at the mall. Not that he had shopping to do—his gifts to his family had been mailed ten days ago. He would go to try to catch some holiday spirit. He would enjoy seeing frazzled shoppers rushing madly from store to store looking for last-minute gifts as he leisurely snacked his way around the food court. The holiday decorations and the music were just what he needed to lift his spirits. As for Christmas Day, his friend Leonel managed the Rappahannock Inn. Leonel had suggested Kevin partake of their magnificent holiday buffet. Kevin figured it was either that or eat at a Chinese restaurant. He was leaning toward the buffet.

As Kevin looked around his dark house, he regretted not putting up a tree or decorations. Christine had always taken care of decorating for the holidays when they were married. After the divorce, Kevin had spent the holidays in Florida with his parents, so there had been no reason to go to the trouble and expense of decorating. He wondered briefly if there were any trees left on the lots at this late date. He might see what was left tomorrow. He could not remember where the Christmas decorations were stored, or if he even still had any. Christine may have taken them when she left, but Kevin knew that was unlikely.

Kevin felt lonelier than ever before. He poured himself a glass of eggnog and settled into the comfy recliner in his den. Reaching for the remote, he spied the Bible Mark had given him. When Kevin accepted it, he had intended to read it as Mark had requested. He had not gotten around to doing that. Maybe he should.

Kevin opened the Bible to the bookmarked page and began to read. He read the first chapter. *That was not so bad.* Kevin had expected the Bible to be dry and boring, but what he read so far was actually quite fascinating. John the Baptist was a pretty interesting character. Kevin was touched by the love God declared for Jesus. He could relate to a loving father being proud of his son. And who would not be proud of a son who went around the country performing miracles? Kevin decided to read another chapter. Before he knew it, Kevin was reading of Jesus' arrest, trial, and crucifixion.

"How could they treat Jesus like that?" Kevin cried aloud.

Jesus had done only good. Yet he was treated like a common criminal. Kevin kept reading. By the time he reached the end of the book, Kevin was convinced that Jesus was truly the Son of God and that he had died for Kevin's sins.

Mark had told him he needed to ask God for forgiveness. Kevin was not sure how to go about that. He would have to ask Mark. Kevin looked at the clock. It was 1:00 in the morning. Too late to call Mark now. Kevin picked up the pamphlet to put it back into the Bible.

"The ABCs of Salvation." Maybe he did not need to call Mark after all.

"'Admit you are a sinner,' Kevin read. "Pastor Mark made it pretty clear that I'm a sinner. 'Believe that Jesus died for your sins.' I'm good there. 'Confess that Jesus is your Lord.' Hmm. Not quite sure how to do that."

He looked at the pamphlet again and read, "If you confess with your mouth the Lord Jesus and believe in your heart that God has raised Him from the dead, you will be saved.' Romans 10:9. Okay, God, I confess that Jesus is my Lord and I do believe."

It seemed too easy, Kevin thought. Mark had told him that salvation was a free gift given to anyone who accepted it. Maybe he should say that.

"God, I accept your free gift of salvation."

Kevin felt a peace come over him that he had never before experienced. Mark had said that Christians had peace in their lives. Kevin smiled, and then he laughed right out loud. He wanted to tell someone—check that—he wanted to tell Mark. It was nearly 1:30. He hoped Mark would forgive him for waking him in the middle of the night.

Kevin dialed Mark's cell phone number. To his great delight, Mark answered on the second ring.

"Hello." Mark sounded like he was awake.

"Hi, Mark. It's Kevin. Did I wake you? I know it's late, but I have something I really want to tell you."

Kevin paused, allowing Mark to reply. "No, you didn't wake me. It's not so late in California."

Right. Kevin had forgotten that Mark and Janet were spending Christmas with Jenny and her family.

"I did it, Mark. I read Mark—the book of Mark, I mean—and I read the ABCs, and I asked God to forgive my sins and I believe Jesus died for me and I confessed Jesus is Lord. I did it, Mark."

Despite getting to bed in the wee hours of the morning, Kevin set his alarm to rise at 9:00. Mark had been overjoyed with Kevin's news and had encouraged him to attend both the morning worship service and the Christmas Eve candlelight service. Now that Kevin had joined 'the family,' as Mark put it, he was anxious to learn more about his new faith.

Hector Perez was ushering. He greeted Kevin with a handshake and a pat on the back.

"I haven't seen you lately. It's nice to have you back in church."

"Thanks. It's good to be back."

Hector showed Kevin to a pew near the back where Christine sat with Kim and baby Josely. Kevin did not utter a word of protest.

He knew it was useless. Besides, he was getting used to sitting with Christine every time he was in church.

It had been six weeks since Kevin had last seen Christine. Her belly seemed enormous. Instinctively, Kevin reached over and placed his hand on Christine's belly. Her eyes widened in surprise, yet she gave him an encouraging smile. The baby kicked. Kevin pulled his hand back in reaction. Christine laughed and Kevin found himself joining in with her. He settled back in the pew, his leg nearly touching Christine's, and slid one arm behind Christine. It felt so natural sitting here with her.

"May I take you to lunch?" he whispered in her ear, just before the music minister opened the service.

"I'd like that."

Scott McAfee delivered the sermon. Christine explained to Kevin that Scott was the associate pastor. Before he closed the service, Scott invited anyone who wanted to invite Jesus into his or her heart to come forward for prayer. Although Kevin had done that last night, Mark had encouraged him to go forward in a public profession of faith. Kevin wasted no time in rising from his seat and making his way to where Scott stood in front of the congregation. Another adult and two teens joined him.

Scott spoke individually with each of them to be sure they understood the commitment they were making before leading them in the sinner's prayer. Then he asked for each of their families to come forward to pray for their loved ones as they began their new life of faith. Kevin was surprised when he felt Christine slip her hand into his. Karen and Greg Marshall and Robin and Chris Jennings encircled the couple. Chris prayed aloud, thanking God for saving Kevin and Christine. He praised God for using Christine's accident to bring about so much good and asked God's blessing on the unborn child Christine was carrying.

Christine sat across from Kevin, picking at her salad and struggling for the right words to say. She had been carrying a heavy burden of guilt since Mark had relayed Kevin's message to her. It was time to lay it down.

"Kevin," Christine began haltingly, "I am so sorry about..."

"You don't need to say it, Christine. I know."

"I do, Kevin. I destroyed our marriage because I didn't trust you. I am so sorry. I should have trusted you."

Kevin let her have her say. When she was done, he reached over and covered her right hand with his left. "Yes, you should have trusted me. I would never deliberately do anything to hurt you. However, it wasn't all your fault. I made mistakes too."

"Will you ever be able to forgive me?" Christine choked back tears as she spoke.

Kevin raised Christine's hand to his lips and gently kissed it. "I already have, Christine. I already have."

The tension of the moment was broken when the server arrived with their meals. While they ate, Kevin filled Christine in on all the changes in his life.

"I've felt so lonely the last few weeks, with Josh gone and my family busy with their own plans. Mark was the only person I could turn to when I needed to talk."

"Mark and Janet are wonderful," Christine concurred. "They have really helped me. Janet told me that although God has forgiven and forgotten my sins, I still have to deal with them. She said women like me, women who've…had abortions often need counseling to…what was the word she used…reconcile, that's it. She said I needed to reconcile my feelings about the abortions so that I could begin the healing process."

"How do you do that?" Kevin hoped that Christine could see that he was genuinely interested in her healing process.

"Talking about it helps. Mark and Janet paid for me to go to a weekend retreat a couple of weeks ago. The attendees were all women who had abortions. They let us talk about our feelings and prayed with us. We did exercises to get rid of anger we had toward those who hurt us. They helped us to see that God forgives abortion, just as he forgives our other sins."

"Josh told me about your second abortion. I had no idea…" Kevin was unable to finish.

"I really messed up, Kevin. I guess he told you Richie was the father."

"I broke Richie's nose," Kevin confessed. "I thought it would make me feel better." He shrugged. "It didn't."

Christine rubbed her belly.

"Do you feel alright?" Kevin asked.

Christine nodded. "I can't imagine how much bigger I will get in the next three months."

"Are you happy about the baby?"

"I am now. Once I could feel the baby move, it hit me that I'm really going to be a mother. I am excited about being a mother. Although I don't know how I'll take care of a baby and support myself. Mark says I shouldn't worry about it—God will take care of everything."

"I'm sure He will,' Kevin concurred. "After I felt the baby kick at the wedding, I started wishing I could be a father one day. Of course, that will never happen. You were right about that."

"I wish I hadn't been. You would be a great father."

By the time Kevin left Emily's house after dropping off Christine, he had received and accepted invitations to accompany Christine to the Marshall's house for Christmas brunch and to the Clark's for Christmas dinner. He needed to purchase some gifts, and there were only four shopping hours left in the Christmas season. Kevin knew the mall and Central Park would be utter madness yet he felt nothing but excitement.

Chapter 35

Kevin awoke on Christmas morning with an expectancy that this would be his best Christmas in years. He was amazed at how much his outlook and life had changed in just two days. He rose early and headed to the cottage Christine shared with Emily.

Chad and Emily had gone to the Marshall's at the crack of dawn to watch the children open their gifts, leaving Kevin and Christine to exchange their gifts in private before joining them. Christine had crocheted a scarf and mittens for Kevin—in burgundy and gold, of course.

"I love them," Kevin told her, as he slipped the scarf around his neck.

Kevin drew a slender jeweler's box from his pocket and handed it to Christine.

Christine's eyes misted as she looked at the strand of pearls. "Your grandmother's pearls. Kevin, are you sure about this?"

"Absolutely. Grandmother would have wanted you to have them. You were always her favorite." He gave her a playful peck on the cheek.

Brunch with the Marshall clan was a joyful, albeit chaotic, affair with four young children, a teenager, and three sets of grandparents, in addition to Chad, Emily, Kevin, and Christine. The Butlers and the Harpers were up from Chester for a few days, and the Sullivans had driven over early to be in on the celebration.

Karen had prepared a delicious spread and insisted that all of the children make at least a brief appearance at the table before returning to their toys. The adults lingered over hot coffee, warm white chocolate cranberry scones, and sausage-cheese strata.

"Aren't you done yet?" Kyle asked for the third time.

"Kyle, don't be rude," Karen admonished.

"Sorry," the six-year mumbled. "We want to show Christine our gifts."

"And Kevin," Austin added. Karen's middle son was the sensitive one in the bunch.

"I know you're excited, Kyle," Greg told him. He pulled the boy into his arms and gave him an affectionate squeeze. "But we don't want to leave this mess for your mother. Since she and the girls cooked, why don't we men clean up?"

Kyle hugged Greg's neck before picking up an empty platter and carrying it into the kitchen.

All three boys pitched in to help Greg and, in short order, everyone had gathered in the den. Kyle, Austin, Bethany, and Brittany happily displayed their gifts for their guests. Trevor seemed pleased when Kevin asked him what he received.

"Austin and Kyle have something for you, Christine," Karen told her.

"I promised you we would make sure you got presents," Austin said quite seriously as he handed Christine a beautifully wrapped gift. Kyle snuggled up against Christine on the couch and plopped his gift on top of her belly. They watched intently as Christine unwrapped a maternity sweater and a journal. Kyle seemed a bit worried until Christine expressed her delight.

"Thank you, boys. I love my gifts."

"We told mom to buy you toys," Kyle informed Christine.

"Toys are nice," Christine agreed, "but I love sweaters. This one will keep my baby warm. As for the journal, I will use it every day when I'm having my devotions."

Austin stood before Kevin, looking glum. "I'm sorry we didn't get you anything."

"Actually, we do have a present for Kevin." Austin turned at his mother's words to find her holding a Christmas tin. "Would you please give this to Kevin?"

"I hope it's your maple walnut fudge," Kevin told her.

It was. "You remembered!" Kevin was touched. "Thank you. I will definitely enjoy this."

Kevin ate two pieces and offered a piece to Brittany, who was sitting beside him on the settee.

"No, thank you," she answered politely. "We have lots more."

"We helped Mom make it," Bethany piped in.

231

"No wonder it's so good. It's the best fudge I have ever eaten."

Both girls beamed.

Christine had been busy with her crochet hooks. She had made scarves for each member of the Marshall family. She had also crocheted stars to hang on the Christmas tree. Tom and Gretchen helped the children hang the stars on the tree. The girls were delighted with their scarves and modeled them for everyone. The younger boys thanked Christine politely, but without enthusiasm.

Trevor scolded his younger brothers. "You should be more grateful. Christine worked hard to make you those nice scarves."

"I guess so," Kyle answered, but he displayed no signs of appreciation.

"You will be happy you have it when it snows," Trevor told him. "It will keep your neck warm so you can stay out longer."

The thought of snow brought a smile to Kyle's face. He hugged Christine.

"I will wear your scarf when it snows."

"And I will wear mine to school," Trevor told her. "It's the colors of my team—blue and gold."

Kevin was impressed by how much Trevor's demeanor had changed since the spring. Trevor had been unhappy that Kevin was dating his mother and had made no effort to hide it. Today, however, Trevor was polite and even friendly. Trevor asked his brothers if they wanted to watch his new DVD.

"That reminds me," Kevin said. "I brought a present for you all."

The boys shrieked. "Can we open it now? Can we? Can we?"

"Give me a minute to get it. I left it in the car."

Kevin returned with a huge gift bag. The boys pulled out the tissue paper and peered inside.

"Popcorn!" shouted Austin.

"And candy!" added Kyle.

Kevin reached into the bag and pulled out a large popcorn bowl overflowing with boxes of popcorn, bags of candy, individual popcorn-box shaped containers, and two movies. Assuming the family owned all the latest releases, Kevin had purchased two classics, both favorites of his when he was growing up.

Christine and Kevin stayed to watch "Toby Tyler" with the boys. They promised to return to watch "The Incredible Journey" another time.

Kevin was apprehensive about their next stop. He and Christine were going to spend a couple of hours with Christine's family. They would pick up her mother on the way to her sister's house.

"I thought you were avoiding your mother," he had responded when Christine asked him at lunch Sunday to accompany her.

"I was until Mark encouraged me to contact her. He said I can't show her the love of Christ if I never see her."

"That sounds like Mark. What happened between you and Carly? I was surprised that she didn't come see you when you were hurt."

Christine and her younger sister, Carly, had been close despite a six-year age difference. Carly had been encouraged by her paternal grandmother to continue her education after high school and had become a dental hygienist. She was happily married to Jack, a plumber, and had two daughters. Carly was the only member of Christine's family with whom Kevin had enjoyed a pleasant relationship.

"After I left you, she decided I was a bad influence on her girls. She said I was turning into Momma. We had a big fight and didn't speak until a couple of months ago."

"How did you get back together?"

"Jenna—from work—is a friend of Carly's. They trained together. Jenna mentioned that I was working at the office, and Carly called me."

Kevin pulled up to the unkempt single-wide trailer which Christine's mother called home. It was in only slightly better condition than the one to which he had taken Christine after their first date so many years earlier. The yard was littered, and a couple of cats slept on the steps. Kevin had no desire to see the inside. He stayed in the car while Christine knocked on the door and helped her mother into the car.

233

Darlene Miller was barely fifty, but she looked much older. Her face was prematurely wrinkled from years of smoking. She was gaunt and pale, and she favored her left side when she walked. Christine had told Kevin she needed a hip replacement. If Darlene was surprised to see Kevin, it did not show in her face. She seemed oblivious of Christine's condition.

Despite Kevin's unease around Darlene, the time spent with Carly's family was pleasant and passed quickly. They caught up on each other's news and exchanged gifts. Kevin had purchased some movies and a board game for Carly's daughters and a snuggie for Darlene. Christine had crocheted gifts for the family.

The couple spent the remainder of the day with the Clarks. Donna and Bill made the couple feel like part of the family. They had also purchased a couple of gifts for Christine and presented Kevin with homemade treats. Christine had crocheted ornaments and coasters for the Clarks, and Kevin gave them a basket of assorted coffees and chocolates.

Kevin was off the day after Christmas, as it was a Tuesday. When he awoke, his first thought was that he wanted to spend the day with Christine. He quickly realized that she was working. He mentally ran through his schedule for the upcoming week, and he realized that the only day each week that neither of them was scheduled to work was Sunday. Kevin had finally acknowledged Felicia's observation about his feeling for Christine to be correct—he was still in love with Christine and he desired to have a future with her. He also recognized that the future he desired would only be possible if he adjusted his work schedule to align with hers.

After prayer and a heartfelt discussion with Mr. Wilson, Kevin adjusted his work schedule to be off on evenings and weekends. He acknowledged that he would not be able to retain his dominance as Wilson's top salesman, and he realized he was fine with letting someone else have that distinction.

Kevin was thrilled when Christine called him on Thursday to ask if he had plans for New Year's Eve.

"I'm having a small dinner party to thank everyone who helped me so much after my accident," Christine explained. "I'd love for you to come."

"Yes, of course, I'll be there." Kevin tried to keep his voice from revealing the hope that was building in him.

"After dinner, I thought we could go downtown with Chad and Emily for the First Night Celebration," Christine continued.

A date for New Year's Eve. Kevin recognized God's hand in giving him hope for the year that was about to begin. He spent a few minutes in prayer after the call ended.

Christine was putting the finishing touches on dinner. Kevin had offered to help, but Christine had banished him to the den where he was watching the Sun Bowl. Chad and Emily were in the living room looking at a catalog of wedding invitations. They had announced their engagement at Thanksgiving; now that the holidays were over, they were busy planning their May wedding. The ringing of the doorbell alerted them that the last of the guests were arriving.

"That must be Mark and Janet," Emily called out. "I'll get it."

Chad accompanied Emily to the front door of her cottage.

"Welcome Pastor. Janet." Emily gave each of them a big hug.

"Great sermon this morning, Mark," Chad said, as he shook hands with Mark and gave Janet a friendly kiss on her cheek. He took their coats.

"Christine says that dinner is almost ready." Emily led the way into the dining room.

Kevin and Chad joined them as Emily appeared from the kitchen with a platter of hot egg rolls.

"I hope you all like Chinese. Please be seated. Kevin, I could use a hand now, if you don't mind?"

In short order, everything was on the table and Mark blessed the meal. Christine had made pepper steak, moo shu pork, steamed rice, and egg rolls, all from scratch. Christine demonstrated how to eat the moo shu.

"It's a bit like a Chinese burrito," she told her guests.

The moo shu was a big hit.

"So, Mark, how was your California Christmas?" Chad asked.

"It was a bit warm for my taste. We had a wonderful time with the grandchildren. They were so grateful that Christine

235

'bullied' me," Mark winked at Christine to let her know he was teasing, "into flying out there for the holidays, they made her a thank you card."

Janet retrieved the card from her purse. "My favorite part was watching the children opening their gifts on Christmas morning."

"And attending church services with Jenny and the children," Mark interjected. "They went with us both Sundays we were there."

"Even Peter attended the Christmas Eve service," Janet chimed in. "The Christmas Eve service is my favorite one of the entire year."

"The minister was an old schoolmate of mine," Mark continued. "The church is not more than ten minutes from Jenny's house. We are praying that Jenny will take the children to church there regularly. The kids enjoyed it and want to go back."

Janet was all smiles. "God's working on Jenny. Getting her to go to church was a step in the right direction."

"I heard some talk about a youth group activity tonight," Kevin said to Mark. "What are they doing?"

"They're having a lock-in."

Seeing Kevin's puzzled face, Mark explained further. "They will spend the night in the gym. The evening begins with food and fellowship, followed by worship and a time of sharing their goals for the new year. They will spend a concentrated hour of prayer from 11 until midnight, to start the year off strong. After midnight, they'll play games, snack, and talk all night. Some of the ladies will fix breakfast for them in the morning. Then they'll go home and sleep all day."

Mark and Janet left around 9. They were going to spend some time with the youth before heading home. Mark planned to be snug and warm in his bed when the New Year rang in.

Chad, Emily, Christine, and Kevin headed downtown right after the Vinsons departed. The First Night events were well underway by the time they arrived. Bands were playing, dance troupes were performing, and children were being entertained with games and stories. The night air was cold and clear. Throngs of people, many of them families with young children, packed the streets.

The foursome watched a performance of "A Christmas Carol," took a ride in a horse-drawn carriage, and swayed to St. George's Jazz Ensemble. They were listening to a string quartet as the old year drew to a close. The First Night Lantern would be lit on the stroke of midnight.

Kevin and Christine joined in the countdown.

"Five, four, three, two, one. Happy New Year!"

All around them people were cheering the arrival of the New Year. Chad smothered Emily in kisses. Kevin hugged Christine. As he released her, he looked deep into her eyes and tilted his head toward hers. He waited for her permission. She nodded ever so slightly and moved a bit toward Kevin. Kevin stroked her face gently and pressed his lips to hers. He felt her shudder, as her lips responded to his.

"Happy New Year, Sweetheart," Kevin whispered, as he drew Christine back into his arms.

"Happy New Year, Darling," Christine answered.

Chapter 36

Mark headed to his office for a few moments of quiet reflection before beginning the service. The first Saturday in April was promising to be a glorious day. In a few minutes, he would baptize Kevin and Christine as a testimony of their membership in the family of God. In the few months since they had given their hearts to the Lord, Mark had witnessed tremendous spiritual and personal growth in each of them.

Seven weeks ago, the couple had been reunited in marriage. In celebration of Valentine's Day, Mark had offered his congregants the opportunity to recommit their marriage vows. Five couples participated. Three of them were nearing significant anniversaries and desired to reaffirm to their children and grandchildren that they were still very much in love. One couple had encountered a rocky patch in their marriage and had toyed with the idea of divorcing during the past year; they used the occasion to celebrate their decision to work through their differences and go forward together. And then, there was Kevin and Christine.

The couple was officially joined in holy matrimony in a small, private ceremony held in Mark's office on Valentine's Day. Two days later, on Sunday morning, Mark had held the renewal of vows ceremony. Kevin escorted his very pregnant bride down the aisle in a lovely cream maternity gown. Kevin's entire family had flown in for the "wedding." Carly and Joe and their two daughters were in attendance. Carly was delighted that her big sister was finally getting her life back on track. Christine had invited her mother but, not surprisingly, Darlene Miller had not shown up.

Joseph Kevin Peterson was born on the first day of spring. Tomorrow, Mark would officiate at a dedication ceremony. Kevin and Christine would dedicate themselves to raising baby Joey to know and love the Lord. Before doing that, though, they had wanted to heed Christ's command to follow him in water baptism. Thus, the ceremony today.

Mark was looking out of his office window as he pondered all that had transpired over the past eight months since his "chance" encounter with Kevin Peterson. A bright orange Spark turning left onto Riverside Drive caught his attention.

"How ironic," he said, chuckling.

"What's ironic, dear?" The question drew Mark from his reverie. He pointed out the window, as he turned his gaze toward his wife.

She spied the car and smiled. "I think it's a reminder that God moves in mysterious ways."

"He certainly does," Mark agreed. "But who would ever have thought that He would use a bright orange car to bring us here today?"

Restored Hearts

~

Book 1

~ ~ ~

Restorations

It's been two years since Karen Harper's husband died. Karen knows that he would still be alive if she hadn't…well it's just too painful to think about. Karen knew her actions were wrong but she never imagined the pain they would cause. Hoping to escape her past, Karen moves to Fredericksburg with her three sons for a new start.

Things seem to be going well. She has a new job which she loves and a new man who seems to be "the one". Then the nightmares start. Karen realizes that she will have to deal with her past before she can hope to move forward with her life.

Will Karen finally be able to forgive herself? Will she allow God to begin restoring the broken relationships in her life?

Restored Hearts

~

Book 3

~ ~ ~

Revelations

While visiting her son's family in Fredericksburg, Edna Clark suffers a stroke and falls into a coma with little hope of recovery. Her family prays for her healing and, more importantly, that God will reveal Himself to Edna and give her another chance to make Jesus Christ her Lord and Savior.

A search for Edna's will and end-of-life instructions reveal long-hidden family secrets. How will these secrets impact Edna's children and their relationships?

Revelations will be published in the summer of 2022.

Thank you for reading *Reconciliations*. I hope that you enjoyed it and that it encouraged you to let Christ heal your hurts and reconcile your heart to him and others in your life from whom you are estranged. God wants to bless you and allow you to be a blessing to others. He helped Kevin and Christine to find forgiveness and reconciliation, and He wants to do that for each of us.

If you enjoyed this book, please go to Amazon.com and leave a review. Thank you.

~ ~ ~

God loves you so much that He sent His only Son to bear the burden for your sins. If you do not know Jesus Christ as your Lord and Savior, I urge you to commit your life to Him today. Accepting the free gift of salvation is as easy as ABC.

A: Admit that you are a sinner. "For all have sinned and fall short of the glory of God." Romans 3:23

B: Believe that Jesus paid the price for your sins. "Believe in the Lord Jesus, and you will be saved—you and your household" Acts 16:31

C: Confess your sins: "If we confess our sins, he is faithful and just and will forgive us our sins and purify us from all unrighteousness." I John 1:9

If you are ready to accept this free gift that God is offering you, then pray this simple prayer:

Dear Lord,

I confess that I am a sinner and need Your forgiveness. I believe Your son Jesus died on the cross to save me from the just punishment of my sins. I ask You to come into my heart and forgive my sins. Thank You for saving me from my sins. Thank You for loving me. From now on, I will live for You. I ask You be the Lord of my life. Please guide me and direct my path that I may walk each and every day with You, Lord.

In the precious name of Jesus, Amen.

About the Author

Susan Ball has been married to her high school sweetheart, Steve, for 40 years. They have three grown sons and eight grandchildren. After graduating from Mary Washington College, in Fredericksburg, VA, they married and moved to Gainesville, FL. They lived in Florida for twenty years before returning home to Virginia. They currently reside in Fredericksburg, which provides the settings for *Reconciliations*.

Susan has been involved in the Girls Ministries program of the Assemblies of God for more than 40 years, working to instill in girls a love for God and a heart for service. She is passionate about teaching girls that God has a wonderful plan for their lives. She also wants them to know that they can find forgiveness and reconcile with God if they have strayed from the path.

By occupation, Susan is a small business counselor. She has worked with hundreds of business owners and assisted them with starting and growing their businesses. Susan authored a Bible study, *Honoring God with Your Money*, which is available for purchase on Amazon. She publishes a blog and newsletter that encourages Christians to be faithful stewards of their time, talent, and money. You may sign up for Susan's newsletter on her blog or by emailing her at susan.ball5@aol.com.

Blog post: susaneball.blog

Website: susaneball.org

Facebook page: https://www.facebook.com/AuthorSusanBall